It was for the best she was leaving at the end of the week…

Kelsea stopped and glanced back at the store as the sign was changed to *Closed*. "I forgot to buy the hat."

"No one should leave Violet Ridge empty-handed." Will passed her the parcel, as concern he might have overstepped his role as a client crossed his mind.

She squealed at the present. "For me?"

"A thank-you for dinner."

She unwrapped the hat and snowflake pin, and her mouth dropped open. She traced the fine filigree of the silver, her eyes soft with wonder. "This is beautiful. I love it."

"Yeah, well, dinner was nice."

He groaned at his choice of words. Sunsets were *nice*, but Kelsea was like a Colorado sunset. You could see one anywhere in the world, but in Violet Ridge against the backdrop of the Rockies, the oranges and pinks popped with an added dimension he'd found nowhere else.

Sunsets here weren't just nice—they were unforgettable and exquisite.

Same as Kelsea.

Dear Reader,

Welcome to Violet Ridge, Colorado! For my new series, I especially loved researching ranches and cowboys. Their rugged spirit and fierce determination enthrall me as does the way they merge independence with community. This trilogy centers around three rodeo performers who cherish the strong bond that binds them together like family. These are also my favorite friendships in life.

In *Caught by the Cowgirl*, the first in the series, Will Sullivan leaves the rodeo behind after inheriting the Silver Horseshoe Ranch, which is in dire financial straits. A hard worker, Will doesn't believe in dreams or get-rich-quick schemes, whereas his uncle Barry believes a brighter day is always around the bend. He wants to help Will turn the ranch around but, even more, he wants his nephew to find happiness and love. Enter Kelsea Carruthers, a dreamer who believes in new beginnings and happy endings. These two opposites may not seem to have much in common, but they both discover first appearances can be deceiving.

I love to hear from my readers. Please check out my website, follow me on Facebook (TanyaAglerAuthor) or Twitter (@TanyaAgler), or email me at tanyaagler@gmail.com.

Happy reading!

Tanya Agler

HEARTWARMING

Caught by the Cowgirl

Tanya Agler

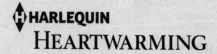

HARLEQUIN
HEARTWARMING

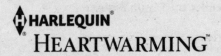

ISBN-13: 978-1-335-58496-0

Caught by the Cowgirl

Copyright © 2023 by Tanya Agler

Recycling programs
for this product may
not exist in your area.

For questions and comments about the quality of this book,
please contact us at CustomerService@Harlequin.com.

Harlequin Enterprises ULC
22 Adelaide St. West, 41st Floor
Toronto, Ontario M5H 4E3, Canada
www.Harlequin.com

Printed in U.S.A.

Tanya Agler remembers the first set of Harlequin books her grandmother gifted her, and she's been in love with romance novels ever since. An award-winning author, Tanya makes her home in Georgia with her wonderful husband, their four children and a lovable basset, who really rules the roost. When she's not writing, Tanya loves classic movies and a good cup of tea. Visit her at tanyaagler.com or email her at tanyaagler@gmail.com.

Books by Tanya Agler

Harlequin Heartwarming

A Ranger for the Twins
The Sheriff's Second Chance
The Soldier's Unexpected Family
The Single Dad's Holiday Match

Smoky Mountain First Responders

The Paramedic's Forever Family
The Firefighter's Christmas Promise

Visit the Author Profile page
at Harlequin.com for more titles.

For my father, Neal Zollars.

One of my biggest regrets is that neither of my parents lived long enough to hold one of my published books. A veteran, my dad loved rooting for the Georgia Bulldogs and made the world's best French toast. His love and encouragement continue to inspire me. I miss you and love you, Dad. This one's for you.

CHAPTER ONE

WILL SULLIVAN SMELLED snow on the horizon, something not uncommon on the first day of May in Colorado. Wet sticky flakes would make for a slippery ride to the northeast pasture in the morning. Even if it didn't snow, the hard freeze might ice up the cattle's water station. He'd have to break the ice to stave off any chance of dehydration, or worse. He couldn't afford any more mishaps this close to the end of calving season.

Best to rise earlier than usual and get a head start on his late father's reliable quarter horse, Tuxedo. That was if the ground was firm enough for riding. He hoped that was the case. He didn't want to have to use the ranch's only utility terrain vehicle, held together with spit and duct tape.

Only a few more chores before dinner. He shoveled fresh hay into Tux's stable stall and checked the water troughs. His dependable ranch border collie, Rocket, barked and rushed past him.

"Will! Are you in here?" His uncle's voice echoed from behind. "You'll never guess what I found!"

Although Uncle Barry celebrated his sixtieth birthday a month ago, his energy seemed boundless. A good thing, too, since he cooked for the five cowhands and Will. A Sullivan through and through, there was never a dull moment with his uncle, who retained the family penchant for dreams. Those never paid the bills, though.

"Can this wait? I have to sweep the tack room before dinner."

Uncle Barry waved a yellow bone in the air. "This is it. The big one. I'm about to call the university and see if they'll send out a paleontologist ASAP. Maybe they'll find a T. rex on our land. Better yet, they could discover a new species and name it after us."

Will removed his Stetson, which had belonged to his grandfather. He played with the brim. "Let me guess. You rode out to the lake and found this near the fence."

His uncle's gap-toothed smile widened. "You feel it in your bones, don't you? This is it. The one that'll put the Silver Horseshoe on the map. We'll sell tours. Tourists who visit Violet Ridge and the dude ranch will stop here. I can see the gift shop now—T-shirts, mugs and dinosaur toys."

"I gave that to Rocket last week." How an experienced rancher couldn't tell the difference between a dog bone and an ancient dinosaur fossil was beyond Will.

A month ago, Barry had caught mining fever. Will had been forced to explain the difference between his uncle's newfound galena rock and actual silver. Barry had just enough time to cancel a visit from the geologist with the mining corporation he'd contacted. Two months ago, they hadn't been so lucky. An oil company sent out a representative who'd been quite upset when the famed puddle stemmed from the UTV's burned out piston ring rather than a gusher.

"Are you sure?" The more Barry waved the bone around, the more excited Rocket became. "I was sure this was big. Really, really big."

Will nodded, and he threw his arm around his uncle's shoulders. "Maybe next time."

Although he hoped there wouldn't be one. Still, he granted his uncle some slack. When Will's parents died in an accident eight months ago, Barry had quit his position as a cook at another ranch and returned to the Silver Horseshoe. Same as Will had left the rodeo for good and come home.

"Why don't you give Rocket his bone?"

The color drained from Barry's ruddy cheeks, and he threw the bone in a perfect arc. Rocket caught it in midair and trotted away, his black-and-white tail wagging with aplomb. "I was sure that would solve our money problems."

Barry removed his wire-rimmed glasses and stared at them. Will squeezed his uncle's shoulders. "Thanks, but I'll manage that with determination and muscle work, okay?"

Barry replaced his glasses and scratched his forehead, the gray in his hair far more plentiful than the dark brown that matched Will's. "You're doing more than the rest of us put together." Will kept listening, but scowled. "You need a day off."

"Ranchers don't get days off." Still, Will far preferred working here every day to being stuck in a cubicle without a view of the expansive Rocky Mountains. This land was the reason he woke before sunrise. This land was part of his blood.

"Maybe so, but there are six of us. We all pull our weight." Barry rolled up his flannel shirtsleeves.

"Thanks, Uncle Barry. I appreciate it." Now, if only that effort translated to results, Will might sleep for more than five hours a night.

"Dinner will be ready soon. I'm whipping up my special jalapeño corn bread as a side for the chili." Barry scooted toward the exit. "Next time, though, I promise I'll hit on something really big."

Will replaced his Stetson on his head and patted Tuxedo. "I can hardly wait," he muttered under his breath.

"Hello?" A woman's voice caught Will by surprise.

A blonde in capris and a frilly floral tank top waved at him from the open entrance. Those strappy sandals with three-inch heels were inappropriate for the weather, let alone a stable where a horse's hoof could inflict serious damage. Slender and shivering, she didn't hail from the Centennial State. He was sure of that. She'd probably taken a wrong turn and ended up at the Silver Horseshoe instead of the nearby expensive dude ranch.

"After you return to the main road, head north for fifteen miles. You can't miss the entrance to the Lazy River Dude Ranch." He pointed north, casually dismissing her.

Rocket, however, had other plans and greeted

the pretty visitor. She held her hand to the dog's nose. His loyal ranch dog allowed her to pet him. The stranger then straightened and smiled, her dazzling white teeth nearly perfect except for one small chip on her upper right canine. Now, why would he notice that? "Isn't this the Silver Horseshoe Ranch?"

The slight Southern lilt of her voice was another giveaway she didn't hail from around here.

Another shiver took hold of her, and Will shrugged off his jacket. "Here. It's better than nothing."

She drew closer and accepted it. The brightness of the woman's blue eyes reminded him of his mother's favorite bluebells. This was the first spring since he'd learned to ride that he hadn't presented Mom with a bouquet of wildflowers on her birthday.

"Thank you kindly for the loan." She sniffed the air. "Whoa! That's a mighty fragrant cologne." Her chuckle told him the horsey aroma didn't offend her.

While the jacket fit him like a glove, it was more like a dress on her.

"Tell the manager of the Lazy River it's mine. He'll return it to me." Will pointed at the tack room. "If you'll excuse me, I have chores to do. During calving season, every minute counts."

"Aren't you Mr. Sullivan, the owner of this ranch?" She snapped the buttons of his jacket while he nodded. "I know I'm late, but I have a good excuse."

"Late for what?" Rocket sidled up to the woman again, and Will whistled for him. "Rocket, stop being a nuisance."

"He's not, and I promise I have a good reason for missing our appointment. It's been thirty hours of constant layovers and airplane cancellations. On the bright side, I spent the night at O'Hare International Airport and enjoyed my first real Chicago hot dog. If the plane hadn't been delayed, I wouldn't have experienced that."

Somehow, eight seconds with this woman were even more dizzying than bull riding in the rodeo. For the life of him, he didn't understand why.

He whistled once more and patted his leg. With reluctance, Rocket returned to his side. "What's your purpose at the Silver Horseshoe?"

He still hadn't caught her name.

"Didn't you get my texts? You didn't return any of them."

Will scowled, his suspicions rising. "It's

calving season, and I've been occupied in the northeast pasture all day. I didn't make any appointments."

"Aren't you Barry Sullivan, the owner?" She pulled up the jacket sleeve and offered a slender hand with four silver rings and a manicure. "Pleased to meet you."

He folded his arms, the flannel shielding him from the slight nip that was gaining in intensity. "I'm his nephew, Will."

"Oh, the foreman." That smile widened once more. "You have a charming uncle."

Speaking of charming uncles, Barry returned to the stables, a jalapeño in one hand and a block of cheddar in the other. "Hey, Will. Do you want my special extra hot corn bread or just the plain boring kind?" He glanced their way and executed a swift U-turn.

Will wasn't fooled or deterred. "Uncle Barry, you have a visitor."

Barry's shoulders went up as if he knew he was busted. "If this is who I think it is, this could be big, really big. It could be the answer to all of our money problems. Don't say no yet."

Why not take an ad out on the front page of the *Violet Ridge Weekly Gazette*? Better yet, Barry could plaster Will's economic status on the internet.

The woman looked at Barry, then her gaze met Will's. "I don't understand. Could someone please explain what's happening? And you should be expecting me. I'm Kelsea Carruthers with EverWind, the nation's fastest growing wind turbine supplier."

"Will, I may have exaggerated my position to EverWind a little, but I haven't steered you wrong yet. This is the opportunity of a lifetime."

Will bit back his groan. He'd heard those words from his uncle's mouth too often. Thank goodness his father left him sole ownership of the ranch. Otherwise, Barry would have signed over the land for some daring deal that promised a huge return. The Sullivan family dreamed big and schemed bigger.

He went to jam his hands in his coat pockets, only to remember he'd lent this woman his favorite jacket. She'd come to Colorado woefully unprepared. "I'm the owner of the Silver Horseshoe."

With his rodeo earnings almost gone, he wasn't sure how much longer he'd claim that title.

"O-kay." That Southern drawl kicked up again. "You're the sole owner of the ranch, and you're the uncle?"

She pointed at Will, then Barry, and each of them nodded in return.

"I have a mountain of work to do. If you'll excuse me, the road will take you back to the highway." Dismissive words, but this was calving season, the most vital time of the year. This could make or break his ability to keep the ranch going.

A small but forceful hand grasped his arm, stopping him in his tracks. "Then my business is with you. Besides, I'm wearing your coat. You wouldn't want me taking it back to Georgia, would you?"

Her grin matched the light lilt of her voice.

He didn't have time for wild schemes that wouldn't pay off. "Once you warm up in your rental, you can leave it on that post."

Even with his harsh tone, she didn't flinch or cower. He gave her credit for that. Maybe the butterfly had a backbone of steel. Too bad he wouldn't be able to find out what she was made of, but he had a tack room to clean. He tipped the brim of his Stetson in her direction.

"Good day."

DESPITE WHAT HER father believed, Kelsea Carruthers wasn't a quitter. She hurried after Barry Sullivan and found herself in a spacious kitchen fitted with sunflower-yellow appliances and mahogany cabinets. The faded wallpaper took her back to cooking lessons at her grandmother's house.

Mr. Sullivan bustled around the area where the spicy aroma of cilantro and cumin filled the air. "Make yourself at home."

She removed Will's jacket and hung it on an empty hook near the mudroom. Somehow, she had to win an audience with the gruff rancher. The wind turbine would surely sell itself once Will heard about its environmental attributes and handsome payout in exchange for the use of a small parcel of his land.

Last year, she'd faced tougher customers than Will at the Georgia bar where she'd waited tables for three months. Then one night, she'd arrived for her shift, only to find herself replaced with the manager's girlfriend. Her father had stared at her with disappointment over her latest dismissal, but she couldn't be blamed for that, could she?

Before that, she'd lasted for a week as a short-order cook at a seafood restaurant. The first evening she sampled the manager's special and ended up in the hospital. Turned out she was highly allergic to catfish. Who knew? Not her, since fish of any kind was never her favorite. The owner told Kelsea she could continue working there, but why risk another ER visit? Prior to that, she'd enjoyed a short stint as a gift wrapper for a department store. Seasonal jobs and serious allergic reactions were genuine reasons to pursue other employment. At least to her, they seemed reasonable. To her father? Dr. Preston Carruthers simply shook his head and pursed his lips when she told him she'd lost yet another job.

Preston had taken it upon himself to aid with her career path. To anyone looking in, his phone call to his college roommate, asking about a position for Kelsea, would seem like an act of filial love. The problem was Preston never did anything of the sort for her two perfect half siblings. Her half brother, Adam, had followed in Preston's footsteps in medicine while her half sister, Alexis, was about to graduate with her doctorate. Kelsea had never seen her father look at either of them with the same disappointment.

For the past six months, EverWind had gainfully employed Kelsea as their newest assistant project manager. Reporting to their training facility outside of Atlanta, she studied ecology and the different models of wind turbines. She'd burned the midnight oil poring over machine specifications and plat maps to check on land boundaries and divisions. Then she'd visited several existing facilities where Ever-Wind's field engineers taught her how to gauge the factors in site selection. Her probation period depended on her leasing land for the company's turbines.

Intent on making her father as proud of her as he was of her half siblings, Kelsea intended on keeping this job. Her future depended on Barry Sullivan signing his name to a contract. *Scratch that.* Now she'd be dealing with his nephew, Will, the rightful owner of the Silver Horseshoe. He hadn't given her time to introduce herself and plead her case. She intended to change that. But how?

The best path to Will seemed to be through Mr. Sullivan.

Kelsea approached the older gentleman and tugged on her winsome smile, the one that didn't have any effect on her father but otherwise got her out of tight jams. "Mr. Sullivan, it's a pleasure to make your acquaintance."

"Call me Barry." He laid the cheddar and the jalapeños on the chopping board. "Sorry you've come all this way for nothing."

She chuckled. He didn't know her if he thought she'd give up that easily.

"I don't have anywhere else to be." She pointed at the cheese. "Are you making supper?"

"Yep. Please stay and eat with us. That is, if my nephew didn't scare you off. It's the least I can do for giving you the wrong impression about the Silver Horseshoe." His wide cheeks reddened beneath his circular wire-rimmed glasses. "Okay, I lied, but I thought Will would come around once he realized how big this is."

"How can I help with supper?" She picked out a pink gingham apron from the hook.

"You're our guest. Can I get you anything?" Barry opened a cabinet and produced a cheese grater. "Would you like water or pop?"

"No thanks. I find cooking and talking go hand in hand. If nothing else, I might learn something new about your ranch operations." Or, at the very least, uncover some way to penetrate his nephew's prickly defenses.

"Can you grate cheese while I mince jalapeños for corn bread?"

She donned the apron over her capris. Yesterday, she'd paired her spring outfit with a light sweater, perfect for a hot and humid Atlanta morning. Delays from a weather system led to hours of waiting at the airport. In desperation, she had accepted a flight with a layover in Chicago. There the airline had bumped her for a medical emergency. Somewhere along the line, she'd misplaced her sweater. On top of everything, the airline lost her luggage, and she was stuck in these clothes for the time being. When no one at the ranch answered her texts, she drove straight through without stopping to buy necessities. Depending on what time she arrived at her hotel, she'd be sleeping in these clothes.

At least the kitchen was warm. In more ways than one. She chatted amiably with the older gentleman while grating cheese. He accepted her minor change to his recipe with thanks. Soon, the corn bread was baking in the oven.

Barry hustled around the kitchen, pulling out flour, butter and other ingredients. "Can you peel and slice peaches for cobbler?"

"My grandmother would turn over in her grave if I couldn't." Kelsea accepted the peeler and reached for a plump peach. "What's the deal with your nephew, Will?"

"My brother and his wife died last year, and Will inherited the ranch. My nephew is rather strong willed and doesn't take any time to enjoy what's around him." He whisked the dry ingredients together.

"How so?" Kelsea finished peeling her first

peach and reached for another, her hands already sticky with juice.

"He prefers to do everything himself. It makes it rather hard to do anything, even court someone." He reached into the refrigerator and pulled out a stick of butter.

"Him or you?" Kelsea's curiosity was piqued.

Mr. Sullivan's ruddy face turned a bright red. "I've been sweet on someone for quite a while. Ever since her divorce, she's steered clear of dating."

"How long has she been divorced?" She handed him the peeled peaches.

"Ten years." He found a saucepan and added sugar and salt to the fruit. "Listen to me blabbering away to someone I just met. Mind you, it's safe to tell you all this as you won't be staying much longer although 'tis a pity."

His brown eyes seemed to size her up. For once, she didn't find herself feeling like she was lacking. "Why do you say that?"

He stirred the peach compote and then stuck the cold butter in the microwave. "You'd be good for my nephew, although he'd be the last to admit anything of the sort." The microwave dinged. She wiped her hands and handed him the melted butter. "Thanks."

She'd only been there five minutes but already ascertained quite a lot. Kelsea had had enough of playing second fiddle in her life, and she'd never settle for coming in last in a relationship or anything else.

"Thanks, but I'll stick to business. When's a good time tomorrow to deliver my sales pitch to Will? If you have any tips about breaking down some of his barriers, I'd be grateful."

"The peaches are done. Now, about my nephew."

He added milk to the dry ingredients and then poured the batter into a cast-iron skillet. With a measured hand, he layered the fruit above that and sprinkled cinnamon over the top. Then he traded the cobbler for the corn bread, which he placed on a trivet. The warm smell filled the air.

She waited for some pearl of wisdom. "You're drawing a blank, too, huh?"

He chuckled. "Maybe you can figure him out over dinner and enlighten me."

The cobbler baked, and Barry gave Kelsea a tour of the house. They returned as the oven timer dinged. A tall lean cowboy walked into the room. It wasn't Will.

He removed his hat and held it near his chest. His longish brown hair was streaked with gray, the same as his bushy mustache. "Howdy, ma'am. I'm Steve."

Barry inserted his hand into an oven mitt and removed the cobbler. The scent of cinnamon and peaches made her stomach grumble. "Steve's the ranch foreman."

Kelsea introduced herself, and Steve hung back. "Calico cut her leg, and Will's cleaning the wound. He wants you and your guest to eat dinner without him."

"Calico belonged to Will's mother. That mare is the sweetest paint horse around." Barry wiped his hands with a dish towel. "Is the vet on her way?"

"The scrape isn't deep enough to need stitches. Will's concerned about the possibility of swelling. I told him his father would have trusted me to tend to Calico, but he had none of that. Said she's his responsibility now." He dipped his head in her direction. "Ma'am."

Steve departed, the spurs on his boots jangling behind him. Will's excuse sounded manufactured to her. That didn't deter her. She'd regroup and try again tomorrow.

"The cowhands will be here in about fifteen minutes for dinner, Miss Carruthers."

Kelsea reached for her phone and the rental car fob on the counter. "Thank you for the kind dinner invitation, but I need to check in at my hotel." And buy a toothbrush and maybe a spare set of clothes and pajamas. Fatigue from her extended series of flights was catching up fast, and the logistics of possessing only the clothes on her back loomed large.

While she wasn't giving up, Will's attitude was a definite setback. How could she convince him this deal would benefit them both if she couldn't get near him to talk?

Barry reached into the refrigerator, pulling out sour cream and scallions. "I'm sorry I dragged you all the way here for nothing. When do you return to Atlanta?"

"Not for a week. This isn't over by any stretch of the imagination."

"Would you like some chili and corn bread to take with you? Least I can do."

"Thanks, but save it for tomorrow. I'll be back." Patience might not be her strong suit, but she'd learned it from the master, her neurosurgeon father.

Barry walked with her to the front porch. Goose bumps immediately pebbled her skin, the temperature dropping fast. She rubbed her arms for warmth.

"You're welcome to eat here any time while you're still in town. Make sure you drink plenty of water tonight. Higher elevation, you know." Barry's advice was cut short as they saw Will Sullivan, all six feet of him, heading their way.

Will wore his thick brown hair an inch or two longer than stylish back east, but in Colorado that length was most likely the gold standard. The hint of dark stubble across his firm jaw might be menacing to some, but not to Preston's daughter. Fierce determination shone in Will's brown eyes, recognizable since she was equally resolved that he team up with EverWind.

Most people took one look at her long layered blond hair and dismissed her. Then they discovered she wasn't as easy to detach from her objective as they believed.

"Hello, Will. Lucky for you, my calendar's wide open." She raised her phone and opened to her schedule. "What time tomorrow works best for you to hear my pitch? I'm staying at the Violet Ridge Inn, and I have a rental car."

"Before sunrise, Rocket and I are heading to the northeast pasture and moving the cows and calves to fresh grass. Won't have time." Will glared, but Kelsea wasn't deterred.

"You have to eat, don't you?" She broadened her grin and tried to meet his gaze.

"Your father always made sure everyone was well-nourished around calving season." Barry pushed up his wire-rimmed glasses with his left index finger.

Will's nostrils widened, and he scuffed the ground with the toe of his dusty boots. "You might want to approach the Double I Ranch or even the dude ranch. They might be interested in whatever you're trying to sell me."

This was the final straw. There was busy, and there was just plain rude.

Kelsea thanked Mr. Sullivan for his hospitality. "If you'll please give me a minute with your nephew." Will wasn't the only one around here who could insert steel in his voice when needed.

"Try to get her to stay for dinner," Mr. Sullivan addressed Will and then entered the house, muttering something under his breath.

Kelsea waited until the older man was out of earshot. "Your uncle has done nothing but be kind to me. I wish I could say the same about you, but you're not running me off that easily. I'll be back every day for as long as it takes. Mr. Sullivan extended me an open invitation for meals."

"Then I'll eat in the stables where boots are required. I don't allow anyone in there wearing those strappy thingies, no matter how attractive their ankles are." He stopped short, as if he'd crossed a line by admitting he'd noticed her ankles.

While part of her was flattered, part of her was steaming at his words. "For your information, the airline lost my luggage. They'll hopefully deliver it to Violet Ridge in the next few days. These strappy sandals are easy to get in and out of during security, but thank you for the compliment about my ankles. I'm proud I spent eight years as a cheerleader, four in high school and four in college. Cheering is a sport that requires agility, balance and poise. I can tumble with the best." Her cheeks grew warm despite the cold that was starting to impact her toes. "I'm guessing your father and uncle are cut from the same cloth. They extend guests a warm welcome."

His swift intake of breath showed she hit a nerve. "You're right about one thing. My uncle is like his late brother when it comes to finances. It's all I can do to turn this ranch into a successful enterprise."

As much as she'd have liked to continue this conversation, she needed the car's heater and a hot meal. "Then listen to my pitch for Ever-Wind tomorrow."

"I can't afford whatever you're selling." His

voice strained as if he were admitting some kind of defeat.

"If you'd listen instead of jumping to conclusions, you'd find out EverWind wants to lease your land. We'll be paying you." She brushed past him and kept going. "Until tomorrow."

CHAPTER TWO

UNCLE BARRY SCRAMBLED onto the fence railing of Domino's corral. Will stationed his stallion from his rodeo days in a separate area from the ranch mares and geldings.

"Am I setting seven or eight plates for dinner?" His uncle didn't mince words, and his normally cheery demeanor was anything but.

Domino paced on the other side of the corral while Will refilled the horse's water bucket. "Seven sounds about right."

He straightened and brushed the hay off his jeans. Kelsea's last line had intrigued him. Could this EverWind company spare him from cutting the ranch's operation? His five cowhands varied in age from fifty to sixty, often considered too old to start over anywhere else. His father had promised them work and a place to live until they decided otherwise. Will intended on fulfilling that vow, even if it meant listening to Kelsea's pitch.

Kelsea. The last person he'd expected to arrive

on his ranch was a Southern belle who seemed as out of place as his prize bull at a cheerleading camp. Who wore capris and high-heel sandals to a Colorado ranch? Okay, he conceded she had a good excuse given the airline lost her luggage. But whoever heard of anyone being happy her flight was diverted just to eat a hot dog?

His mother would have done the same thing. His whole family, except for him, was known for attempting to weave gold thread out of a pile of straw. Too often townspeople would bring up the name Sullivan with a chuckle not far behind.

His uncle jumped off the fence railing, away from the corral. "If you change your mind, her proposal might do the ranch a world of good." Barry pointed out the obvious while Will shoveled fresh hay into Domino's feed trough. "An apology from you would go one better."

Will rested his arm on the shovel. As far as he was concerned, he was the injured party, considering his uncle had lied about being the ranch's owner. "Why are you making me into the bad guy?"

"You could redeem yourself in a hurry by helping me out." Will stilled at the energetic and feminine voice behind him. "My rental won't start."

He turned and locked gazes with Kelsea. To his surprise, she didn't give an inch. His uncle grinned and walked toward her. "This is an obvious sign you should share dinner with us." He glanced at Will, his eyebrow inching upward. "Right, Will?"

Domino trotted over and nudged Will's arm as if urging him to agree. There seemed no way out. "You're more than welcome to eat with Barry while I check on your car."

"You two talk while I find Kurt, our maintenance expert." Barry patted Kelsea's arm. "Kurt can fix anything. Then your mind will be at ease during dinner."

"Only if it's no trouble. Otherwise, I'll call the rental agency. I don't know how long it will take for someone to arrive since I rented the car in Grand Junction." Kelsea focused on Domino. "What a beautiful horse."

"That settles it." Barry rubbed his hands together. "Will can introduce you to Domino while Kurt and I examine your car."

Barry hurried away, and Will rubbed the back of his neck. Kelsea jerked her thumb in the opposite direction. "It's my rental. I should be there."

"Kurt and Barry will figure it out faster without you looking over their shoulders." Domino whinnied and pranced around as if waiting for Will to introduce him. His rodeo horse always put on a show for a pretty woman.

"Why is Domino over here and not with the other horses?" She shielded her eyes from the sun and then glanced toward the main stables. "Don't they all get along?"

"He's a stallion, so it's best to keep him away from the mares and geldings." Will rubbed his hand along the stallion's flank. The American quarter horse nickered and pawed the dusty brown dirt with his front left hoof. "Domino was my rodeo partner. Watch."

Will set aside the shovel and performed some hand gestures. Domino galloped around the pasture before returning and stopping on a dime. The horse lived for the roar of the crowd, his big personality suited for competition and the ring. Even now, he staged quite a show for Kelsea's benefit. This was the most lively Will had seen the stallion in weeks.

"He's a character, isn't he?" Kelsea laughed from the other side of the fence. "What's the best way to say hello to Domino?"

"That's a good question. Saying hello is important to a horse." He approached her while frowning to himself. Was EverWind reputable if it sent a ranch newbie to sell him a wind turbine? He'd investigate their angle tonight. "Walk toward him with some confidence and extend your knuckles toward his muzzle."

She made a fist and showed Will. "Like this?" He nodded, and she approached Domino.

"Now bump him gently, and then stand back." Kelsea did as directed, and Domino gave a soft whinny of contentment. "That's his way of saying hello back."

Her smile was a welcome reward.

She faced Will with her hand extended, her blond hair blowing in the breeze. "Hello, Mr. Sullivan. I'm Kelsea Carruthers, and I'd like to talk to you about EverWind. If you show me around your ranch, even though it's calving season, I'll determine the best location for the wind turbines and see if we can form a partnership."

Her cheeks flushed a pretty shade of pink. Before Will could respond, Barry approached and wiped his hands on an oily rag. "You were out of gas. Kurt filled up your tank, and the rental started."

"Well, that's rather embarrassing. All that beautiful scenery kept me so occupied that I didn't realize how far I'd driven from the airport. Three hours never went by so fast. Thank you so much!" Kelsea hurried over and shook his uncle's hand. Then she turned back his way. She hesitated and wound her arms together, rubbing them for warmth.

Where had the jacket he'd lent her earlier gone? Without a word, he shrugged out of his spare and handed it to her. Her fingers were like icicles. He should have realized she might be cold standing in the open elements. She smiled and snuggled into the inner layer of flannel, her happiness at such a simple gesture obvious.

"Dinner's ready. There's nothing like a bowl of chili for warming your insides." Barry stared at him in an obvious ploy for him to echo his sentiment, but Will was reeling at this closer contact with Kelsea.

That feeling wouldn't do at all, especially if she held the answer to infusing much-needed funds into the ranch's bank account.

"There's always plenty," Will said.

"That's a ringing endorsement if I've ever heard one." Kelsea laughed and rubbed the jacket's outer layer of suede. "Thanks, but I want to check in to my hotel. I'll return your jacket tomorrow afternoon."

After she left, his uncle's stare turned into a full glare. "I expected more from you. Your parents were always the picture of hospitality and graciousness."

Too bad they hadn't been good business managers, leaving a bank balance near zero. Shame at the harsh thought shimmied through him. He missed them every day, and the suddenness of that fateful UTV accident had robbed him of any chance of saying goodbye. He shoved his hands into his pockets, forgetting that was his cue to the stallion that his favorite snack was coming. Domino headed over and nudged him. Will produced a piece of watermelon rind and held it out to the horse. His muzzle tickled the palm of Will's hand. "Don't worry. Kelsea is coming back tomorrow."

"Why she'd be a sucker for punishment that way, I don't know," Barry fumed. "At least not with the Double I and other ranches around that would open their doors to her in a heartbeat. This could be big, Will, really big. Listen to her sales presentation with an open mind." He stormed off toward the ranch house.

A hunger pang gripped Will's stomach. Or maybe that was desperation. Uncertainty bit at the corner of his mind as to whether his uncle wouldn't feed him dinner tonight and possibly for weeks to come, unless he listened to Kelsea's pitch. If EverWind paid him, that could help Will save the ranch and the jobs of the five cowhands.

There was one way to find out, but his gruffness might have driven Kelsea away for good.

THE CHARMING AMBIENCE of the Violet Ridge Inn captivated Kelsea. Welcoming sepia leather couches flanked a stone fireplace where a cozy fire blazed. The same flat stones graced the front of the reservation desk. The smell of lavender soothed her ruffled spirit. Peace at last.

That, and a mattress with her name on it for a good night's sleep, was all she needed.

She stopped at the little convenience store off the lobby and picked out a toothbrush and toothpaste, along with a few bottles of water. Her stomach rumbled. She threw in some trail mix and protein bars for good measure and carried her purchases to the front desk. No one manned the area, so she rang the bell on the granite counter.

A harried employee with her auburn hair pulled into a ponytail bustled out of the back room, her hands loaded with towels. "Are you the guest from Room 205? How did you get here so fast?"

"Because that wasn't me." Kelsea flashed her brightest smile and pulled her wallet out of her purse, noting Martha's name from her ID badge. "I have a reservation under Carruthers."

Martha placed the towels on a nearby chair and pressed keys on her keyboard. "Can you spell that for me?"

Kelsea obliged while pushing her purchases front and center. "Can you add these to my tab? And is there room service?"

"Yes, and the kitchen closes in an hour. The restaurant's already closed for the night."

Kelsea didn't mind at all. She'd have her order placed before she opened a bottle of water. "Thank you."

The clerk frowned. "I don't see a reservation under your name, and we're booked solid because of the rodeo later this week. Ty Darling's coming to town. He's a huge draw after winning the finals last year."

A light bulb clicked on. "It must be under the corporate name, EverWind."

Martha's frown deepened. "Are you sure you have a reservation?"

After sleeping in the airport terminal last night, Kelsea hoped she was at the right hotel. She pulled up the reservation on her phone. "Here's my confirmation email."

Martha's expression changed to the same look Kelsea's hairdresser gave her when she chopped off her long hair following her first college breakup. "Oh, hon, this reservation started yesterday."

"My flight was delayed, and I spent the night in an airport chair not meant for sleeping." She stretched her back, loosening the knots in her muscles.

"You didn't check in." Someone cleared their throat behind Kelsea, and Martha reached for the towels.

Kelsea moved aside while the guest accepted the towels. She felt envious. That woman might be about to step into a steamy shower or stretch out on a soft billowy bed.

She returned to her place in the line, now considerably longer, with more people coming in the door. "I didn't see the point of checking in until I arrived."

"It's the hotel's policy to cancel reservations when the guest is a no-show," Martha said in a monotone voice. "We're booked solid. No vacancies."

Customers behind Kelsea started muttering about the wait. Her frustrations grew stronger, but she wasn't budging.

"I'm not a no-show. I'm here." She might as well have directed her protests to a brick wall, so she changed tack. "Can you recommend another hotel in Violet Ridge?"

"Every motel and camping ground for fifty miles around is booked solid because of the rodeo. Have you seen a picture of Ty Darling?" She fanned herself with her hand. "Colorado's favorite son."

"Can't say as I have." Kelsea jerked her thumb toward the couch. "Can I park myself over there for a few minutes?"

Martha's frown returned. "You don't have a room…"

Desperation made her plead her case. "Please. I need a few minutes to regroup. The airport lost my luggage. They found it in Graz, Austria, rather than Grand Junction. I arrived for a business meeting in this outfit," she plucked at her tank top, "and my last meal was a bowl of oatmeal I purchased at an airport kiosk."

"Are you going to be all day? My family's waiting for me to check in," a man grumbled from behind her.

"I'll be right with you." Martha tilted her head and sent the customer a smile. "You can stay until I'm done with this line."

Kelsea grabbed her phone and hurried to the spot closest to the fire before Martha changed her mind. She sank into the sofa's comfortable cushions, wishing she could just park herself here for the night. However, she needed some place to stay and soon. She consulted her phone app. Martha wasn't exaggerating. The closest hotel with a vacancy was back in Grand Junction, a good 120 miles away. How was she going to drive all that way on an empty stomach and a light head? Searching for a nearby restaurant that was still open reminded her she'd refused a perfectly good dinner at the Silver Horseshoe.

Her pulse raced as she thought of her first visit to a working ranch. Will measured up to her preconceived notions of what a cowboy should look like on the outside. Handcrafted dark brown leather boots with fine stitching matched the cowboy hat adorned with a silver horseshoe buckle. Too bad his sullen personality didn't match the handsome exterior.

Will had mentioned something about riding Domino in the rodeo. She checked out a video clip of him on her phone. There he was, roping a steer in mere seconds. Mesmerized, she watched until the end when he charmed the journalist in his interview.

Was this the same man? She viewed it again. Yep, it was.

That side of him, hidden as it was, must explain the inexplicable tug of attraction she'd felt toward him.

Business professionals are not attracted to potential clients.

But if she discovered the disconnect between the rodeo performer and the rancher, that could seal the deal for EverWind. Otherwise, she'd have to explain to her boss why she couldn't convert the easiest sales prospect on the list. If EverWind fired her, her father would never let her live it down.

First things first. A good night's sleep was in order. Then she'd be ready to conquer the world, or at least Will's defenses. But where would she stay? Grand Junction, it was. She peeked over at the desk where Martha had her hands full. No one would notice if she closed her eyes for a wink before she tackled that long drive.

Someone tapped her shoulder, and Kelsea bolted awake. "Sorry, Martha. I'm leaving right now."

Then the vision in front of her became clear, and she stiffened. What was Will Sullivan doing here?

More to the point, how long had she been asleep?

"You've been called a lot of names in your time, but never Martha." The cowboy beside him poked Will before tipping his dark brown

Stetson at Kelsea. "Pleased to meet you, ma'am. I'm Lucky Harper."

Kelsea rubbed her eyes before standing. Hunger gnawed at her stomach. "Likewise. I'm Kelsea Carruthers." One glance at the long line at the reception desk staunched any hope someone might leave their room unclaimed tonight. She glared at Will. "Why are you here?"

"You mentioned where you were staying. I came to talk to you and ran into my best friend, Lucky." Will removed his cowboy hat and rotated it in his hands. "Can you spare a minute?"

"Will you be doing the talking or the listening?" She might not have the added inches of those boots, but she wasn't Preston's daughter for nothing.

"Sounds like you two don't need a third wheel." Lucky patted Will's shoulder. "I've saved you seats for the rodeo."

"I'm not going. There's too much to do at the ranch," Will said.

Lucky muttered something unintelligible under his breath and departed. Will concentrated on his hat. "Do you have time to talk now? Maybe we should start over."

Hunger and fatigue staved off any discussion as far as she was concerned. Let him stew about his behavior overnight. "I'm leaving for

Grand Junction. I hope I can find a fast-food restaurant that's open this late."

Will scowled, and it wasn't fair that his scowl wasn't the least bit scary. On the contrary, it only made him that much more attractive. A funny flutter gripped her stomach, but this time the feeling had nothing to do with food.

"You're leaving? I thought you were staying through the week."

"My hotel reservation disappeared in a cloud of red tape." She picked her purse off the maroon, tan and azure rug woven with a traditional Native American design. "I'll be at your ranch tomorrow afternoon."

"If you don't have experience driving that road to Grand Junction, it might not be best to travel at night." Concern replaced his scowl.

She hiked her purse strap in place. "Thank you, but I'll manage just fine." Martha looked her way with an arched eyebrow, and Kelsea waved goodbye. "Nice meeting you, Martha."

Kelsea brushed past Will.

"There are potholes," he called after her. "Sometimes a cow escapes a fence and ends up on the highway."

"Our roads are safe for driving." Martha sought to reassure the customers and sent Will and Kelsea an exasperated look. "Please take this discussion somewhere else."

Like a chastened student, Kelsea hurried outside. The frigid mountain air hit her at once. She shivered. Will shrugged out of his jacket, this one a rich forest green with a fleece lining, and handed it to her. "Good riddance. I never liked this jacket, anyway. I'm used to this weather. You're not."

"Then why did you see the need for the coat in the first place?" But she didn't hand it back. Instead, she put it on and reveled in the feel of the wool still warm from his skin. This time, a pleasing woodsy scent clung to the fabric.

"I drive my truck with the windows down."

"I can't return this until tomorrow." One advantage of heading to Grand Junction tonight was the selection of shopping venues. By the time she was back in Violet Ridge the next day, she should have all the essentials. She'd even take a page from his book and roll down the windows. That was, once she was dressed for the fickleness of a Colorado spring. "I don't think whatever I buy will be half as nice as this, but I'll have fun shopping."

He shuddered and stuck his large hands in his pockets. "*Fun* and *shopping* are two words that don't belong in the same sentence."

"They do when your luggage ended up on a different continent." She smiled and reached inside her purse for the car rental fob. "At last I found a positive spin about today. Now if you'll excuse me."

"What if you found a place to stay in Violet Ridge?"

"I'm quite capable…"

He held up a hand. "I'm discovering you are very capable of whatever you set your mind to, but the potholes around here are deep. You also wouldn't know what to do if you found a cow in the middle of the road."

"Do you have a connection with one of the local hotels?" She'd listen to anything he had to offer. She was rather tired, more than she cared to admit.

"I was thinking you could stay with me."

CHAPTER THREE

WILL USHERED KELSEA into his living room and had to admit Barry did an excellent job of making it feel cozy. A roaring fire greeted them, and ambient lighting bathed the room in a soft glow. Will almost didn't recognize this picture of domesticity. Was it the place or the person beside him? Could one person change a house into a home just by her mere presence?

"Thanks for driving me here and letting me spend the night." She stepped back and yawned. "I don't think I'd have stayed awake all the way to Grand Junction."

Considering she'd fallen asleep before they left the hotel parking lot, that wasn't an understatement.

"You might want to wait on those thanks until you see your room. For all you know, you could be staying out in the pasture with Domino or in the stable with the cats and horses and Rocket." He sure didn't recognize the light banter coming out of his mouth.

"How do you know your uncle didn't put you in the stables and let me have your room?"

She made a fair point, one he'd do well to remember in light of Barry's earlier admonition.

She glanced around the room while rubbing her hands together in front of the fire. "Will I disturb your renovations? It looks like you're getting ready to paint."

After his parents' accident, he'd taken down his mother's beautiful watercolors. Around the holidays, he finally noticed the dinginess of the walls. He'd bought paint, intending on sprucing up the place. Last year, though, dealing with probate and issues popping up on the ranch occupied all his time. He'd never even started prepping the room.

He'd get around to it eventually. The ranch and the cowhands were his responsibility now. As far as he was concerned, duty came before something as mundane as painting.

"I'm not renovating. Keeping the stables and grounds in good shape takes priority over my living quarters." Now he looked around as if seeing the room through Kelsea's eyes. After calving season, he'd make the time to get this done.

"Oh." She walked over to the floor-to-ceiling

windows. "When it's daylight, the view must be beautiful."

"I need to upgrade those windows against the winter cold." An expense he could scarce afford with a pile of bills as long as Domino's legs.

"You're lucky to have that magnificent view of the Rockies. I'll make sure to get up early to see the sunrise. It must be gorgeous with all those rich colors." She traced the outer wooden frame, offsetting the glass. "A cup of coffee and that view, and I'd be set for life. It's a lovely place to dream up your next adventure."

"Did I hear the word *dream*?" Will's least favorite word of all. Barry entered, a bowl of chili in his hands. "Ah, there's nothing like a dream and a roll of duct tape for a lifetime of happiness."

Kelsea licked her lips and pointed to Barry's bowl. "You wouldn't by any chance have a spare serving of that, would you, Mr. Sullivan?"

"Please call me Barry. Welcome to the Silver Horseshoe, Kelsea." Barry handed her the bowl. "This is the last of the chili, and it has your name all over it. I set a nice sizeable chunk of corn bread aside for you."

She squealed with glee and plopped on the leather couch. "Thank you, Barry." She swallowed a mouthful and closed her eyes, a smile spreading over her pink lips. "Real Western chili. This fulfills one of my wishes for the trip."

Daydreams and wishes were no substitute for spit, hard work and steely determination. While Kelsea was a breath of fresh air, she was cut from the same cloth as his uncle and his father, dreamers who'd never had two nickels to rub together. Will wanted more for the ranch, starting with it becoming self-sustaining so he could then tackle the myriad of necessary improvements.

He sat across from her on the matching couch, expecting her to wolf down the chili. Instead, she slowly savored every bite. When she cut the chunk of corn bread and slathered on Barry's honey butter, he seized his opportunity to talk shop. "How long have you worked for EverWind? Why my property? Why not the Double I Ranch or the dude ranch?"

She paused, the corn bread halfway to her mouth. "Uh-uh. Not tonight. It's late, and I'm tired. I have something at stake, same as you, but tomorrow is soon enough for my presentation." She looked at her outfit. "After I go shopping. When can you take me back to Violet Ridge so I can retrieve my rental?"

He faced his uncle. "Can you run her into town after breakfast?"

"Don't you remember?" Barry scratched his chin and frowned. "Jody, Jerome and I volunteered for the rodeo setup. We're heading out early for the arena. Jody's on the electrical end, while Jerome is building the chutes. I'm baking sheet cakes and brownies. The organizers are expecting us around seven, and we won't be back until sunset."

Even though it was smaller than the rodeos in Greeley or Gunnison, the event required a huge number of volunteers. The organizers had recruited Barry right out of the gate, along with Jody, Will's groundskeeper, and his brother, Jerome, whose specialty was carpentry and fence repair. Trouble was Will would be down three cowhands at the tail end of calving season.

Kelsea brightened and raised the last bite of her corn bread. "If your desserts are half as good as this meal, I'm there."

"Have you ever been to a rodeo?" Barry paused while Kelsea shook her head. "Will's a former competitor. You won't find anyone better to explain what's happening."

Delight registered on Kelsea's face. "My first rodeo. How exciting." Then her eyes widened. "Is it dangerous?"

"Chances are strong someone will get hurt during the season," Will said, "but the competitors train hard and understand the risk. It's about endurance and not quitting. Mental toughness plays a major role." He missed the sport to his core. His parents' sudden death ended any possibility of going back. The sport demanded intensive training, and he had no time to spare.

He'd said three permanent farewells in the span of twenty-four hours.

"I'm in," Kelsea said.

"I'm not attending." Will had come to terms with what he'd left behind, and that was enough. There was a ranch to run while everyone else had fun.

"Don't listen to him. Of course, he's going." Barry waved away Will's protests. "My nephew will show you to the guest room."

Barry scurried off, leaving Will alone with Kelsea. She popped the last bite of corn bread in her mouth. Her content smile left little doubt she was enjoying herself. "So, what time works for you tomorrow?"

"For the presentation?" Down three cow-hands, he didn't have a spare minute. "Since you're staying for the week, how about we talk the day after tomorrow?"

"No, for shopping. I've lived in these clothes for thirty-six hours, and they're going to start taking on a life of their own soon." She waved her hand under her nose. "I didn't expect to sleep at an airport, in a hotel lobby and in a rancher's truck when I selected this outfit for my flight."

"I'm moving cows tomorrow." Which would come even earlier than usual with the late night and the possibility of snow. Add in a reduced staff, and he'd be lucky if he slept between now and the end of the rodeo.

"I don't imagine there's a local rideshare program or bustling taxi service in town, is there?" He shook his head. His mother had spent many afternoons driving anyone who needed a ride to the doctor's or the store. "I'll be ready to pick up my rental whenever you finish your chores."

As hard as it was to admit it, she was right. When he drove her to the ranch in his truck, he assumed responsibility for getting her back to her rental. "How's early afternoon? I'll make a list of everything I need and conduct my errands before I head back to the ranch."

"If you want to leave a little later, I'll throw in dinner in exchange for a personal introduction to Violet Ridge. I have an expense account, and I'm not afraid to use it, especially considering how much you're saving my company for lodging."

Will got the impression Kelsea wasn't afraid of much. Whether or not that impressed him, he wasn't quite sure. Problem was, there was too much about Kelsea that was impressing him. He didn't have time for vivacious blondes. "We'll see."

"Most people find me quite persuasive." She yawned, her eyelids lowering ever so slightly. "I'd offer you everything I own for a bathroom and some spare toiletries. That is, if I thought you could use my few meager possessions."

She shrugged, and he held back a chuckle.

He'd best show her the guest room before Uncle Barry sent him to spend the night outside with Rocket and the cattle. He shuddered to think about what life was going to be like after a week with her on the ranch. She'd already made quite a mark around here, and he'd stay on guard that another goodbye wouldn't leave a permanent scar.

CLEAN CLOTHES, *fresh minty breath and a full stomach*. It was amazing how little things could be such huge morale boosters. She marveled at the Rockies and then turned toward Will, who concentrated on driving his truck with the same determination he seemed to devote to everything. Then again, the roads were rather slick after a night of sleet and howling winds, but he navigated them with ease.

If she knocked out this shopping trip in a few hours, she'd start discussing the advantages of EverWind to Will tonight. After telling her boss about the layovers and the rodeo, he'd granted her an extension, making it a two-week visit. She'd also broach the subject of an extended stay at the ranch during dinner. For now, though, she intended to make the most of every minute in Violet Ridge.

"How do you get any work done? I'd be staring at the gorgeous scenery all day long." She adjusted the heat, thankful Barry had lent her a sweatshirt before leaving for his volunteer shift.

Will glanced over, his face as stony as the rock precipice they'd passed a mile ago. "Animals and staff depend on me."

"I can't even keep an African violet alive." She'd done most of the talking during the past fifteen minutes since they'd started for town, but she didn't mind. Silence was worse than hearing herself chatter. "And here you keep a whole ranch running."

"The cowhands do their part, and the cattle do theirs."

"You make it sound so simple." She gained her first glimpse of Violet Ridge's downtown district in the daytime. The charming atmosphere didn't disappoint.

Sidewalks bustled with tourists who'd arrived early for the rodeo. Half of them wore coats, while the other half had already discarded the extra layer of clothing. She supposed that had something to do with the sunshine peeking through the clouds, the rising temperature a most welcome taste of spring after a blustery morning. On either side of the street, storefronts rose a mere two stories. A plethora of bright colors greeted her. Weathered blue, burnt sienna and creamy yellow predominated, and one green structure caught her eye. "Saucy Sal's Green Chili Specialty Sauces." She chuckled at the sign over the awning. "That's cute. I could spend days browsing."

He only grunted before he pulled into the hotel lot alongside her rental car. *Good gravy.* Her rental Ford Mustang looked as though she'd driven it through the desert and back again, a fine layer of dust obscuring the dark paint.

"Is there a place you'd recommend for a car wash?" If she turned it back into the rental agency like this, they'd charge her account extra. While it wasn't her dime, she wanted to use EverWind's funds responsibly.

"That's Colorado for you. I'd wait and have

it detailed in Grand Junction when you return it in a week."

"About that." With that type of lead in, there was no time like the present to spring her news on him. "My boss granted me an extension, since we need some soil samples."

"How long?"

"I'll be here for two weeks. I can check into the Violet Ridge Inn once the rodeo is finished." This was no time for hesitation, but this was a mighty big imposition. "In the meantime, can I stay at the ranch? Or would you prefer I check into a hotel?"

A muscle twitched under his jawline, and then his shoulders relaxed. "It's a big ranch house, and Uncle Barry likes your company."

Was Barry the only Sullivan who liked her company, or was she growing on Will, too?

"Thanks." She kept her hand on the passenger door. "Any insights about the best places to shop?"

"Violet Ridge's niche businesses depend on tourists year-round. There's skiing in the winter, fly-fishing and rock climbing in the summer. Not to mention this rodeo, which marks the start of the season for the local circuit, and the dude ranch. Gunny's your best bet if you want a box store." Four sentences at once. That was a record.

She opened the door and hopped down. "Hopefully Gunny won't be as jammed as downtown."

"Gunnison's the next town…normally a thirty-minute drive. Longer in this traffic."

Great. More time spent in a vehicle and less time on her presentation. Once Will approved, she'd tour the ranch and collect soil samples for determining the best place to install the turbines.

But the scenery was breathtaking. That was the proverbial upside. She smiled. "Don't wait up for me. Thanks for the ride."

"Kelsea." She stopped short of shutting the door, noticing a softness in those dark brown eyes of his. "The feed and seed here is like a general store. You should find enough there to hold you over. If not, you can leave early for Gunny tomorrow morning. The traffic won't be as intense. Get back in."

She didn't wait for him to repeat himself, as that wasn't his style. "I've never been to a real feed and seed before. How exciting."

"Hold your judgment until you see the place."

"Do they have cowboy boots? I'll buy my first pair." One thing struck her as odd. "Why'd you change your mind? You could have just left me at the hotel to figure this out."

He headed back toward the downtown district. "You can't sell me on EverWind if you're driving back and forth from Gunny. I promise I'll listen to the idea as soon as the ranch cooperates."

She caught a glimmer of a smile, which had the impact of a stampede of mustangs on her. Smiling shaved ten years off his age, and she guessed he was closer to thirty than forty.

Trees with silvery bark lined the sides of the street. "What type of trees are those?"

"Aspens. Those small flowers herald spring, and the catkins release cottony seeds." Will navigated the turn into the Over and Dunne Feed and Seed, a long low-lying building with an exterior of harvested timber. "I'll drop you off at the front. My order's around back."

The car behind them honked. Kelsea scurried toward the building, keeping clear of the traffic. Already she missed the warmth of the truck's cabin. A long porch with rocking chairs greeted her, and a patio heater made the scene that much more appealing. A trio of older gentlemen rose when she approached the empty rocker.

"May I interrupt your gathering and sit with you?"

They blinked and then grinned, the spurs on their cowboy boots jingling.

"I've never minded when a pretty woman asks to sit by me." The first man, his wrinkled face open and friendly, rose. He removed his cowboy hat and revealed a thick thatch of white hair. He motioned for her to take the seat closest to the heater. "Glad you're joining us for a spell."

"Thanks." Kelsea reveled in the warm welcome and settled on a rocking chair.

"I suppose you're here for the rodeo." A thin man with a brown bandanna tied around his neck scratched his chin, his weathered face not as lined as the first gentleman's. "Most everyone who's shopped here today is. You're the first who's talked to us, though."

The three of them nodded, and Kelsea liked them on the spot. She'd never known either of her grandfathers. These men seemed like the type who'd make their granddaughters feel special. Then she caught sight of the rodeo logo on the sweatshirt Barry lent her. "Oh, I have business with the Silver Horseshoe. I'm not with the rodeo. I'm Kelsea Carruthers with EverWind.

I borrowed this since my luggage took a ride without me."

While she had a captive audience, should she ask about Will Sullivan? Maybe find out what made him tick?

The three men exchanged glances. The second gentleman tugged on his brown bandanna. "It's a shame about the accident that claimed Rick and Polly Sullivan. They ran the ranch for some thirty years. Nicest couple you'd ever want to meet. Rick gave me this bandanna off his neck when I complained about the heat."

A low gasp alerted Kelsea to Will's presence. She turned and found an inscrutable expression shielding those dark eyes.

"We were just talking about your parents," she said.

The first gentleman rubbed the brim of his hat. "This is one of Rick's Stetsons. He gave it to me after a late night call to Polly's mare, Calico. Sweetest horse around."

"I didn't know that, Doc." Will nodded, his voice terse. "If you'll excuse Kelsea and me, I'm in a hurry."

"Rick always had a moment to shoot the breeze. I miss his laugh." The second man rose and patted Will on the shoulder. "He was so proud of what you accomplished in the rodeo."

Will separated himself from the group and tipped his hat. "Didn't know that, either, Marshall. Have a good rest of your afternoon."

Will walked inside, and Kelsea rose from her rocking chair. The three gents followed suit. She'd like to know them better. She'd especially like to find out if the third one ever spoke. "I hope we meet again before I leave Violet Ridge."

Doc scratched his chin. "Are you staying long?"

"A couple of weeks, give or take."

"I'm Doc Jenkins. I was the only horse vet in these parts for a good forty years. Retired now. This is Marshall Bayne." The gent with the brown bandanna smiled and nodded. "And that's his brother, Glenn."

"Nice to meet you." She rubbed her hands in front of the heater before wishing them well.

Kelsea entered the feed and seed. A cowbell above the wooden doorframe jangled, and the smell of alfalfa and tractor oil, not altogether unpleasant, assailed her. Rows of feed in big bulky bags occupied space on metal shelves. She spotted Will at a display of products near the front cash register. She wouldn't bother him unless necessary.

The back of the store caught her eye with its

selection of Western apparel and other goods. She headed in that direction but hadn't progressed far when an older woman, who could just as easily be sixty or forty, came her way.

"Welcome to Over and Dunne." The woman's appraising blue eyes made short work of Kelsea's sweatshirt and sandals, and she swung her coppery long braid to her back. "Let me guess. You're one of Ty's biggest fans, and you came for the rodeo. Whatever you don't find here, you can look for at Larkspur and Lace downtown."

Kelsea guessed her sandals and capris made her stand out more than most. "No and no."

"Hi, Regina. This is Kelsea. She's staying with Barry and me." Will approached from behind.

The clerk's eyes softened. "How's your uncle? He hasn't been around for a good month. If I didn't know better, I'd say he's been avoiding me."

"I'll tell him you asked after him and make sure he picks up the order next time."

"You do that." She smiled at Kelsea. "You let me know if there's anything I can do for you."

Kelsea headed toward the first display, the dull colors not to her liking. She moved on to the next rack. She flipped through the women's flannel shirts with a flick of the wrist.

"What's wrong with this one?" Will held up a yellow, orange and fuchsia plaid flannel shirt.

Kelsea winced. "It's a bit loud."

"I'm surprised. Since we've been in here, I haven't heard one *marvelous*, *wonderful* or *great* from you."

"I must be the touristy tourist ever to show up in this town." She glanced at her capris and sandals, which marked her as an outsider. Finding herself this isolated reminded her of her childhood and feelings best left in the past. "I want to blend in and have folks invite me back."

"Tourists come and go, although Violet Ridge does pride itself on repeat visitors."

Then she must be the problem. Suddenly, she didn't feel much like shopping.

She grabbed the first three shirts and then stopped. Was this a business expense? She didn't feel right charging clothes on her corporate credit card. "That Larkspur and Lace that Regina mentioned doesn't happen to be a consignment store, does it?"

"It's an upscale women's boutique." Will pointed to the front of the store. "Do you need a cart?"

"No, I'm good." She covered her left arm with two of the shirts and returned the third to the rack. With any luck, the airport would deliver her luggage to the ranch by the weekend and she'd have her clothes again.

But then again, she hadn't packed any flannel shirts. Considering she intended to travel to other ranches in the future, she'd best invest in three of them. She grabbed a basket from the end of an aisle and headed toward the hat display. She pressed the tag with her fingers. "Two hundred dollars?"

"A good Stetson lasts forever." Will cast a critical eye over the display and headed over to a rich, buttery-looking hat with a braided leather ribbon around the brim. "This one should fit."

Regina rolled a cart in their direction. "It looks like you need this." She faced Will. "My manager informed me about your order being incorrect. Sorry about the mix up. He's working on it, and it'll be ready when you are."

Why was a clerk apologizing for the manager? Her quizzical look must have caught Will's eye. "Regina's the owner."

Kelsea placed the three shirts in the cart. "Do you have anything on sale?" She stroked the supple leather on the brim before replacing it on the shelf. "Or on consignment?"

"Once someone buys one of these, they keep them pretty much forever, especially a Stetson. They're made in Colorado." Pride laced Regina's voice.

"You know." Kelsea's mind went back to the six weeks when she worked as a visual merchandiser for a department store until the holiday season ended. That had been her favorite of her former jobs. Dealing with colors and fabrics was soothing and fun. "If you reconfigured this space, it would be more aesthetically pleasing to the eye. Then, if you added some consignment items, I bet you could double your sales."

"Most of my business is from repeat customers. I haven't heard any complaints." Regina's arched eyebrow might have given others pause, but Kelsea wasn't daunted.

She forged forward with nothing to lose. "It's May, but you only have flannel shirts on display."

"Colorado has long winters, and this time of year, we have all four seasons in one week." Will and Regina exchanged a knowing glance.

He nodded as if to back up Regina's statement.

Four seasons in one week sounded good to her. She loved her home state of Georgia, but winter snow was as rare as a sale on her favorite heels. "I know, but look around your beautiful outdoors. Color is exploding around us, and that's reflected in our clothing choices. Some of your repeat customers might appreciate more affordable clothing. They might even make an extra trip if you display seasonal offerings."

The intercom system squeaked and buzzed, and then someone announced Regina's name overhead. "I'll keep that in mind." Regina pursed her lips and left.

Kelsea turned her attention back to the Stetson. The hat better last forever. Then she looked at the boots. If she wanted to make her way around the ranch, boots were a necessity. She narrowed down her selection to two.

"Which ones would you buy?"

"Both are good quality. I'll lend you some socks. We have plenty of extras. You want thick heavy socks while you break them in. You need to scuff them up so there's less chance of your feet getting blisters. Anything to bend and stretch the leather." His face flushed, as if he was uncomfortable offering that advice. "At least that's what my father always told me. Never had a blister from new boots yet."

Buying new shoes and then making them look old? It made little sense to her, but he was the expert. She selected the more colorful pair of turquoise boots with delicate white stitching that reached mid-calf.

She rolled her cart to the front of the store.

A comfortable silence took root and expanded. She realized that was Will's nature, and she found herself enjoying his company. The time with him was passing too quickly.

There was one customer ahead in line. She faced Will.

"What about dinner—"

"Did you find everything—"

Their voices overlapped. A worry line, one way too prominent for someone Will's age, creased his forehead. Whether she was the cause of that or overwork, she wasn't entirely sure. She'd find out the answer before she left. There was already quite a bit she knew about him, even though they hadn't been acquainted with each other for long. He preferred moments of quiet action, getting fully involved rather than standing on the sidelines and giving advice.

She motioned for him to go first.

"It's not fancy, but Howard's Grocery at the edge of town sells some toiletries. You can't miss it."

"Let me buy you dinner first. Some place where we can eat before the sun sets so I can drive my car back tonight."

"Some of the order's perishable. It has to be

refrigerated immediately, so I have to get back to the ranch. Do you have my number?"

"Don't forget. You have to drop me off at my rental first." She added him to her list of contacts and then paid for her purchases. "Thanks for taking time out of your day to introduce me to your hometown and Regina. My first taste of the real West." There was something about this country that called out to her. She loved soaking in the brightly colored buildings and the rugged spirit of the individual. "Since you're too busy to eat at one of Violet Ridge's dining establishments, I'll help you with your chores, and then we can cobble something together for dinner since Barry's out setting up the rodeo."

The surprise on his face as the cashier handed her the bag with her purchases was priceless. He was hosting her and allowing her to stay at his ranch. The least she could do was pull her weight. She'd learn about ranching and talk to him about the benefits of allowing EverWind to lease his land.

Then he'd sign the contract, and they'd go their separate ways.

WHILE WILL WAS gone that afternoon, someone, or something, had opened the gate to the goat pen behind his house. Most likely that would have been one of the two Nubian goats, which lived there with a miniature donkey who kept watch over them. Churro the burro was the only reason the animals hadn't escaped deeper into the ranch environs.

So far he'd led one of the goats and the donkey back into their pen, but Flake was, by far, the most stubborn of the three. He'd responded best to Will's mother. Over the past few months, he merely tolerated Will.

"Come on, Flake." He held out a handful of honey nut cereal, intent on luring the Nubian goat back into the pen.

Flake had other plans. He was above accepting a mere bribe in exchange for his newfound freedom.

It was almost as if the goat had a mind of his own.

Which he did.

Something butted him from behind, and Will spun around and found Snow there with a gleam in her blue eyes. The bits of cereal fell on the ground, and Snow gobbled them.

Goats 2. Will 0.

He closed his eyes, needing some time to compose a plan that would outwit the pair. He opened them upon hearing amused laughter. There in the fading glow of the setting sun stood Kelsea, her blue-checked flannel shirt worn over a plain white T-shirt and paired with jeans. She looked as comfortable in this outfit as she had in her capris, and her natural beauty shone through. She scuffed the toe of her new turquoise boots in the dirt.

"It seems wrong to get new shoes dirty." Kelsea frowned as she examined one boot, then the other.

"This speeds up the expansion of the leather quicker than general wear and tear. You want the boots to be durable for whatever ranch life throws at you. One of the best ways to scuff up boots is with sandpaper." He clicked his tongue for his next attempt to lure the goats back into their pen. "You've worked on a ranch before, haven't you?"

EverWind wouldn't have sent a total novice here. Would they?

"There's a first time for everything. So far, I'm loving the experience."

Will stopped chasing the goats and faced Kelsea, surprised at her being out here. Chasing butterflies seemed more her style than chasing goats. "How long have you worked for this company? How many contracts have you negotiated on their behalf?"

Had she intended for his uncle to be an easy target for her first sale?

If the company had sent a novice, what sort of service would they provide? This deal was looking worse by the minute, and he had half a mind to send her on her way without listening to her pitch.

The brown dirt flew off the toe of her boot. "I've spent six months learning the ins and outs of EverWind. During that time, I've traveled to wind turbine facilities near the Great Lakes. The company paid for my continuing education, including training in foundation planning and construction. It's gotten to the point where I see soil analysis in my sleep. Rest assured, I'm fully qualified to explain the advantages of EverWind over other companies of equal stature."

"And I'm supposed to trust a company that sent a salesperson with no prior experience on a ranch?" He lunged for Flake and almost fell flat on his face.

"Yes, you can trust them. EverWind is currently the fourth largest renewable energy supplier in this country. Their accomplishments are verifiable on the internet. Besides, how am I supposed to gain experience without someone giving me a chance?" She kicked the dirt with the tip of her boot again, and Flake scooted over to her. He sniffed her like he was searching for his next meal. She reached out and petted his side. Flake lapped up the attention like a lap dog. "Who's this sweet fellow?"

"Goats aren't normally referred to as *sweet*. That's Flake." He gestured to the one gnawing her boot. "And this is Snow. They belong in there rather than out here."

Recognition lit up her face. "Snowflake. How adorable. I love their names." *Of course she did.* "Did you name them?"

A while back, when Will had missed out on qualifying for the national year-end rodeo by two spots, he arrived home, out of sorts. Then he and Mom witnessed the goats' birth with the first snowflakes of the season drifting from the sky. That had pulled him out of his doldrums.

"Naming the animals was something my mother always looked forward to doing. She didn't name the cattle, though. Only the animals that have a permanent home on the ranch."

"What happened to her and your father?" Genuine concern radiated out of her. "If you don't mind telling me."

"She and my father were in a UTV accident last fall. Neither survived."

"I'm sorry."

That concern magnified into full-blown sympathy, and he sought an escape. It was time for those goats to return to their home, but he could say the same for Kelsea. "I'll be back in a minute. Make sure they don't go any farther."

Enough was enough. He ran to the shed for a length of rope. If food wouldn't lure them, he'd lead them into their pen on a tether. When he arrived back, they weren't there.

"Over here." His jaw dropped when he saw that Kelsea had corralled them without benefit of food or a rope. "By the way, I'm sorry if I made you feel uncomfortable."

"My story had nothing to do with my leaving. I went to the storage area and fetched this." He held up the length of rope. "Food wasn't getting me anywhere."

He was rather upset with himself that it took him so long to set aside his pride and go for the easiest solution.

Kelsea approached the miniature donkey. "What's this fellow's name?"

"Her name is Churro." He motioned for Kelsea to follow him to the supply area.

Cutting up a pear, he handed Kelsea a couple of slices. "Feed her these, and you'll be her new best friend."

Delight lit up her face. No, he couldn't fall under her spell, unlike the three animals in this pasture. She'd be leaving soon, maybe tomorrow. However, his uncle would banish him to the meadow with the cattle if she departed before he listened to her sales pitch. Still, he'd have to stay wary. He had some doubts about EverWind.

"They're adorable." She stayed near Churro's side, petting the miniature donkey. "I can see why you love this place so much. How large is your ranch?"

"It's a little over seventy-five-hundred acres, but the cattle need the room. I have three thousand Herefords with about thirty new calves."

Although if Will had his way, he'd like to expand. This past month he'd spent late nights coming up with a plan to introduce elk to his spread. With less of a carbon footprint and a high tolerance for the local environment, their easy manner was a natural choice for the area.

Elk would look mighty good in this valley, and the extra income would bolster the ranch's bottom line so he wouldn't have to lay off any of his cowhands. He'd mapped out a way for the cattle and elk to roam on different parts of the ranch. He'd also crunched the numbers. Even with an initial output for the animals, he should break even and show a substantial profit the second year. While paperwork wasn't his strong suit, he'd endure that for the sake of saving the ranch.

Flake must have been jealous of Churro. The goat butted Kelsea's leg, wanting a snack. "Hey there, I'm looking out for you. Is he allowed pear slices?"

"This is Flake's favorite treat." He transferred a handful of honey nut cereal into her palm, the softness of her skin rubbing against his. Awareness of her spread through him.

The goat nibbled at the treat, and her smile broadened. "It tickles."

Snow came over, looking for her share of the snack.

That smile. It brightened everything around her. This was crazy. He'd known people for a sight longer than a day and didn't yearn to see their smiling faces.

Take Lucky, for instance. His best friend was the younger brother he didn't have, but he never craved seeing his smile.

Oh, no. Will was supposed to meet Lucky at Domino's corral. He'd been so distracted by

Kelsea he'd forgotten all about his friend making a special trip out to the Silver Horseshoe.

This wouldn't do at all. He'd best get his mind off his fine guest and back to the ranch where it belonged.

CHAPTER FOUR

LUCKY APPEARED AT the gate. *Whew.* His best friend didn't look upset at Will's forgetfulness. Then again, his even nature was why he was so popular on the rodeo circuit. Lucky let himself into the pen and quickly shut the gate behind him. "Glad I found you. When you weren't at the corral, I figured something had come up."

"It slipped my mind that you were coming," Will admitted.

"Kelsea, isn't it?" Lucky doffed his Stetson and smiled at her. "It's a pleasure to see you again."

"Will's been wonderful in allowing me to stay at his house. Otherwise I'd be driving five hours a day to and from Grand Junction." Kelsea returned Lucky's smile. "Can I come with you to visit Domino?"

It wouldn't surprise Will if Kelsea turned out to be a horse whisperer like Lucky, who had a reputation around the rodeo circuit as one. She sure had a way with animals. She was pretty and smart—and Will didn't like the direction his thoughts were heading.

"That's a good idea." Lucky placed his hat back on his ruffled blond hair. "I'd like to see Domino around someone he doesn't know."

Will would do pretty much anything to find out what was troubling his stallion, even spending time with Kelsea. Then again, getting to know her personally wasn't a sacrifice.

With a stiff nod, he led them to Domino's pasture. The stallion whinnied and trotted over to Will, nudging his arm with his muzzle. He stroked his favorite horse's silky coat. "Hey, there."

Will reached into his coat pocket for the bits of watermelon rind he always kept there. The stallion loved the snack, but it seemed like the horse was taking it to be polite rather than with gusto. He transferred the pieces to Lucky, who stood back, his arms folded, his gray eyes discerning. "How long has he been like this?"

"About six months." *Give or take*. That was when he'd finally arranged for Domino to come live on the ranch. There were times he'd spruce up, but then he'd lapse back into this dejected state.

"He seems forlorn." Lucky stepped aside and watched Domino approach Kelsea.

A flicker of the stallion's tail was more than Will had seen in some time. Even the lights in Domino's eyes seemed brighter. The horse looked around Kelsea and then quieted once more. Will glanced that way and found his foreman, Steve, riding away on Calico.

Will turned back to Lucky. "The vet can't find anything wrong with him. He's physically sound."

Lucky ran his hand over the horse's flank. "He's lost weight since you left the rodeo."

If Will didn't spend almost every waking hour taking care of some aspect of the ranch, he might have had more time to miss the rodeo and notice his horse's downward spiral. As it was, he hadn't much time to do anything but ride range. He ached at not saddling the stallion and taking long rides at night after completing his chores, but Domino wasn't trained for ranch life. Maybe it was time to call the farrier and change his shoes for this setting.

Or did Domino miss the rodeo? Too often, when they arrived at a new site, Will unloaded the quarter horse from the trailer and then gauged his condition. Domino appeared calm and stoic instead of rippling with excitement. Will always fretted that the stallion had caught some equine illness. Then, when it was showtime, Domino came alive and acted like a different horse. His ears perked up, and the desire to win coursed through him. He lived for the excitement of the rodeo and the roar of the crowd.

Was it selfish to have him stay on the ranch rather than let him live his best life? Had Will been relegating him to a life that wasn't right for him?

Reining in Domino's personality would be more damaging in the long run. Will had to consider the horse's well-being first.

He swallowed the rock in his throat. "Lucky, do you think Domino would benefit from returning to the rodeo?"

Lucky glanced at his friend. "Are you considering running the ranch and riding in the rodeo? I know that's done—"

"No," Will cut him off. "I'm just considering what's best for him."

If that meant the stallion returned to his natural environment with another rider, so be it.

"The bond between you and Domino is as obvious as the horns on Flake's head." Kelsea scuffed her boot in the dirt. "I don't understand something. Why won't you attend the rodeo in town?"

Lucky came over and bumped Will's elbow.

"I thought you were joking. Sabrina will be devastated if you don't come."

"Who's Sabrina?" Kelsea asked.

"She's like a sister to us and the best rodeo clown around," Lucky said. "She and Will can turn a horse on a dime."

"It's calving season." Those repetitious words were starting to sound like a weak excuse, and Will didn't want to disappoint his best friends.

Lucky glanced at his watch. "I have a meeting with my advertising sponsor. I'll check in later." He fed the horse the rest of the watermelon rind and glanced at Kelsea, then Will. "I'll reserve two tickets instead of one. You need a little fun now and then."

No sooner did Lucky exit through the gate than Kelsea turned to him. "Your friends expect you to go."

The light breeze caught her blond hair. It already seemed as though she fit right in, but she didn't have ties to this place like he did. Those ties had been the subject of an argument between him and his father the last time he'd visited before the accident. Dad had taken in Jody and Jerome, two new employees. Will had vehemently objected, pointing out all that needed updating. And that pretty much covered everything on the ranch. Even the tractor was held together with parts from the older one.

Jody and Jerome need this, Will. Never underestimate what a person will do for a chance and a warm bed. I promised them a home, and a man's word is his bond.

Will had scoffed at the sentiment. He jammed his hands in his pockets and stormed away. He'd headed inside the ranch house, wanting to rest up for the end of the season. The next day, he left for the rodeo without setting things right with his father. A few weeks later, he received Steve's call delivering the fateful news.

The stern words to his father could never be taken back. Hadn't he learned anything? After the accident, Will had vowed to himself that he'd carry out his father's pledge, adopting it as his own. He dialed back his attitude and resolved to make good on his own promise to Kelsea about EverWind.

"I'll see if Uncle Barry can take you to the rodeo. Once he and the cowhands are finished with their duties and the rodeo's done, the ranch will be operating with a full staff again. Then I'll be able to listen to your sales pitch about the wind turbines."

"With an open mind?"

He extended his hand, and she clasped his,

the contact going on too long for his liking. Something about her challenged him when he needed all his energy focused on plans to make the Silver Horseshoe the best midsize ranch around. Under his guidance, he wanted it to thrive rather than getting by on duct tape and dreams. These turbines could provide extra revenue, so he could do just that. That alone made Kelsea's presentation worth his time. "You have my word."

"I'll hold you to that." She pumped his hand once more. Tingles sparked up and down his arm on account of this optimistic dynamo. "In return, you have my word I'll knock your socks off with my presentation. In the meantime, can I walk around the ranch and get a feel for the land? Collect some soil samples and pictures?"

He agreed, and she took her leave. Why had he added another vow to his long list? He already had enough promises to keep.

Kelsea passed the shed where the UTV was stored, along with the ranch's mechanical gadgets and gizmos. Lyle, a ranch hand, was loading the vehicle with a toolbox, and Rocket bounded over to her.

"Evening. Barry just returned from the arena and sent me out here to tell you he's making dinner tonight, after all. It'll be ready in an hour." Kelsea called out.

Nearing sixty and tall, Lyle turned his neck from side to side and then realized she was addressing him. His ruddy, tanned cheeks contained a hint of red. "Evening, ma'am." He tipped his hat in her direction, a thatch of gray hair crossing his forehead. "Thank you kindly for the message, but I'm headed to the southern part of the ranch to repair some fence."

"Then I should tell Barry not to expect you for dinner?"

"Hmm." He hefted the toolbox into the back of the vehicle. "It won't take long. Ask him to set a plate aside for me. I'll be back in a couple of hours."

"Can I go with you? Will granted me permission to do some soil sampling." She pointed toward the ranch house. "I need to grab my kit, but I can be back in two shakes of a lamb's tail." Or a donkey or goat, as the case may be.

He seemed like a deer caught in the headlights but recovered. "I'll check with Will first." He reached inside the UTV for something that looked like a walkie-talkie.

"What's that?" Kelsea asked.

"It's a satellite phone."

A new concept for her, she listened as Will

approved Lyle's request. Kelsea motioned to Lyle she'd be right back. Thank goodness she'd brought the kit in her carry-on or she'd have had to request a new one. With her camera loaded in her backpack alongside her kit and water bottle, she returned in record time. Relief that he hadn't left without her reassured her of how much this job meant to her.

"So, Will gave his okay to my going with you?"

"Yep. He can't come with us since he's checking on a cow that's been off her feed. Said not to wait up for him."

Lyle ordered Rocket to stay behind, and the border collie's tail lowered in disappointment.

The breeze ruffled her hair while Lyle drove the UTV. The evening sun created a glow over the meadows. "It's so beautiful here." Lyle grunted his assent. A man of few words, he seemed like the uncle everyone counted on for a sage opinion. "Have you ever seen such vivid colors anywhere else?"

"Desert's mighty pretty, too." He swerved around a pothole, and Kelsea held onto the dash. "Colorado beats all, though. And this ranch is pretty special. Rick Sullivan was a good person. Same as his wife, Polly."

Kelsea thought to ask him about Will, but

held her tongue. Problem was she could find herself getting attached to Colorado and its residents quite easily. That wouldn't serve her purpose.

"How long have you worked at the Silver Horseshoe?"

"Going on ten years. This was the fifteenth place I applied to. Rick promised I could stay here long as I like." He parked the UTV near a fence that needed repair, the gaping hole obvious even to her untrained eye. "I'll watch out for dangerous wildlife. If you see any snakes slithering on the ground, whistle. I'll do the same. Also, look out for coyotes or wolves. Anything of that sort. Those are the main predators in these parts."

That was a pretty frightening list, but she thanked him for the heads-up. He hurried toward the fence with his toolbox. Kelsea collected her gear and snapped pictures. Right away, she had a strong feeling this part of the ranch wouldn't suit EverWind's needs. But she wanted a feel for the whole ranch before she came to any conclusions. Still, she'd wait for confirmation from the lead engineer.

Once she finished collecting the soil samples, she whipped out her cell. Thankfully, the coverage extended out here. She texted her manager and the engineer the best of the photos and received an out-of-office reply. Then she double-checked her voice mail and texts. Her father still hadn't replied. A busy neurosurgeon, he often relegated tasks like that to his assistant, but neither had responded to her. Frustration bubbled up at the slight.

Converting the time difference, she decided to call him. No answer. She dashed off a text, letting him know she was now staying at the ranch and starting on her new assignment.

Lyle motioned he'd finished, and Kelsea glanced at her phone one last time before meeting him at the UTV.

THE DAY HAD started with Lyle informing Will of the hole in the pasture fence. Over coffee, Barry had let him know they needed him, Jody and Jerome at the arena again. Seemed as though they'd all be occupied until the start of the rodeo.

Short-staffed, Will then headed out on Tuxedo for the daily chores with the calves. With Rocket's help, he'd moved them and the cows to a grassy incline and checked each, making notes on their progress, including the one who'd kept him out late last night. After he got her to other side of the pasture, she began eating again. Now he wanted a hot shower and dinner, but caring for Tux came first. He stopped and checked on the ginger stable cat, Endora, who allowed a brief spell of attention before meandering her way to the loft. Then he removed Tux's saddle and placed it on the rack. He hung the bridle reins before giving the quarter horse a thorough brushing. "You did good today. Dad would have been proud."

He fed the gelding a carrot and patted his rump. The soft whinny let Will know he'd been doing his job without expecting any reward.

"What do you think, Tux?" Will started mucking out Tux's stall. He disposed of the old straw and returned with a fresh bundle. "Why didn't Dad tell me how much trouble the ranch is in?"

His father hadn't confided the extent of the financial downfall and the omission had stuck with Will. He fluffed the bedding with a pitchfork and prepared feed for the eight horses in the stable. Water splashed in the trough when a voice came from the doorway.

"Hey, there, pardner. I heard you have a room for a tired traveler."

At last, his friend Sabrina, more like a sister really, had arrived. Good thing as the rodeo started tomorrow and no doubt she'd be busy.

He set down the water bucket and faced her with a grin. She never changed. Her long chestnut hair was pulled back in a braid, and she stood tall in her boots. That familiar jean jacket with bright turquoise embellishments was worn at the elbows. "Where have you been keeping yourself?"

"Here and there." She dropped her duffel and carefully laid her Stetson on the bag before rushing over and embracing him. "Like I wouldn't come and visit my favorite rodeo star."

"I won't tell Lucky you said that." He laughed and hugged her. "You're a sight for sore eyes. I've missed you so much."

Will caught sight of Kelsea entering the stable, and he broke away from Sabrina. "Hi, Kelsea."

"I was walking back from the bunkhouse when I saw a car pull up." Kelsea's smile reached her eyes. "I was wondering whether I should set one more place for dinner."

"I'm Sabrina MacGrath. Nice to meet you. If you have extra, I'd love to stay for dinner." Sabrina moved toward her duffel, but Will beat her to it, hefting it over his shoulder. Sabrina glanced at Will, then at Kelsea, unasked questions all over her expressive face. "Are you new to the Silver Horseshoe?"

"Yes. I'm here on business. I'm Kelsea Carruthers, and I work for EverWind." Kelsea crossed over and shook Sabrina's hand. "My company wants to lease some of the ranch land for wind turbines. Will and Barry are being generous hosts and allowing me to stay here since the hotels are full on account of the rodeo."

"Will's like a brother to me. Lucky, too. They're my good luck charms." Sabrina winked at Will.

"He and Lucky speak highly of you."

Sabrina glanced at Will. "He hasn't mentioned you to me." That dare in her brown eyes was one of the reasons she excelled as a rodeo clown. There weren't many women doing the job, although, that number was now growing by leaps and bounds as it should. "Will, this is what I'm talking about when I ask you if there are any exciting developments at the ranch."

His defenses prickled. "You're a hard person to track down, Sabrina. I expected you yesterday." He couldn't have been more protective of her if she'd been his biological sister. "Glad you finally arrived in one piece."

"Not so fast, mister. I've been talking to Lucky. What's this about not attending the rodeo?" Sabrina faced Kelsea again and donned her Stetson. "But maybe we should eat dinner first and then talk."

"For the record, I also think you'd regret not attending the rodeo tomorrow night." Kelsea tapped her boot on the topsoil.

How was he outnumbered at his own ranch by two women who hadn't met each other before?

"I think we're going to be best friends. Of course, any *friend* of Will's is a friend of mine." Sabrina grinned and tipped back her cream-colored hat.

"I'm his business associate, and EverWind's newest sales representative." Kelsea asserted her title, giving Will some pause. He'd mistaken her interest in the ranch for something more personal. He'd best remember she was here on business.

"Uh-huh." Sabrina nodded and glanced at Will. "We have a lot of catching up to do."

"Starting with why you're a day late and didn't return my texts." Sometimes a good offense was the best strategy to deflect attention away from yourself, and Will wanted to shed this unwanted scrutiny.

"First, have some pity for an old friend and feed me. I'm starving." Sabrina clasped her hands in supplication as thunder rumbled in the yard.

"After I check on Domino, I'll fire up the grill if the rain hasn't started." Down three cowhands, Will had a responsibility to his animals before he fed himself or his guests.

"Oh, I cooked dinner." Kelsea walked over to Tux and clenched her fist, lightly bumping his muzzle the way he'd taught her. Tuxedo must have liked the attention, as he nudged her in a blatant attempt for more affection. "Thank goodness my luggage finally arrived today. While I was in Grand Junction, I picked up some staples. I made my grandmother's chicken potpie as a thank-you for letting me stay. I took the bigger pie over to the bunkhouse, and Lyle and Kurt gave me a tour. No matter how many times I tell them to call me Kelsea, they still say ma'am. They're so sweet."

Sweet wasn't usually a word he'd use for rough cowboys. If he didn't do something, and soon, the cowhands would vote to keep Kelsea on the ranch and send him packing. In no time, she'd entranced his uncle, his cowhands and his horses. All that on top of being pretty and smart. Somehow, he had to prevent her from working her magic on him as well.

Sabrina planted her hat on her head and then

glanced at Kelsea. "No matter why you're here, I think you're a great addition to the Silver Horseshoe."

Sabrina's eyes gleamed. He'd better think of a new offensive strategy for after dinner, and fast.

CHAPTER FIVE

THE NEXT MORNING, Kelsea stumbled sleepily into Will's kitchen, the fresh aroma of coffee infusing her with quiet happiness. Not that she needed caffeine to bolster her excitement level. Tonight was the first night of the Violet Ridge Roundup Rodeo, and she had a front-row ticket thanks to Lucky and Sabrina. Warm apple muffins with cinnamon streusel occupied space on the table, and whole eggs rested in a bowl on the counter. The crisp bacon sizzled on the stove, close to being finished. Her gaze locked on the full coffeepot. She reached for an earthenware mug but paused and glanced around. The genial Barry was nowhere in sight, although she was sure that was his phone next to the coffeemaker. "Barry?"

No response. She repeated his name. A bleary-eyed Barry appeared with a tissue in hand. "Is the bacon ready?" He honked into the tissue and threw it in the trash. Then he reached into his jacket pocket for another one.

"Are you sick?" She went over, and his forehead was burning up. "You shouldn't be cooking. You need to go back to bed and rest. Does Will know you're ill?"

"Will always makes his own breakfast. He's already out tending to the calves. Sabrina made the muffins before she departed for the arena." Barry leaned against the doorframe, looking as though a stiff wind would knock him over. "I have to finish making the eggs and bacon for the cowhands."

"I've been a short-order cook and a waitress." And too many other jobs to count. "I'll handle the cowhands, and you rest."

"I'm not sick." Barry sneezed and wobbled before Kelsea reached him.

She guided him into the living room. "You most certainly are. I'll fix breakfast and take it over to the bunkhouse."

"They're fussy about their eggs." Barry sat on the couch and wheezed. "I need a minute, then I'll be good as new."

"You need at least a day in bed. If you get any worse, call your doctor." Kelsea handed him the box of tissues from the mantel.

"I have to frost the Texas sheet cakes at the arena and decorate the booth for tonight's fundraiser. We're raising money for early childhood education in the county. The kids are counting on me. This is big for them. Really, really big." He reached for the tissue and popped out two, followed by a third.

"You're in no condition to do anything of the sort. I'll frost the cakes and help with the booth." Frosting cakes or spending the day in the zoning office examining the maps for egress routes? That was a no-brainer. She much preferred interacting with the customer and his world than poring over dusty maps.

She enjoyed working with one person in particular, the enigmatic cowboy who owned the Silver Horseshoe. Once the rodeo was over, she hoped to wow him with her pitch.

Business professionals should keep a healthy distance from their potential clients.

"I can't ask you to do that." Barry's eyelids lowered to half-moons, and he looked as though he would fall asleep sitting up on the couch.

"You're not asking; I'm volunteering. Now, how do the cowhands like their eggs?"

She thought she made out something about sunny-side up before Barry's eyes closed. She found a nearby blanket and covered him. Humming, she prepared the eggs and removed the bacon from the stove. Gathering the food, she headed to the bunkhouse. Jody and Jerome answered the door.

"Morning, ma'am. Where's Barry?" Jody tipped his Stetson in her direction.

"Kelsea, not ma'am." She was fighting a cattle stampede, so she gave up for now. "He's not feeling well."

She held up the basket and delivered it to the brothers. "Thank you, ma— Um, Kelsea."

"That's much better." A wide smile spread across her face as Jerome snatched a muffin from the basket. "I don't suppose either of you could help me at the arena today?"

The brothers glanced at each other and shook their heads. "Sorry, ma— I mean Kelsea. We volunteered earlier this week, but we have to get back to our ranch duties." Jody moved the basket so his brother couldn't snatch a second muffin. "I'll be riding range today and Jerome will be mixing the feed. When he's done with that, he'll take over the cooking for the next few days."

"Got it." She started down the steps of the bunkhouse but hesitated, her hand on the rail. Then she turned back around. "Tell Will about his uncle, okay?"

Kelsea checked on Barry, who woke when she entered the room. "Ah, that power nap hit the spot. I'm on the mend."

A wheezy cough betrayed his lie.

"Where am I supposed to go when I arrive at the arena?" Kelsea said, putting on her best stern look to match her voice.

"It's too much for one person if you haven't done it before." Barry lay back on the couch. "You won't finish in time if I'm not there to help."

Then she'd simply have to recruit more workers. While it would have been fun to have Will beside her, his seriousness balancing out her more happy-go-lucky self, the ranch would keep him busy until he attended the rodeo tonight. A plan shaped up, and she had a sneaking suspicion of where she could find three workers.

"Leave it to me." She retrieved his phone from the kitchen. "My only request is that you send me your frosting recipe."

She changed from her maxi skirt into more serviceable jeans and flannel. Something was off about her outfit. She rifled through her suitcase until she found a silk scarf with a bright pattern and wove it through the belt loops for a touch of color. The larkspur on her nightstand caught her eye. She picked one and wove the purple flower into her hat brim.

After reviewing the recipe with Barry, she drove her rental to the Over and Dunne Feed and Seed. This day away from the ranch would give her a chance to get acquainted with the townspeople. In the long run, better connections with the community would benefit Ever-Wind as much as the contract itself.

At least that would be her story if her boss asked about the latest delay. She only hoped Mr. Mulroney agreed about the positive PR campaign.

She walked toward the entrance of the feed and seed. Sure enough, the three gents, as she called them in her mind, already occupied their rocking chairs to observe the comings and goings of the day.

"Howdy, ma'am." Doc Jenkins tipped his Stetson in her direction. "Always a pleasure when a pretty lady visits us, especially at the start of the day. Did Regina's new employee mess up Will's order again?"

They remembered her, and that made her happier than it should have.

"That's not why I'm here." She held up the

basket of muffins and a thermos of coffee. "I come bearing gifts in exchange for favors."

She lifted the napkin, allowing the aroma of freshly baked muffins to waft in their direction. They listened while she explained her mission for the day. Then they huddled in the corner, their voices too low for her to hear.

Doc separated from the group, a hank of his white hair visible under the Stetson. "You drive an easy bargain, and we'd love to help."

The other two came over and nodded. The man with the dour expression pursed his lips. "Doc and Marshall outvoted me." He flexed his gnarled hands. "It won't be the last time."

"Don't mind my brother. Glenn's ornery, that's all. We should be thanking you, what with muffins and cake coming our way." Marshall, the jovial one with twinkling blue eyes, plucked off the top muffin. "We're getting free cake, right?"

She chuckled, and they joined in the laughter. Doc accepted a muffin and savored the first bite. "Shaking things up will be good for us. Change of scenery won't hurt, either. Thanks for asking."

"I didn't expect you to be this amenable." This type of tight-knit camaraderie wasn't what Kelsea was used to, but she liked it. "Thank you."

"I'll drive the three of us in my truck." Doc nodded to the other two, and they followed Kelsea.

With her volunteers accounted for, she headed to the arena. Within minutes, the four of them settled into a rhythm in the clubhouse-concession kitchen area. The rest of the morning passed by in a blur. The three gents baked cakes while she prepared the fudgy icing. After frosting the last corner of the cake, she licked the spoon, the delicious chocolate smooth and creamy. Then she placed it in the dishwasher. She loved getting to know the three gents, even Glenn with his slightly sour disposition.

After they finished cutting the cakes into smaller square pieces, they loaded the carts and rolled them from the clubhouse to the concession stands. Kelsea stood back and frowned. At the farthest end from the entrance, their booth, sponsored by the town of Violet Ridge, was rather blah. It needed pizzazz, something to stand out in the crowd. Glenn and Marshall stood to the side, enjoying their squares of Texas sheet cake, so she pulled Doc aside and ran her idea by him. He nodded, and they went to work.

Less than two hours later, she smiled at the

improvements when the first people filed into the rodeo.

"Free cake! Get your free cake!" Marshall hawked their booth and turned to Kelsea. "Bet you didn't know I worked as an auctioneer for fifty years, did you? Remind me to tell you about the time I sold someone's dentures along with their sheep."

"Not that old story again. I've heard it twenty times," Glenn grumbled while unpacking plastic-wrapped spork and napkin sets.

"Kelsea hasn't heard all my stories from my auction days." Marshall grinned. He juggled the can for donations at the young man carrying a toddler. "Every dollar goes toward preschool education for those living in town or the sur-rounding counties."

Several such cans and donation boxes occu-pied prominent space at the booth, made more colorful with lights in the shape of jalapeños. Marshall's earlier mention at the feed and seed of getting paid with homemade cake had given Kelsea an idea that she'd passed along to the rodeo management. They agreed with her suggestion of asking for donations rather than charging for the cake.

Kelsea arranged the cake squares on the

counter and tapped her toes to the lively country music from the speakers. What a fun vibe! In Georgia, she'd seen advertisements for the rodeo, but she'd never even dreamed she'd attend one. Her father owned season tickets for the Atlanta Symphony Orchestra, and he frowned on athletic events. He'd always elaborate on the risk of long-term injuries from contact sports. What he'd say about Will and his past participation in the rodeo was something Kelsea wouldn't ask once he finally returned her texts or called.

Business boomed, and they passed out Texas sheet cake to what must have been half the town. A sea of unfamiliar faces swamped the booth, but the sea parted and revealed a steady set of brown eyes attached to a familiar face. Will.

A ping of attraction tickled her stomach. His presence dominated the booth, and he tilted his head at her. "Do you have a minute? I understand if you're busy," Will said.

"I can spare one." She excused herself, leaving Doc in charge.

"I wasn't sure you'd come." Her voice sounded too relieved. She dialed down her joy. Besides, it wasn't that she was happy to see Will; she was happy to see a familiar face, that was all. "How's your uncle?"

He fidgeted with his hat. "Uncle Barry's resting. His temperature's down, and I made him a bowl of chicken soup."

"You could have texted me that." She mimicked that action with her thumbs. Then she softened. "I'm glad he's feeling better, although you didn't need to make a special trip here to tell me that in person."

"Same thing goes for you, but in reverse. Why didn't you text me about my uncle's illness?" Frustration laced his words. She knew that had less to do with her and more with his concern for his uncle.

"I think the two of you need to work on your communication rather than blaming me. If that's impacting your relationship, that's on you. Relationships take two people to work. Trust me, I know that from experience." Her father proved that to her over and over, but Will needed to stop assuming responsibility for everything and enjoy his time at the rodeo. She dragged him back to the booth. "Later tonight, you can tell Barry about some of our changes. The cake is free although donations for the preschool assistance program are welcome. I also set up a T-shirt order form. They'll feature the rodeo logo along with the year and tagline. It'll be another fundraiser for the preschool program. People can order through the scanned code or use the hard copy form. They'll arrive next week."

"Seems to me like you're doing everything except giving me your pitch."

"I went ahead and sent in the soil sample, which should be analyzed soon. And you were the one who asked me to wait until after the rodeo. Taking care of a ranch while you're down three cowhands is a big responsibility. Besides, serving Violet Ridge is part of my job." *In a roundabout way.* "And, the three gents graciously stepped in and helped."

"Who?"

She bumped her head with her palm. "That's what I've started calling Doc, Marshall and Glenn."

A young woman with a toddler approached them and smiled at Kelsea. She held up her slice of cake, and her toddler lunged for it. "She'll be in preschool too soon, and I love this idea. What a win for the community. Thank you."

The woman moved on to the next booth. Marshall caught her eye and held up both thumbs, leaving her little doubt he'd been raving about her. That suspicion was confirmed when another person also came over and congratulated her on her idea. Kelsea flushed. She wasn't doing this to receive accolades; she'd done it for Barry and because the town was growing on her.

Country music stopped blaring through the speakers for an announcement about the night's high school rodeo exhibition. Excitement welled up in her.

"Since your uncle's improving, I hope you stay and experience the rest of the rodeo. You've been doing so much at the ranch. You need some fun. And when it's all over and you have everyone home again, maybe you can show me around the acres so I can better prepare my remarks tailored to what I see. I'll be gone before you know it."

Another reminder of her limited time in Violet Ridge even though it already appeared that she'd made more progress finding a place to belong here than in carving a niche in her family for the past twenty-seven years.

"I promise you I'll show you the ranch as soon as possible."

Will's word meant something. Trouble was

the cowboy was beginning to mean something to her. She wouldn't have responded the same way to seeing Barry or any of the cowhands. She had to stem this growing attraction since she'd move on to a brand-new adventure too soon.

"Then I promise if you come to the main event tomorrow night, it'll be an evening to remember. You can teach me about the rodeo, and I'll make sure you smile at least once," she said.

Will needed some levity while she was here. Maybe she was the one who could provide some spring sunshine in his life.

ON THIS COOL Saturday evening, Will entered the fairgrounds for the Violet Ridge Roundup Rodeo. Last night had marked the first time since he'd started shaving that he'd entered the rodeo grounds as a spectator rather than a participant. If it weren't for Kelsea and his friends, he'd be back on the Silver Horseshoe, rounding up the cattle. A certain blonde was very persuasive when she wanted to be. That concerned him almost as much as his absence at the ranch for two consecutive evenings.

Maybe everyone was right, though, about him needing time away from the ranch. How had his father managed the ranch and retained his sense of humor?

Overhead speakers blared an instrumental country music song, heavy on the fiddles. Hay lined the mucky topsoil, absorbing the moisture from the chilly rain that had fallen overnight. Smiles lined the faces of almost everyone pouring into the Irwin Arena on the outskirts of town.

Kelsea passed through the metal detector, and then he showed his ticket to the attendant for scanning. The female security guard inspected Kelsea's purse, then they forged forward. Kelsea didn't blend into the crowd; she stood out like a thoroughbred. Nearly everyone else matched their jeans with a T-shirt and flannel. Like others, he wore a silver belt buckle from winning the all-around event at a regional rodeo last year. In contrast, Kelsea's breezy style made her noticeable like fireweed, one of his favorite flowers. She paired a casual floral dress with a denim jacket and her new cowboy boots. The effect was spectacular. When they'd met at his truck a half-hour ago, his jaw had almost dropped. He'd opened the passenger door for her before heading to the driver's side, muttering about goodbyes before he did something foolish like tell her how beautiful she looked. She didn't live here in Violet Ridge and would be departing in a short while. Goodbyes always came way too soon.

Kelsea reached for Will's arm, her soft skin caressing his flannel shirt. "My first rodeo! Yesterday evening I only heard the goings-on since I was at the booth the whole time. At last, I get to fully experience it. Isn't this the best night ever? What's first?" She sniffed the air. "Please say it's dinner."

His stomach growled at the tangy scent of barbecue. "We have enough time for our meal before tonight's main draw."

She led the way toward the concession area where people congregated around picnic tables, their plates filled high with barbecue or bison burgers. Vendors hawked everything from chili to barbecue to prairie oysters. Tonight the community booth where Kelsea had given out free cake last night was occupied with workers giving out miniature toy horses and horseshoes.

She squealed with delight at a nearby booth. "I didn't expect seafood. I love oysters, and that would hit the spot."

He neared her ear, and explained that prairie

oysters had to do with a certain part of a bull's anatomy rather than seafood.

She shuddered. "Those are a hard pass from me then."

After ordering barbecue sandwiches, they found two unoccupied seats and settled in. Will tried hard not to stare at the blanketflower she'd woven through her hat brim. Where she'd picked one that bloomed this early, he didn't know, as they usually started blooming next month.

She asked plenty of questions about ranch life while eating their food. He wasn't surprised she loved her meal.

"Make sure you drink plenty of water." What he'd hoped would sound like a casual comment came out rather harsh.

Kelsea paused with her bottle of water poised in front of her mouth.

"I can't tell if you're only brusque with people you like or don't like." She sipped her water until the bottle was empty.

She crossed to a recycling container, and then they headed to the main arena. They settled in their seats, and she turned to him. "Well, which is it?"

He wouldn't pretend to not know what she meant.

"I—"

Three people filed past them into their make-shift seats on the other side of him and Kelsea, which prevented him from answering. Everyone started settling down while an announcer thanked the local sponsors.

A scratchy squeal came through the loud-speakers, eliciting groans. The announcer finished his remarks while a cowboy checked the barrels in the dirt-packed oval. Will waited for some feeling to sweep over him, some pull of regret, but it was almost a relief to be in the audience rather than in the chute.

His hips certainly didn't miss the action. That realization brought a sense of something that bordered on pure happiness.

"What's happening?" Kelsea raised her voice, and he consulted his program.

"The timed events. They start with bareback bronc racing, followed by barrel racing and end with the team roping."

The lights went out before spotlights flickered on, showcasing the arena. The crowd became more raucous, and many waved signs of support for Ty Darling. He was currently atop the leaderboard with Lucky in second. The cheering made it next to impossible to think. People clapped while the color guard marched toward the center of the oval, kicking off the nighttime festivities.

"This is so much fun." Her bright smile lit up the place.

"Yeah." To his surprise, he was telling the truth. Some of his tenseness melted away. "I probably needed a night away from the ranch."

"Only probably?" She chuckled. "Barry and Jody would have lassoed you and delivered you to the arena if you hadn't come."

The master of ceremonies tapped the mic. "Five minutes until showtime! Be sure to visit our concessions and stay between events for a special presentation you won't want to miss."

One of the rodeo clowns came out and heckled the emcee before running to the sidelines. Sabrina then drove out in a long white convertible and waved at the crowd. Will chuckled at Sabrina's antics, her features easily recognizable under the layers of makeup. Her checked shirt and baggy pants fit right into the festivities. The audience lapped it up.

"That's Sabrina, isn't it? Why is she dressed like a clown?"

"Rodeo clowns entertain the crowd between acts. She's one of the best. After this, she'll hunker down in one of the barrels, ready in a split second if a contestant falls off and needs her help escaping from a bull."

The crowd roared at Sabrina's act with laughter echoing up to the rafters. While Will had been on the receiving end of her help, he'd had little occasion to see Sabrina from this side of the arena. In the past, he'd always been backstage waiting or in the chute while she delivered her performance.

His calf muscle started aching. Just one more sign he'd left the rodeo at the right time before he incurred any permanent injury. Perhaps a forced goodbye might have a hidden benefit.

The lights went out, and the crowd pummeled the ground with their boots. Tremors rocked the arena. Music blared a loud welcome to the main event, and four show lights circled the red dirt. Sabrina and the car disappeared, and the master of ceremonies greeted everyone. Cheers rose to a crescendo as the first bareback rider took center stage.

Kelsea neared him, her soft scent tickling his nose. She brought her lips near his ear. "Tell me more about the sport."

Will faced her. The happiness in her eyes caught him by surprise. She seemed as taken aback by whatever this was between them as he was. What would it be like to kiss her and see joy reflected there? The noise of the crowd broke the spell, and he blinked back any regret. "Bareback bronc riding is one of the hardest events. It's like he's riding a jackhammer. He's trying to stay on the horse for eight seconds, and he's judged based on his technique. They take agility, speed and power into account. I predict he'll score around an eighty."

The crowd greeted the seventy-nine on the scoreboard with whistles and approval, and the next rider prepared for action. In less than four seconds, he fell off his horse, landing on his head. Sabrina shot out of the barrel and distracted the horse until the rider struggled to his feet and hurried over the fence.

"Is he okay? Does he have a concussion?" Her genuine concern came through, and her nails dug into Will's forearm through the layers of flannel.

"He should be fine. His training and experience are paying off. See, he's waving to the audience. There's an element of risk, but there's a connection between the horse and the rider adjusting to and respecting each other that's like nothing else." Bareback bronc riding was adrenaline pumping. Will preferred barrel racing where he and Domino worked in sync, performing for the crowds while pushing their own limits.

Now, he was adjusting to the steady day-in, day-out tasks while he rode under the open sky. That and taking care of what was entrusted to him. Maybe it wasn't the rodeo he missed as much as the close bond between him and Domino, something he'd lost under the weight of the extra responsibility.

Kelsea's words brought him back to the arena. "My father would check his pupils and ask him to recite every sixth letter of the alphabet."

"I'm not sure I could do that, and I'm in the audience rather than participating. Why would your father do that?"

"F-l-r-x." Kelsea released Will's arm and sat back while the announcer introduced the next rider. "That's every sixth letter. My father is a neurosurgeon, and his life revolves around medicine, including sports injuries."

At that moment, the announcer introduced Lucky. Kelsea jumped to her feet and raised two fingers to her mouth, letting out a huge catcall whistle. Then she glanced at Will. "Get on your feet! It's time to support your friend."

She was right. Even though Will no longer rode professionally, Lucky did, and support was everything. He jumped out of his seat and waved his Stetson. "Come on, Lucky! Make it to the bell."

Lucky shot out of the chute. The seconds dragged by, too long for Will's liking. Still, Lucky executed the ride perfectly. The bell sounded. The crowd rocketed to their feet, and Will admitted he'd never ridden better himself. A score of ninety showed the judges approved as well. That score put him atop the leaderboard for this event, second overall.

After the last rider finished out the bareback bronc riding, the emcee occupied center stage and tapped the mic. "Tonight we have a special presentation, and here to help me is last year's finals champion and fan favorite, Ty Darling."

The crowd went wild, jumping to their feet. The noise reached a fever pitch. Ty emerged from the other side of the fence atop his horse, waving his arm, his grin as wide as the Black Canyon of Gunnison.

"Howdy." Ty dismounted and held the reins

of his magnificent quarter horse. "I want to thank the fine folks of Violet Ridge for hosting the first rodeo of the year. The sponsors and the volunteers have worked together to put on quite a show, don't you agree?"

More cheers, and the emcee waved for silence. "On behalf of the organizers, the Violet Ridge Roundup Rodeo is changing things up this year. First, we'd like to recognize a new sponsor, who signed on yesterday. EverWind is committed to renewable energy. One of their employees is in town and displayed real Violet Ridge ingenuity and spirit. Her idea for free cake stunned us at first, but you fans delivered and doubled last year's amount. Thanks to her, we have our biggest donation yet to early education in this county."

The emcee handed the mic back to Ty, who grinned. "Ladies and gentlemen, let's give an enormous hand to the newest addition to Violet Ridge, a special someone I know you'll be proud to call one of your own now. Give it up for Kelsea Carruthers, this year's rodeo princess and honorary cowgirl."

The spotlight landed on Kelsea, her pale skin a testament to her shock at the honor she'd just received. Polite applause greeted her as she waved from their front-row seat. Ty mounted his horse and rode toward them, handing Kelsea a ribbon and shaking her hand.

Ty smiled for the cameras and then shook Will's hand. "Miss you on the circuit, but you're a mighty lucky fellow to have such a fine lady at your side."

Will's jaw clenched, and he wanted to clear up any misconceptions. He hadn't made any commitments to Kelsea or EverWind, outside of an open mind for her presentation. The choice about what was best for his ranch might have been decided already in this arena tonight.

He wasn't quite sure how he felt about that.

CHAPTER SIX

NEAR THE FENCE about a mile from the stables, Kelsea capped the last soil sample. She straightened and leaned her elbow on the nearest post. From here, she could see the Double I Ranch, owned by the Irwin family. Her muscles were stiff from her work, so she stretched her neck and back, maneuvering into her favorite yoga poses on this bright morning. The Rockies were the perfect backdrop for her routine, a moment of calm in the midst of the proverbial storm swirling around her.

Two days ago, out of nowhere, she'd received the honor of becoming this year's rodeo princess by the one and only all-around champion of the Violet Ridge Roundup Rodeo, Ty Darling. The publicity would be a boost for her career and draw attention to EverWind. A huge win, indeed.

At that moment, though, she'd seen the color drain from Will's face, and no wonder. Her victory strained their business relationship, leaving her unsure about her place at the ranch. Was she an interloper or a welcome newcomer? Saturday night had muddied those waters and left a dark morass of a mess.

This type of community support she had was unheard of in her experience, and she couldn't help but love how special it made her feel. Too bad she couldn't say the same about Will's reaction. He clammed up after that. Any progress in making the enigmatic cowboy lighten up had been halted in its tracks.

One minute everything clicked at the Silver Horseshoe with something pure and lovely coming to the surface, bringing out a part of her she hadn't known existed. The horses were an accepting lot, and she loved interacting with them and Rocket. The same went for the cowhands who went out of their way to be friendly, or maybe they just liked her corn bread.

It would be easy to cut her losses and run with the other new leads. This morning the company's chief executive officer, Dave Mulroney, had called about the influx of queries, all positive. In his eyes, the rodeo endorsement was a rousing success, an opening in this part of Colorado for years to come. Using all her resources, Kelsea convinced Mr. Mulroney to allow her to follow this lead rather than the one for the Double I Ranch next door. There was only room for one set of wind turbines in the immediate area, and she wanted Will to have the first chance at the contract. Perhaps it was a sense of loyalty, since Will and Barry had allowed her to stay here when there was no room at the inn. Perhaps it was something else.

No, she couldn't let anything distract her. She couldn't let whatever she was feeling amount to anything more than a business partnership. Yet another reason to present her ideas to Will and hope the turbines sold themselves. With the soil samples now finally in hand and things returning to normal here at the ranch, it was only a matter of time. He'd either accept or reject the offer. Then she could get out of Dodge.

She collected the supplies in her EverWind kit. Two figures on horseback caught Kelsea's eye. Sabrina arrived first on Calico, and Will followed on Tuxedo. The brunette dismounted and then Will did the same. Rocket brought up the rear and bounded over to Kelsea. She bent over and petted the border collie's bristly black-and-white fur.

"Good morning." And it was, the brisk air cool enough to make her comfortable in her coat, but not freezing. Hints of spring surrounded them. The nearby meadow was a veritable treasure of wildflowers. Earlier she'd whipped out her phone and used an app to identify many of the types that caught her eye: Indian paintbrush in a rich carnelian red, columbine in vibrant blue, and her new favorite, the Rocky Mountain bee plant, in a gorgeous shade of purple.

"Hi, Kelsea." Sabrina held the reins of the sweet mare and walked along the fence border. "It's a beautiful morning for a ride."

"Oh?" Kelsea looked at Will, rather disappointed at yet another delay that prevented him from showing her around the ranch.

"I've been riding herd since four this morning. It took longer than anticipated because I ran across an injured cow. I attended her hoof and arrived back fifteen minutes ago when Sabrina told me she's leaving this afternoon for the next rodeo." Will obviously picked up on her dismay.

Sabrina touched her forehead. "I might hang around an extra day if that's okay. I could be coming down with whatever Barry had. I'm not feverish, though."

Concern etched Will's face. "Why don't we head back so you can rest?"

What would it be like to have Will be that

conscientious about her? Sabrina waved him off. "I haven't had a horseback ride with you in a long time. Besides, you mentioned there was something on your mind about the northwest pasture."

Kelsea looked at Sabrina, her concern rising for the pale brunette. "Will's right. You do seem a little under the weather."

"I thought Calico would be the best medicine of all. She's such a sweet mare." Sabrina inhaled and patted Calico's side. "But a nap sounds really good. An extra hour of sleep should make me as right as rain."

"We'll talk another time. I don't think you need to be out riding if you're sick." Will sounded firm.

The foreman, Steve, drove the UTV toward them, and Will waved him over.

"Everything okay, boss?" Steve asked Will.

Sabrina noticeably wobbled in the saddle, and Steve helped her dismount. Will kept astride Tuxedo, frown lines popping out on his forehead. "Steve, can you ride Calico back?" He faced Kelsea. "Can you drive a UTV?"

"I can drive my father's golf cart."

"I'll be fine." Sabrina's protests sounded hollow, and she gave up the fight. "You're right.

I'll head to the house with Kelsea. Thanks for looking out for me."

Steve agreed to ride Calico over to the stable and handed Kelsea the keys to the UTV. Will answered his cell and hung up. Then he faced Kelsea. "Can I take you to the pasture tomorrow?"

"I realize you have things to do, so maybe you could head to the stables with us? Once we get Sabrina settled, we can continue on to the pasture. I can talk to you on the way." She stretched and soaked in the beauty of the spring day. There was something about this place that was reeling her in. Okay, that was only part of what was drawing her to the ranch. She was attracted to Will. Reminding herself about her purpose here was good for all of them, especially her.

"Hold that thought." Will whipped out a walkie-talkie, and Kelsea heard Jody's muffled voice. "There's an issue with a couple of the calves. I have to go now." He rubbed his eyes with his hand and then dismounted. He walked alongside Tux and talked to Kelsea. "I'd appreciate it if you accompany Sabrina, so she can get that rest. Please text me with an update.

If I'm back by lunchtime, I'll take you on that personal tour then."

"No problem about the text. I can do that." She hefted her backpack into the back of the UTV and clasped the keys. "A new adventure. I can't wait. I'll hold you to this one."

While she thrived on excitement, she had a feeling Will was one adventure she'd best bypass.

WITH THE CALVES improving after a slight scare that turned out to be a case of dehydration rather than anything more severe, he headed to Domino's corral. He hadn't expected to find Sabrina there with Lucky. He rushed to her side. "What are you doing out here?"

"That nap was a lifesaver. I'm on the mend. I must have eaten something that disagreed with me." Her reassurance, along with her improved color, gave credence to her statement. She patted his arm. "Will, I'm okay."

He let out a breath, willing to take her at her word. They turned their attention to the stallion. Between the three of them, they should be able to diagnose what ailed the quarter horse. He'd bought Domino as a yearling and trained him from early on. They'd ridden in eight years of rodeos together, always coming back to the Silver Horseshoe at the end of the season. That exposure to ranch life had given Will hope he'd adjust to residing here permanently.

If Domino continued going downhill, Will might have to resort to drastic measures. He might have to sell him to Lucky and let him go back to the rodeo.

Lucky slipped a halter on the American quarter horse and led him around the corral. Sabrina's gaze didn't leave Lucky, the look of yearning different from any he'd ever seen on her face before. It took everything for him to keep his mouth from dropping.

His two best friends together? He waited and absorbed the idea. Surprised, he expected some kind of envy to take root, but none came. He was happy for them. With their rough childhoods, they deserved the best. Finally, something was going right. He leaned toward Sabrina. "I approve."

"Of what?" She kept her focus on Lucky.

"I see the way you're looking at him. If you two are afraid of my reaction, you don't have to be. I'm happy for you both."

Sabrina faced Will, a sad expression on her

generally cheerful face. "I love Lucky." Will knew it. "Like a brother. Same as you."

The three had grown close over the past ten years. He and Lucky met first when the younger man, who'd been shuffled from home to home in his teen years, didn't have anywhere to go for Christmas. Will invited him to the Silver Horseshoe, cementing their friendship. Later, Sabrina, who'd been raised by her grandparents, made their trio complete.

"Didn't you meet up with Lucky last night?" He'd heard someone coming in and out. Barry snored loud enough for Will to know it wasn't him, and he'd passed Kelsea, who smiled at him while carrying a cup of hot cocoa to her room.

Sabrina's cheeks turned bright pink. "You know I went out?"

She confirmed what he'd already guessed. "I know you, Sabrina. You're the first rodeo clown out of the barrels. You love green chilies, and you fall asleep earlier than anyone else I know. I can set my alarm clock by your sleep schedule. If you left without telling me, it must have been important. I didn't say anything because I respect you and wouldn't want to overstep unless you wanted me or needed me for anything, of course."

"You don't have to worry about me leaving tonight." Sabrina's fists clutched the wood of the fence so hard her knuckles turned white.

"I'm concerned about you."

"Before you hear about it from anyone else, I've asked for a transfer to the women's rodeo circuit." Sabrina kept her gaze on Lucky and Domino.

"What? Why? You love your job."

Lucky looked their way at Will's loud voice, and Will motioned everything was fine.

"I also thought I was in love with Ty Darling. He said he loved me until a few days ago when he told me I'd be better off in the long run without him. He walked away and won't answer my emails."

The sweetheart of the rodeo and the heartbreaker? No wonder Sabrina was devastated. He reached for her hand and squeezed. "You deserve better."

"Darn right I do. Too bad I didn't fall for you or Lucky. That's why I was looking at him." Sabrina's small smile let him know she'd be okay. "That shouldn't stop you from going for it."

He frowned, unsure of what she was saying. "Huh?"

"Kelsea. She's making you look like the contented cow that swallowed the clover. At least I think she's the reason you're smiling more."

That wasn't good, considering the newcomer was leaving soon, maybe as soon as the conclusion of her presentation. If he said no to the turbines, other ranchers would jump on the bandwagon if today's texts asking him to send Kelsea their way were any indication. He couldn't imagine saying yes and losing valuable acreage. It would come down to the income stream she offered. Extra money would sure come in handy. "She's only here on business. There's nothing between us."

Sabrina nudged his side. "Don't be so sure about that. Her lightness and positivity could counter your broody side."

"Thanks. I tell you about the best parts of you, and in return, I'm broody."

"I'm serious. There's something between the two of you. It's as obvious as my clown nose." She released his hand and jumped from the fence. "Now, if you'll excuse me, I'm heading to Violet Ridge for a visit to the Blue Skies Coffeehouse and Bakery. I have an awful hankering for one of their chocolate éclairs. I'll be back before sunset. Do you need anything?"

He shook his head and she left. He watched

her as he absorbed the shocking revelation about her and Ty. Then Lucky headed his way with Domino. "You look like you've just seen a yeti."

"Nope."

Lucky glanced at Sabrina's retreating figure. "What's with Sabrina?"

Their friend's relationship with Ty Darling was her news to tell. "You know what she's like when she wants a chocolate éclair."

Lucky laughed. "Say no more."

Will focused on Domino. "How's he doing?"

"He's missing something, but I'm not convinced it's the rodeo. It might be that he's attuned to you. Have you thought about another run?"

Yes, but not in the way Lucky meant. Domino needed the crowd and adventure in his life, things he wasn't getting here at the ranch. With Lucky leaving in a few hours, this was the best time to broach the subject he'd been hoping to avoid. "Your Appaloosa, Blackjack, is a dependable presence, but Domino would have cut inside faster in the tie-down roping event and shaved a second off of your time with his instincts. That would have made the difference between finishing in second place like you did or breaking through to the top." Will was convinced Lucky had all the elements in place for this to be his year.

"What are you saying?"

Domino was part of his family, but then again so was Lucky. This was the best solution Will could find to keep Domino close and allow him to return to competition. Will took a deep breath. "I think you should consider making Domino your permanent rodeo horse."

CHAPTER SEVEN

TAKING CARE THAT the goats were occupied on the other side of the pen, Kelsea opened the gate and pushed the wheelbarrow inside the enclosure. She stopped and fastened the fence latch behind her. Then she parked the wheelbarrow next to the three-sided goat shed. With a wave to the goats and Churro, she removed the printout with Barry's instructions for cleaning the shed from Will's jacket pocket. *Scoop out all the pine shavings and sweep the little nooks.* Snow came over and playfully butted Kelsea.

"I'd much prefer having fun, too, but whew!" Kelsea fanned her nose with her hand. "Good gravy, you'll thank me for making it smell better around here."

One Saturday she was the rodeo princess and the next Tuesday she was the goat keeper. That was the way ranch life went, she guessed.

While Barry was on the mend, she'd offered to help him. Little did she know this was today's top priority, but hey, she'd offered…

Churro the burro watched from a distance, patrolling and protecting the area. Obviously, she didn't see Kelsea as a threat. Kelsea started shoveling old hay into the wheelbarrow when Snow and Flake came over, searching for snacks. She threw a handful of their favorite honey nut cereal on the ground. Then she hustled the full wheelbarrow through the gate, taking care to close it quickly. She stretched her muscles, including the ones she didn't know she had.

Ranch work was a lot harder than she'd have believed a week ago. A strong gust of wind knocked the wheelbarrow over. Smelly hay spilled out. She groaned at the mess. This wasn't on her bucket list, but it was still an adventure. She started shoveling again when her phone rang.

Her caller ID flashed on the screen. Her mouth dropped. Of all the times for her father to return her six voice mails, it would have to be now. As much as she'd like to send him to voice mail, who knew the next time he'd deign to call?

"Hi, Dad." She picked out a pellet of what she hoped was goat feed from her hair. It wasn't. Will probably never found little pellets in his hair.

"Kelsea." His voice sounded gleeful. If she'd

known absence would make his heart grow fonder, she'd have attended cheerleader camp in California rather than the one within commuting distance. "What's so important that you needed to leave six messages?"

Ah, there was the Preston Carruthers she knew and loved.

She leaned against the fence, watching Snow and Flake gobble up the last of the cereal. "I'm in Colorado. I'm safe and sound, and I missed you." As improbable as that sounded, she did.

"Kelsea." Too often she'd heard her name said with this level of disappointment, and she braced herself. "You didn't lose this job already? I promised Dave you would take this opportunity seriously."

She waited as he delivered the familiar speech about how Dave Mulroney had been the best man at his first wedding and would have been at his second if her mother hadn't insisted on a simple civil ceremony.

When he stopped for breath, she reassured him. "I still work for EverWind. Thank you for putting in a good word for me." Even if it wasn't the career she'd have chosen for herself. What career she would have picked was still a mystery. Something in fashion? Definitely something with color and constant variety. "I'm staying at the Silver Horseshoe, the ranch where EverWind wants to lease land. Mr. Mulroney agreed to a week's extension for my current assignment."

"Why do you need extra time? It sounds pretty cut and dry to me."

Snow came over and nudged Kelsea's hand through an opening in the chain-link fence. "It's calving season, and the rodeo came to town." Neither, though, were genuine reasons she shouldn't already have presented her initial PowerPoint to Will. She'd remedy that this afternoon.

"The expansion into Colorado is important to Dave." *What about me?* Kelsea clenched her hand around the phone and listened to her father once more. "That's not the reason I called."

Her messages weren't enough? She stood straighter, and another pellet fell out of her hair. "Then what is?"

"A leading medical journal accepted Adam's article for publication in an upcoming issue. Your brother is making a real difference in pediatric heart surgery." Which begged the question of why Kelsea couldn't be more like her half siblings. "I just finished talking to Alexis. Her doctoral graduation ceremony is at the end of the month in Boston. That's three Dr. Carruthers in the family. Do you need me to send you money for the airfare to Boston?"

He'd taken Alexis's call but hadn't bothered to return hers until she was covered in dirt and muck. Thank goodness this wasn't a video chat. "I can afford my way. I just can't guarantee the time off."

Her father should understand a strong work ethic. He'd used his career as an excuse around her for years. Tonight, though, Kelsea wouldn't be like him. She'd find time and call Alexis to congratulate her. She touched her hair. That was after a long hot shower with her favorite orange-scented shampoo and deep-cleansing conditioner.

"Your brother already booked his flight."

No matter what she did, she'd always be the child who needed the offer of airfare where her half siblings could do no wrong. "I'll try to be there."

"Don't just try, Kelsea. Book the flight."

"Someone needs me." That *someone* happened to be two goats and a donkey, but they counted. "I have to go."

Her father ended the call, and Kelsea wiped away tears with the back of her hand.

"Kelsea?" Will headed her way, Rocket nipping at his heels. She cringed.

Business professionals don't cry in front of prospective clients.

"Hi, Will." If he noticed something was wrong, he didn't indicate it. "Is it finally time to go on the tour of the ranch now?"

At that moment, Flake butted her from his side of the fence, and she stumbled. Will steadied her, his arms muscular and reassuring. Their gazes met, and something changed. Quivers skittered down her spine. She inhaled his woodsy scent that eclipsed the smell of the goats. His smile was reassuring and promising. What would it be like to kiss Will?

He blinked first and reached out his finger, his callused skin brushing her cheek. The same strong hands that took care of everything on the ranch were gentle to the touch. When he pulled back, he looked down and noticed the moisture there. "Have you been crying?"

She thought about blaming it on the goats, but didn't give in to the easy out. With some reluctance, she nodded, while Rocket tilted his head with concern in those big brown border collie eyes of his. "My sister's graduating. She's the third Dr. Carruthers in my family."

"Then these are happy tears?" Surprise skittered through her that this tough rancher knew the difference.

"Not really, but thank you for asking."

Will stepped closer, that protective nature of his wrapping her in a warm cocoon. He then reached over and pulled a goat pellet out of her hair. "Having a rough day?" She nodded. "Do you know what I do when I have a bad day?"

This softer side of him was novel and off-putting, a distinct contrast to his gruffer side. "Play with goats?"

Snow and Flake did have a winsome appeal.

"I go for a long horse ride." A shadow crossed over his face, and instinct told her she wasn't the only one having a rough day.

"I've never been horseback riding before." The admission wormed out of her, yet another way she didn't belong around here. Rocket nudged her hand with his snout. She obliged and petted the bristly strands of fur.

"Then it's time we do something about that. First, I'll help you finish cleaning out the pen and then I'll formally introduce you to my mother's mare, Calico. She's the perfect mount for a beginner." Will hurried into the pen with Kelsea on his heels, shooing Rocket away so he wouldn't enter. Rocket headed off toward the stable.

"You're a brave man, Will Sullivan. Volunteering to help me clean a goat pen and teaching me how to ride a horse." Flake came over and butted him. "Be on your best behavior, Flake, or he'll think you don't like him."

The Nubian seemed to understand and ambled away to his water trough.

"You're a goat whisperer, Kelsea Carruthers."

That might have been one of the nicest compliments she'd ever received. They worked together, and she was pleasantly surprised at how well their methods meshed. In no time, the pen looked and smelled better. Will shoveled alfalfa hay into the goat's feeding trough while she topped off the water for the three animals.

They arrived at the handwashing station at the same time. Reaching for the faucet, their hands collided. His calluses made a deep impact. He lived out the principles he stood for. In this day and age, that meant something. She pulled back, but he insisted she go first. A gentleman at heart. This type of treatment could go straight to her head.

A few minutes later, Will led her toward the stables. Her excitement about this newest turn in her day soared as high as the eagles overhead.

"You're already wearing boots and proper clothing, but you'll need protective headgear." Will gave her a tour of the tack room, explaining the different equipment, and then went over to the helmets. "Try this one on for size."

She removed her Stetson, placing it on a hook near the other hats. "Why a helmet instead of a hat?" He leveled a look, and she glared right back at him. "I'm curious. This is all new to me and really interesting."

"Safety first. You haven't ridden before, and there's a risk of injury."

Will went over a list of safety procedures, and she noted each of them. "I don't know whether you're helping or making me nervous." She laughed away her discomfort while he fitted a helmet on her head.

When he fastened the strap under her chin, a pool of butterflies took flight in her stomach. As much as she wanted to dismiss them on account of her first horseback riding lesson, she knew that was only part of the reason. Mostly, though, they had everything to do with her rugged instructor.

"We have a good safety record at the ranch. I want to keep it that way." That gruff tone returned, but she was no longer fooled. There were many sides to him, all intriguing. "Does that feel secure?"

She nodded. "It's a good fit." As was the Silver Horseshoe, connecting her to nature and the world around her in a way she never expected it to when she arrived. She wondered if she and Will would also be a good fit.

Business professionals keep their feelings out of negotiations.

While he saddled Calico, she repeated her mantra to herself, hoping she'd start believing it. Learning to ride was a necessity so she could conduct presentations on other ranches. That was why she was here in the first place. This experience was a wise business move, and nothing more. Definitely not anything personal.

Will motioned her over, reins in hand. "Always stay alert. Pay attention to the horse and your surroundings," he said.

Now that Calico was up close and personal in the corral, Kelsea's nerves reared up. "She's so big."

"She's a sweetheart. Each horse has a different temperament. Domino lives for people, the more the better and all the attention that goes with it. Tuxedo will work all day long. They also have tricks when you saddle them. You need to look out for them." Will tightened the cinch. "See how Calico inhaled? Make sure the horse doesn't inhale because the saddle would be loose and you'd fall off."

"You're not making me feel better."

"Wait until you're riding. It's all worth it. Once the saddle is on, stand beside a horse's front shoulder."

"Why do I want to stand there if I'm supposed to say hello to a horse by bumping its muzzle?" She could hear the frustration in her voice. There seemed to be a different rule for everything at the ranch.

Why couldn't this be simple?

But then again, the best things in life never were.

"Horses have a blind spot and a powerful kick." He waved her over another couple of inches, and she complied. "I'll help you mount."

He was so close his breath grazed her cheek. A horse's kick probably wasn't as potent as what she was experiencing every time Will was in the vicinity.

After a couple of turns around the corral, she released her anxiety and took in her surroundings. The breeze ruffled her jacket, and the beauty of the craggy mountains brought back the joy she'd lost talking to her father. Calico gave a soft whinny as if in response to Kelsea's letting go, almost as if to say she preferred an enthusiastic rider to one fretting over everything. Kelsea finally relaxed. "Thank you,

Will. Calico's a beautiful horse. You must be what they call a horse whisperer."

"Thanks, but I'm not. What I know I learned from my father. The first time I fell off a horse, he told me I should only mount again once we were communicating with each other. Dad said it was as important for the horse to feel comfortable with me as I felt with the horse."

"It sounds like your father was hands on and supportive."

She wished she could say the same.

"As I got older, I often disagreed with him about his approach to ranching." He clenched his jaw, and then his face softened. "I'm about to make some big changes."

"Is EverWind under consideration? I'm almost done putting the finishing touches on my presentation."

"Good. Change is the only way to keep the ranch intact. I hope my father would have approved."

Would she and her father ever get to a point where he'd approve of her actions? She hoped so. Calico reared her head up in a gentle manner, as if reminding Kelsea to pay attention, and she relaxed once more.

The ranch foreman, Steve, arrived at the fence and leaned his arms over the railing. He tipped his Stetson, showing some of the gray hair that matched his salt-and-pepper mustache.

"See how Steve didn't wave his arms about or make any sudden noises?" Will pointed out. "That's another important rule. Horses can spook easily, some more than others. Calico's pretty levelheaded. That's why I chose her for you."

Another rule to learn and follow. However, unlike her father's rules, that seemed to favor her half siblings, these benefited everyone on the ranch and kept them safe.

That was Will. He longed to protect, and she was drawn to that. She had the feeling he didn't step back and enjoy the vibrant colors around him very often, if at all. She could help him do that while she stayed here. Problem was she wasn't staying for the long run. There were always new dreams to dream and fresh territory to cover.

She waited with Calico while Will spoke to his foreman. Calico snorted, and Kelsea glanced around. In the far off distance, she saw Domino gallop to the fence and paw at the ground. What was upsetting the stallion? There was only one way to find out. She flicked the reins and approached Steve and Will.

Steve tipped his Stetson in Kelsea's direction. "Sorry to interrupt your lesson, ma'am."

"Don't give it a second thought, Steve. It's always a pleasure to see you. And how many times do I need to remind you? While every female over ten is ma'am in the South, I prefer Kelsea." She loved the wide grin on his weather-lined face but remembered why she'd ventured this far. "Is something wrong with Domino?"

The two men looked in that direction, and the stallion pawed at the ground again. The muscle in Will's neck popped out. "As soon as I teach Kelsea how to clean tack, I'll check on him."

"Then you want me to go to Over and Dunne?" Steve scratched his chin. "This is the third order in a row that wasn't accurate."

Will muttered something under his breath. "I'll have to go and speak to Regina personally about her new employee," he said, not bothering to hide his tenseness. "I'll see to Domino and then head to town."

"I'd like to go, too," Kelsea said. "Can we wrap up the lesson?"

"I'm glad you're learning to ride. Some parts of the ranch are only accessible by horseback. Once you have more lessons under your belt, then you can see more of the ranch."

"Still, you can take me on the UTV for the rest of that tour, and soon."

"You'll want to see it in the daylight. We'll try for tomorrow."

"I'll hold you to that. In the meantime, could I drive into town with you?" Her disappointment at ending the lesson early subsided at the thought of seeing Regina again. After the rodeo, Kelsea had some new ideas for the feed and seed she'd like to run by the owner. "Maybe we can even meet up with Sabrina."

Steve reached for the reins. "Since I'm the one who brought the shortfall to your attention, I'll groom Calico."

"I'd prefer Kelsea learn how to take care of her horse." Will glanced at his watch before catching sight of the plea in her eyes. "The feed and seed closes early on Tuesdays. You can come with me, and we'll cover saddle care and grooming next time. Thanks, Steve."

Kelsea echoed her thanks. Will reached up and helped her dismount. His gaze was tender yet intense. Another reminder he wasn't all he seemed on the surface. He stepped toward the corral gate. Something flickered deep in those brown eyes. Whatever was happening between them wasn't one-sided.

"I'll check on Domino and then be at my truck in fifteen minutes."

She glanced at her hair and clothes, still covered in dirt and more. That wasn't much time, but she'd make it work.

"I'll be there."

WILL TICKED OFF the final minute and exhaled. While he was with Domino, Sabrina had arrived from town and waved her éclair box before she'd headed for the ranch house. There'd been nothing wrong with his stallion. At least nothing wrong to the naked eye.

He glanced around and found no sign of Kelsea. For some reason, traveling by himself to the feed and seed didn't bring him the relief he'd anticipated. He was used to being alone, but he was starting to find it didn't provide the same comfort it had in the past.

"Wait for me!" Kelsea's voice came from behind, and he stilled his hand on the door. She caught up and slid into the passenger seat. "Fifteen minutes on the dot. I didn't have enough time to shower, so I can't say I'll smell like a daisy."

Her light chuckle was becoming too familiar. He liked it and was already seeking ways to hear it. But she was only here on business, so he'd best not get used to her presence.

The truck's slight backfire caused Kelsea to jump. "It's old, but it works. We try to use everything on the ranch until duct tape and spit can't even hold it together."

Another laugh brought a flutter in his chest, and he stopped the truck at the ranch's front gate. Waving him off, she jumped out of the cab. He watched her graceful gait while she opened and closed the gate. She climbed back into the truck, and he turned in the direction of Violet Ridge.

"After we go to the feed and seed, could we stroll downtown? I need to buy a graduation gift for my sister. Perhaps I can start my pitch to you on the drive home."

As much as he'd like to oblige her request, he couldn't.

"The order requires refrigeration. I have to get back to the ranch and unload the medication as soon as possible."

"I understand. What about a preliminary discussion tonight after your usual chores?"

He gave her credit for her persistence. If he signed with EverWind, it wouldn't be a quick in and out. The company would have access to his land, to his heart. If he didn't agree, though, he might have to break his father's promise to the cowhands. Acid roiled in his stomach.

"There's no time like the present to talk. Where does EverWind want to place the turbines?" The more he'd considered it during his daily chores, the more questions he had. "And do you oversee the entire project from start to completion?"

Maybe Kelsea wouldn't be leaving as soon as he thought. That lifted his spirits more than it should have.

"This is how it works. After Barry contacted us and we arranged our appointment, I reviewed online plat maps and consulted with the engineers. We narrowed in on all the potential sites. I've collected some samples, and I'm waiting to send them all in one package so the analysis can take place at the same time. Since it's late in the day, tomorrow would work well for the next soil collection. Then I review the findings with the engineers." She rolled down the window. A soft breeze fluttered inside. "Once that happens, I finish my pitch with a recommended area and the terms of the final contract. Once you sign, I'll be on my way to the next contact."

"So, you wouldn't be staying in Violet Ridge?"

"You'll be rid of me in no time. Oh, I just realized something. The inn probably has vacancies again. I love the ranch, but I'm taking advantage of your hospitality."

This time, it was his turn to laugh. "Considering you cleaned out the goat shed today, I'm the one infringing on your hospitality."

She glanced in the rearview mirror and touched her hair with a slight groan. "I should have tried to tie my personal record for the shortest shower ever. I must look awful."

More like wonderful, but they were establishing business boundaries. He'd respect that. Still, he couldn't lie. "Nope. You look beautiful."

Her blue eyes widened, and his heart started racing. He'd love to see that expression more often, but he couldn't have everything he wanted.

Will dropped her off at the front entrance of the feed and seed. The three old timers on the front porch greeted Kelsea, and Will drove around to the back. A few minutes to gather his wits and keep his mind occupied on loading the fragile pallets onto the cargo bed was just what he needed.

Too soon, the truck was filled to the hilt. No sense putting off the inevitable. He headed over to the porch and nodded to the three gentlemen sitting on the rockers.

"Howdy, Will. That Kelsea sure is a pistol." Doc rose from his rocker, coming closer to Will, staring at his face. "You're looking a little stressed. Your parents would be concerned you're taking on too much. Sometimes you have to sit back and rock a spell. Have a cup of coffee and see what's really around you."

Why did everyone keep insisting he should take time to smell the coffee?

"Barry's cold is starting to go around the ranch. My friend Sabrina was sick. I'm fine, though," Will said. "And I relax. I attended the rodeo this weekend."

Glenn and Marshall Bayne came over as if to add their two cents. The three meant well, but Will had to get that order back to the ranch. He started for the entrance, but someone tapped his arm.

"Sure hope you dropped by the cake stand." Marshall licked his lips. "Kelsea and Barry teamed up for a fine Texas sheet cake. Your uncle's a wonderful cook. Much better than Glenn here."

"I follow recipes to a T. Same as I followed the tax laws when I was an accountant." Glenn pursed his lips and narrowed his eyes at his brother. "It's our old oven. The temperature control isn't great. Same as the broken heater thermostat in our rental. I thought we were supposed to be looking for a permanent place."

"Good talking to you. Kelsea and I need to be getting on the road." Will fidgeted and removed his Stetson. "I've got supplies to unload, and I want to check out the details of the auction coming up in June."

Marshall's eyes lit up. "Auction? The only one around here is for livestock. You thinking of a different type of cattle?"

Of all the things to let slip, he had to mention that. "No."

"Alpaca? Sheep? Elk?" Will gave Marshall points for persistence.

Will exhaled. "Elk." There was a section of land on the ranch, perfect for elk. The intro price was a little hefty, but if he succeeded, he could keep everyone employed without resorting to drastic changes.

Marshall exchanged a glance with Glenn and then rubbed his salt-and-pepper beard. "You know my brother's a whiz with numbers, and I'm good at appraisals."

Glenn's lips turned down into a frown. "It won't work, Marshall. Give it up."

"Give what up?" A funny feeling nipped at Will's heels. He should walk into the feed and seed and be done with this, but it was as if he couldn't budge.

"You need help with that auction, and my brother here thinks we're the recruits." Glenn shook his head, his reputation as the dour brother well-earned.

If Will didn't start changing his attitude, would he be called the dour rancher years from now? "I didn't say anything about help."

"What plans do you have for the elk?" Glenn asked.

Will stared at the three. *What the hay.* It wasn't like he was keeping a secret, like anyone could keep a secret in Violet Ridge, anyway. "My goal is to introduce elk to the Silver Horseshoe, away from the cattle. Elk have a low carbon footprint and other advantages."

Marshall came over and patted Will on the back. "You need the three of us. I have auction contacts. Glenn can crunch the numbers and navigate any sort of paperwork, and Doc is still a licensed vet. We can help with your ranch expansion."

The three crowded around as if waiting for his response. Doc stood stoic yet discerning, Marshall eager and Glenn appraising. Would the three do more good than harm? The ranch could use their expertise, but at what cost? "Why do you want to help me?"

Doc winced and adjusted his cowboy hat. "Your parents were good people. Besides, that's what folks do around here."

"And maybe some of us would like a dinner that wasn't charred, over-salted or raw in the middle." Marshall glanced at Glenn, who glared back. "So, we move into your bunkhouse for a while and earn our keep. In return, we get to share in Barry's cooking. It's legendary in these parts. That's settled, then. We'll turn in our notice to the landlord and be at the Silver Horseshoe tomorrow. You coming, too, Doc?"

Doc scratched his head. "I owed Rick, so yep. I'll get your ranch ready for the elk."

They all walked toward the parking lot, and Will's mouth dropped open. He went from five in the bunkhouse to eight, and he didn't even know how. He only knew he was now responsible for the welfare of three new guests.

WILL HURRIED INSIDE and found Kelsea smiling at the clothing display near the front. "Isn't this great? Regina took my suggestion and moved the rack. Looks like the clothes are selling well if the empty spaces are any indication."

Regina headed over and joined them. "Will,

I'm sorry you had to make an extra trip into town." He wasn't sure yet whether he was as well. He was still in shock about his three newest cowhands.

"Yeah." That one croaked word was all he could get out.

"Kelsea, I have to hand it to you. I found a box of cargo shorts and light fleece vests in the back." Regina cast a shrewd look in Kelsea's direction. "I placed them near the registers, and the vests sold out on the first day."

If Kelsea made a difference in less than a week at the Over and Dunne when the store had remained the same inside and out for the better part of half a century, could she be a positive force at the Silver Horseshoe as well? If so, the wind turbine contract might prove beneficial. There'd be a level of comfort about hitting the pillow without having to worry about the ranch's finances or the fate of the cowhands, now eight in number.

"That's wonderful." Kelsea beamed. "This weekend, I thought of ways your store could create more revenue streams and stay true to your mission. Take right now, for instance. You're wearing a plain black T-shirt."

Regina flipped her braid to her back. "It's too warm for flannel. As soon as I get home tonight, I'll change into flip-flops and cargo shorts."

Kelsea tilted her head, her eyes thoughtful. "Have you thought about selling T-shirts with your feed and seed logo? A small one on the front and larger sized on the back."

"That'd be a waste of money. No one would buy them." Regina scoffed and switched the few shorts that were left on display.

"You'd be surprised. Tourists love buying shirts as souvenirs, and locals will buy one in a show of support. It's also free advertising." Kelsea removed her scarf, bright with geometric patterns, and tied it around the top of the display. "What about a consignment section with scarves and coats in the winter, and boots and hats year-round?"

She retrieved her scarf while Regina shook her head. "Darlin', this is Colorado. You don't get rid of a good Stetson."

A customer approached and nodded his head. "Hats are forever."

"Says the man whose Stetsons have outlasted three marriages." Regina held up her index finger. "I'll be with you in a minute, Vern."

Kelsea faced Will. "How many hats did your father own?"

Before he died. He shrugged. "Ten or eleven."

"Everyone here says Stetsons live forever. Even if you kept one and gave one to Barry, you'd have nine that probably have wear in them. Regina could be a consigner and sell them for you." Kelsea's eyes lit up from within as she went into business details.

"I run a feed and seed," Regina protested and shook her head. "That's what I do and why this place is successful. I don't try to pretend to be something I'm not."

He expected Kelsea to get discouraged, but her face remained vibrant and open. "Adding a rack of T-shirts isn't faking it. It's about change and keeping up with the times. There's a place in every business for dreams."

There was one of his two least favorite words, *dreams*, with the other being *goodbye*. Kelsea was a dreamer, same as the rest of his family, who'd never had two cents to rub together. His father had kept the ranch running on laughter and hope when hard work and consistency built prosperous spreads like the Double I Ranch next door.

"Regina, I really need help finding this salve," Vern pressed his case.

"Hi, Vern. I'm Kelsea." She smiled at the older customer. "Do you have any extra hats you'd be willing to part with in exchange for a little money?"

Vern scratched his chin. "Mebbe, but I need some salve for my prize heifer."

"Regina, I'll come in later this week and talk more." Kelsea waved while Regina accompanied Vern to another part of the store.

"Won't that interfere with your duties with EverWind?" Will picked up some salt blocks.

"I can do both. Making sketches and some plans for Regina will be fun." Kelsea followed him to the register and rubbed her hands together.

That radiant glow was how he felt inside whenever he thought about introducing elk to the Silver Horseshoe. The feed and seed had thrived as a family business for three generations because it was based on tradition and constancy. The plans Kelsea would present to Regina would fall by the wayside and flounder without Kelsea's dreams and drive.

Then again, constancy had flatlined the Silver Horseshoe. The wind turbine idea sounded like a good one, but how much land would he lose to the equipment? Too much and the elk venture might be finished before it even started.

The truth crashed into him. Here he'd thought

he was rising above the schemes and dreams of the rest of his family when, in reality, he had more in common with them than he cared to admit.

CHAPTER EIGHT

WILL RELEASED THE last calf from the chute with a loud hee-yaw. Sweat and bits of dirt and hay clung to his skin and jacket. The aches and pains from a decade of rodeo falls reared their ugly head, and he'd be feeling each and every former injury tonight.

Steve headed over and nodded. "That's the last calf. They're all vaccinated now. I'll drive the trailer with the cows back to the pasture and you can take the trailer with the calves."

"What about taking them to the northwestern meadow instead?" Will raised his voice over the lowing of the cattle.

Steve frowned and removed his Stetson. He scratched his salt-and-pepper hair. "Don't think much of that idea. Normally we wait two years before we reintroduce the cows to overused fields. We used that area last spring."

"I didn't know." His father had still been alive then. "We'll stick to the original plan and return them to the northeastern pasture where they came from. I'll drive the truck with the calves." Neither trailer was large enough to transport all the cows at once. So far, the season had progressed well without the loss of a single calf. He intended to keep it that way.

"The six of us got them vaccinated in no time." Steve nodded, his gaze not veering away from the thirty head of cows and calves, the spring additions to the three thousand Herefords grazing on his other acres. Rocket also kept watch over the livestock. "This morning went easier than I expected, Will. Now that the rodeo's over, we're at full staff again."

"About that. I have news regarding the bunkhouse." How could he explain he'd been railroaded by three of the sweetest, most ornery gents in town? Everyone loved them.

Steve held up his hand. "I already know about Doc, Marshall and Glenn moving in for a spell. They texted Barry and me last night."

That was a relief. Dissension in the bunkhouse would have brought added stress. And this morning had already brought more bills in his inbox. That paled to saying goodbye to Sabrina and Lucky, who were moving on to the next rodeo on the circuit. Sabrina looked too green to leave, but she insisted she wasn't sick or contagious. She was raring to return to work.

Will exhaled as he caught sight of Kelsea and Uncle Barry heading their way, their laughter preceding them. They carried baskets on their forearms.

Steve tipped his Stetson in Kelsea's direction. "Thank you, ma'am, er Kelsea, for bringing those cookies to the bunkhouse last night. They were mighty tasty."

"Were?" Her teasing chuckle revealed so much about her. "They're gone already?"

Steve's ruddy cheeks gave away the answer.

To Will's dismay, everything about Kelsea was making the Silver Horseshoe a happier place. Life would return to normal after she left, but he wasn't convinced that was a good thing anymore.

"After I get the calves back to the pasture, I'll take you on that ranch tour this afternoon," Will said. A promise was a promise.

"I'd appreciate that. Barry explained this morning about how the vaccinations had to happen. But now you and I need to nail down a time for that tour. Maps are useful, but they're not the real thing. I need to see the topography for a sense of the location where the turbines will tie in naturally to the landscape."

"We are headed to the northeastern pasture in a little while…"

Why was he so hesitant to commit to this venture? What was he afraid of? That his uncle, the biggest dreamer of the Sullivan family, was right? Or that he'd lose part of his acreage and have to give up on his plan of introducing elk to the ranch? The latter was a genuine issue, while the first involved his pride and made him sound shallow and petty.

Steve sniffed and pointed to the baskets. "Something sure smells good." And that was saying something as the chutes had a pretty fierce odor. "What did you bring us?"

Barry opened the basket, the aroma of the spices and chicken almost intoxicating.

"Lunch." Kelsea smiled at the foreman. "Barry told me vaccinating the calves makes for a rough work day, and we wanted to make you something special. Hope fried chicken sounds good. It's my grandma's special family recipe."

"Do you have a drumstick? That's my favorite." Will's tough-as-nails ranch manager looked as smitten as a lovesick teenager. "Appreciate you thinking of us. This will hit the spot before we drive the two trailers out to the pasture. It sure is a pretty sight reuniting the calves and their mommas."

"You're driving to the northeast pasture, and

not the northwestern meadow?" At Steve's nod, Kelsea perked up and turned her basket toward Will. "Any chance I can come along with you? Chicken breast or drumstick?"

"I brought my lunch, and that's not a good idea. You could get hurt with all the cattle moving about. I'll take you later this afternoon once everything calms down." Will rejected her cooking and her request in one fell swoop. Barry and Steve both frowned, but he held firm. "The sooner the calves are reunited with the cows, the better."

Kelsea handed one of her baskets to Steve and faced Will. "Can I speak to you for a minute?"

"I'm busy."

"Barry and I can handle the cattle. We've been doing this for years." Steve nudged Will in Kelsea's direction.

He guided Kelsea to a sheltered spot within sight of Domino, who was off his feed this morning. "Make it quick."

Will unzipped his lunch box and munched on an apple.

"I need some consistency here." Kelsea appealed to him with her expressive eyes before unclasping the basket. She handed him a chicken breast. "You promised you'd show me around. Now is a perfect time."

"It takes total concentration for the cows and calves' reunion." Something he might not be able to give with her so close. *Drat.* Of all the women in Violet Ridge, including an available Elizabeth Irwin—a neighbor and all-around good person—why did Kelsea appeal to him? He polished off the apple and threw the core back in the bag for the compost pile. Then he started on the chicken.

"Are those two big trailers the transport vehicles?" He nodded. "I promise to stay out of your way. If I do anything wrong, I'll sit in the trailer. Let me do my job so I can present you the best contract possible. My boss is pressuring me to visit other ranches. I'm keeping that in mind. Still, your cowhands are teaching me so much about ranch life. I'm soaking it up. It'll help me be better at my job."

He chewed while considering her request. "The minute I call out to get back to the trailer, you'll do it?"

"Yes, and how's my cooking?"

"I'm eating my own lunch." Then he glanced at the half-eaten chicken breast and flushed as the flavors snuck up on him. "It's delicious."

"See, that wasn't so hard to admit, was it?" She nudged him and squinted. "You know, even with that stubble on your cheeks, I think I detect some dimples. You should smile more."

She walked away, and he stared at the chicken breast in his hand. Did she just play him?

And did he like the game a little too much?

KELSEA EMERGED FROM the passenger side of the truck and gasped at the beauty. In this nook, the snow-capped Rockies stood stark and majestic against the cerulean sky. The nearby pond glistened with the sun's rays reflecting diamonds on its surface. An eagle soared, releasing a squawk that echoed across the plains of the valley. Grass grew high with fields of wildflowers of purple, pink and white bursting with color while a stand of aspens and other trees dominated the other side of the pond. Even the spring air tasted especially sweet.

She could get used to this life really fast if she let herself.

On the far side of the field, Steve had already arrived and released the cows, who were searching for their calves with plaintive moos.

She slammed the door and made her way to Will, his hand on the lever at the back of the trailer. "You're one lucky man, Will."

He stopped and turned in her direction. "Luck has nothing to do with my current situation. Hard work and determination pay the bills."

"That may be the case, but take a minute to look around." Laser beams were less focused than the man standing in front of her. "Drink in the atmosphere and feel the moment."

"Dawdling doesn't make for an early night." His shoulders stiffened, and then he gazed at her. "I received some unexpected invoices today, but I shouldn't take it out on you. I'm sorry."

"That wasn't so hard, was it?" She smiled.

"Hmm? Apologizing or vaccinating calves? Close call." His tone was light, and she chuckled.

"But cleaning out the goat pen? Snow and Flake are so pungent." She fanned her hand under her nose, keeping her tone equally buoyant.

"You got me there." Chuckling, Will pulled out the ramp extension and acknowledged Steve. "I can handle it from here if you want to head back."

"Yep. The horses need my attention this afternoon." Steve dipped his hat at Kelsea. "Thank you for the chicken, ma'am."

Steve drove away, brown dusty dirt rising behind the trailer. Will motioned for Kelsea to stand aside. She did so, and he released the calves.

Just when she thought the valley was perfection, the cows and calves found each other with Rocket circling the pairs and keeping them from wandering astray. She almost melted from the sheer preciousness and hugged Will's arm. "Look at the reunions."

Then his hard muscular presence registered. *Business professionals did not notice their client's strong arms.*

She cleared her throat. "How do the cows and calves know each other?"

"They know the same way you knew your mom. Her voice, her smell."

"My mother died when I was two months old." She'd heard the story so often it was second nature to her. "She and my father celebrated their first wedding anniversary at a ski lodge. A sudden windstorm kicked up and she ran into a snowbank. She died instantaneously."

Pictures of her mother weren't the same as what a warm hug of love would have felt like. For years, she had been lucky to have her grandmother in her life. Mimi, her grandmother's preferred nickname, had relayed stories about her daughter, Kristy, while showing Kelsea how to soak chicken in buttermilk and make a pie crust from scratch. She'd cherished her Mimi until breast cancer claimed her too early.

Both she and Will had lost their mothers as a result of sudden accidents. They had that in common.

One calf stood bawling, and she turned toward Will. "Where's his mother?"

Will approached the calf. "*Her* mother. She's here somewhere. We'll reunite them." He whistled for Rocket, and Kelsea followed, intent on witnessing a happy ending for the calf.

Reuniting this little one with her mother, finding where she belonged, became that much more urgent with every plaintive moo. Kelsea stepped back while Will and Rocket worked together. He signaled to Rocket, who tightened his circles around the cattle.

On the sidelines, she observed the handsome cowboy at work. Intensity radiated off him, same as it did when he was fighting her every step of the way about letting her into his life. His friendship would be hard to earn, but well worth it.

A funny feeling constricted in her chest. Will wasn't one who struck her as somebody who did anything halfway, unlike her, who almost always left commitments unfinished. Fierce determination stoked his eyes. He devoted everything to the moment. His protective streak intrigued her, and despite his gruffness, he drew people close to him and cared for them. He'd done just that with Lucky and Sabrina. Same with his cowhands and now the three gents. To that extent, he also sheltered all the animals under his wing. That only added to his appeal.

He went from pair to pair, concern etching his face. The calf bleated, the soulful cry distressing to Kelsea. Even Will grimaced. "I'm worried this one was a twin, and the mother's rejecting her."

Kelsea felt for the little calf. If that was the case, she could relate only too well to a parent rejecting a child in favor of another sibling. "What can we do?"

"We keep looking. If no cow comes forward, we take this calf back with us and feed her until she can eat on her own." Will cast a watchful eye over the pasture and gazed long and hard over the entire site. "If that's the case, I'll stay in the stable with her tonight."

So Will would take on the role of surrogate mother and become the calf's family, the same way he'd created a family with Sabrina and

Lucky. That was the type of man he was, and that strength spurred something inside her.

Until Violet Ridge, she never saw herself settling down, but this place sparked a need deep within her.

At that moment, something moved on the other side of the calf trailer, and Rocket ran over there. A black cow lumbered toward them, mooing all the while. The lost calf's bleats grew higher in pitch until the two found each other again. The cow nudged the calf with her head, the reunion as glorious as the surroundings.

Kelsea reached for Will's arm. "Isn't that just the most beautiful thing?"

"That's life on a ranch." He sounded too matter of fact and went to check on the other pairs. How could he take tender moments like these in stride, as if they came along every day?

How could someone with that single-minded attitude occupy space in her mind, and not in a way that revolved around business? When she fell for someone, she wanted poetry and chocolate. Someone who'd cherish her. Someone who didn't disregard her like her father did.

That trite pep talk didn't stop her attraction to him from humming in her veins. As hard as it was to admit it, Will was making her question what she wanted, for herself, not for anyone else.

If she just stayed her course, she'd move on soon enough. She always did. In the meantime, the ranch fostered sweet moments like these. She doubled down on her personal promise of helping him appreciate what he had at his fingertips.

"When was the last time you truly savored these types of reunions? Look around you. Life is beautiful." She pointed to the cow and calf, their happiness at finding each other clear. Then a strong whiff of cattle reached her, and she laughed. "Even the aroma of the cows."

"I love all of this. It's why I do what I do. Every day is packed with something different each hour."

"Just because you see this every day, doesn't mean you really see it." Her father had made sure she'd never wanted for any material object while growing up, yet he'd never seemed to take joy in her accomplishments. Being a part of someone's life and savoring the sheer joy of it weren't the same. "This scenery is breathtaking, and spring is in the air."

"Watch out for the cow patty in front of you."

She sidestepped it and shook her head. "Always practical, aren't you? Tell me what you see when you're out here."

He approached the fence, the sun glistening off the shimmering pond. She neared him, soaking in the wildflowers and the soaring eagle she spotted above. Facing him, she waited for his response. Silence stretched out, and she gave up. She wasn't getting through to him any more than she'd ever reached her father's heart.

After another minute, she turned away. She wouldn't let Will see how much his silence felt like rejection.

"I see animals that depend on a rancher who keeps his head about him. I see a ranch that fulfills a genuine necessity for people." His voice stopped her in her tracks. "I feel a responsibility for my cowhands who've worked hard their entire lives and need a place where they don't have to worry about a boss believing they're too old for the job."

That was the most he'd ever said to her at once. It wasn't lost on her that he'd delivered that speech to her back. With slow deliberation, she turned to face him once again. His hands were jammed in his pockets, determination lining every muscle of his lean body.

"Something can have purpose and be beautiful at the same time. Just because ranching serves a utilitarian purpose, doesn't mean you can't take note of its charm."

"When the ranch can support itself, I'll find time to appreciate everything around me more." He grimaced as if he also heard how futile that sounded.

"Sounds to me like you'll find an excuse then as well. No time like the present." She leaned on the wooden post, already sensing the coiled spring in him, eager to get to the next task. "I know it's calving season, but taking one minute to enjoy what's around you won't hurt the animals or the day. In fact, it might make you stronger."

"On one condition."

She shifted but decided to accept his stipulation. "What is it?"

"You use this minute to evaluate this northeast pasture, then tell me about the turbines."

Her shoulders dropped. His mind had been focused where hers should have been: her job. Six months of training had led her here and provided her a chance to show her boss and her father her true worth.

"Sounds great to me."

They gazed at the lake, the gentle lapping along the shore soothing and melodic. She turned a critical eye over the area. There was no easy access to this meadow except the single-lane dirt road where the trailer was parked. That would make it harder, but not necessarily impossible for the construction vehicles. Aspens of varying size dotted the other side of the shore, a natural windbreak. Without pulling out the vials for soil samples, she knew this wasn't the best site.

"The minute is up." She startled. That moment passed by too quickly. She'd found that to be true of all the hours she'd spent with Will so far.

She faced him, his gaze inscrutable. "Did you see how clear the lake is and how the aspens are a harbinger of spring?" She stared at him, wondering if he'd allow anyone into his thoughts and his heart.

Had he ever let anyone in?

He was silent until Rocket came over, as if expecting another order. Like rancher, like ranch dog. Both letting nothing impede their job.

"I saw a shadow of what the Silver Horseshoe could be in the future if I dream the day away." He shoved his hands into his jacket pockets. "Dreams don't pay the bills."

"Maybe not, but sometimes they sustain us until we can make them a reality." Now for the bad news. "I scrutinized the tract, but this isn't the site the head engineer and I believe is optimal. The one EverWind is interested in has fewer aspens and more open space."

"Why didn't you say that sooner?" Will huffed out the words. "That's on the other side of the ranch."

"Maybe because you've always been busy, almost to the point of avoiding me. But really, this is my first assignment. There's a steep learning curve that wasn't part of the geology lessons or map-reading classes. Those subjects don't teach you about the reality of varying quadrants and the significant differences."

"Point taken," he said, "but we've been alone at the rodeo and during the riding lessons. You could have mentioned it."

"And I've been absorbing everything the whole time. The vaccinations, the issues that come up with predators and cattle hooves. Now I'm more familiar with you and what this ranch needs. I understand I'm encroaching on your time, but this deal could benefit us both. I need you to give a little." She'd had enough of being the sweet, compliant, cheerful person everyone expected.

Except that was who she was and she wouldn't go against herself to get ahead in her career.

Staying true to her genuine nature—that was as necessary as the crisp mountain air. She'd love it if her job landed her in Violet Ridge permanently. Something on this ranch and in the town spoke to her. Surely, the next assignment would spark the same feeling, though.

Will turned back toward the cattle, that tic in his jaw quivering. She followed his gaze toward Rocket, who was running after a cow who seemed intent on testing whether the grass was, indeed, tastier on the other side of the fence. The border collie maneuvered the cow and her calf back to the pasture. That drive and focus sometimes reaped rewards.

"We'll go to the northwest pasture tomorrow. I'll switch duties with Lyle. He was supposed to repair the fencing there while I checked on the cows here."

"How will we get there? I don't know if I'm an experienced enough rider. Barry and Kurt have been giving me more riding lessons, but we've stayed close to the corral."

Will whistled to Rocket, who was amazing in action, his nips at the cows and his circles a thing of beauty. "Lyle can ride Tuxedo out here if the weather cooperates. With dry hard ground, there's no chance Tux will sink in the ground and hurt himself. We'll use the one working UTV. It'll save us time."

"Will driving the UTV be a problem for you?"

He turned and shrugged. "Why would it be?"

"Didn't your parents die in a UTV accident?" The one time she'd asked her father for permission to travel with her cheerleading squad to a ski lodge, he'd refused, saying it was best she stay at home and practice.

"It's a ranch, Kelsea. The UTV has a better center of gravity and more cargo space. It doesn't leave ruts like the trailer." The amber flecks in his brown eyes darkened to charcoal. The way his chest rose indicated he'd been about to add something but changed his mind.

He turned his attention to Rocket, leaving her hanging. She wasn't deterred and stayed beside him, taking care to steer clear of the cow patties. "And?"

"Will you be ready to leave around five?"

She merely nodded. Will called out for Rocket, who circled around the herd once more before approaching the rancher. With everything in order, Kelsea helped Will replace the supplies in the trailer. A sideways glance confirmed what her heart screamed out. She'd best back away from her burgeoning attraction to the rancher, who appealed to her sensibilities on too many levels. He was dealing with grief, and she had a job to do. Then she'd be out of his life forever. She had to keep her eyes on the road ahead rather than get distracted as she'd been too apt to do in the past.

CHAPTER NINE

THE NEXT MORNING, Will approached the UTV with sweat breaking out on his brow. Riding in one had never rattled him before. He wasn't sure if talking about his parents to Kelsea yesterday caused his unease, or if the culprit was Kelsea herself. She walked beside him, her Stetson set back on her forehead, her blond locks ruffling in the early morning breeze. She was throwing him off his game, and considering how many times he'd been thrown off horses in his rodeo career, that was saying something.

Still, a promise was a promise, and he made a vow to listen to her pitch with an open mind. Soon, they were off to the fallow pasture on the northwestern quadrant. The oranges and pinks of the sunrise were a wonder to behold. Dew sparkled on the blades of grass. This was good. A pleasant ride to remind him of the positives of this easy mode of transportation.

It crossed his mind she was the reason this was easier than expected.

She held her hat on her head. "I'll never forget my first trip to Colorado. I feel like I've come home."

He knew exactly how she felt. That was why he wanted to save this ranch. It was more than his family's history, although that was as much a part of him as the long scar on his leg. It went deeper than saving the jobs of his cowhands, although they were as much his responsibility as Rocket and Churro. This was his home, and he'd do everything in his power to keep it intact.

"Where *is* home for you?"

"Atlanta. I grew up there, and my father's medical office is downtown. So is my half brother's pediatric cardiology practice. My half sister is moving back after she graduates." Her normal exuberance was absent from her voice, as if she didn't enjoy discussing her family.

"You're a long way from Georgia."

"EverWind's main headquarters are in Austin, but the East Coast branch office is in Atlanta. They hope to open another location in Grand Junction once the Colorado contracts start piling up." She sounded like she was reading from a script. "It will be a great opportunity for someone, but my home and family are in Atlanta."

That cemented the fact, though, that she wasn't here to stay. Why would she move here? This was just a temporary business assignment.

"Why didn't they send someone from Austin?"

"You sound like you want to get rid of me." That teasing tone was back for a brief second. "I was the sales associate who was forwarded Barry's request for more info."

From what he'd seen, Kelsea had no problem tackling problems. That type of work ethic was most impressive. "Are you enjoying your trip to Violet Ridge?"

They went over a bump, and she reached for the dash, righting herself. "Too much. New places are so exciting."

"I liked the thrill of traveling when I was in the rodeo, but coming home was always best. I just wish I'd have spent more time with my family."

"That's exactly it!" He'd never met anyone who smiled with their voice before. "Still, my father always seems to have more time for my half siblings than me. They're older than I am, and their mother doesn't like me much."

He couldn't understand why they'd reject this warm, vivacious woman who pulled people toward her.

"Their loss." Something stirred at her admission. He valued the respect of the residents of Violet Ridge, but he wasn't sure he'd earned it yet. Kelsea wanted her father's admiration, but it appeared as though the neurosurgeon held back his approval. Why was it that the ones whose respect you valued the most were also the hardest to win over?

Will navigated around a pothole and pulled over, needing a minute to compose himself. A field of wildflowers on this side of the fence caught his eye, stretching out to the rays of the early morning sun. He wouldn't have noticed these a mere week ago. He pointed them out to her, sure she'd love them. "That's larkspur, Indian paintbrush and fireweed."

"Beautiful. Simply beautiful."

He caught sight of her, her cheeks rosy, her smile broad. "Yes, it is."

He wasn't talking about the flowers. Her beauty was as much on the inside as her exterior. At last he continued driving. They approached the far northwest pasture, the one he wanted to use for the elk expansion. Last night, he'd knocked on the bunkhouse door and shared with Doc, Marshall, and Glenn some of his thoughts about elk. They asked concise questions and pointed out a need for a business plan. They'd given him real food for thought.

Cutting the engine, he and Kelsea exited the vehicle. The land with its flat valley and its access to the pond cried out for elk. Rocket jumped out and ran straight for the fence line.

Kelsea gasped. "This is the site the engineer had in mind." She waved her hand around the pasture. "See the wind rippling off the pond."

Will nodded and donned his utility belt. Then he grabbed the toolbox from the rear of the UTV. "My grandfather had big plans for the ranch, and he installed that pond himself."

They walked toward the fence where Rocket pawed at something. Will hurried over with Kelsea by his side. A small hole at the bottom of the fence alerted Will to the presence of an interloper, most likely a wolf. Some nearby tracks confirmed his suspicion. Hopefully it was long gone, but he was prepared if it wasn't. He made a note to tell the cowhands to be on the lookout. Extra patrols for the calves, too.

Rocket's tongue lolled out as he waited for praise, which Will provided. "Good dog."

Satisfied, Rocket began exploring the rest of the fence while Will got down to work. Kelsea touched his arm. "What caused the hole?"

"Some sort of predator. We coexist with a

number of different animals, and we straddle a fine line of respecting each other's presence." As it was, he'd set up rotating shifts for the northeastern pasture with the cows and calves so nothing invaded their space. "I need to fix this fence."

"I'll proceed with my work, too." She laid her pack on the ground, then typed some notes into her phone. Rummaging in her pack, she pulled out a pair of latex gloves and donned them. "Barry provided the written authorization for the soil samples. Can I get your verbal okay, and then you can sign off later?"

This was getting too real. "Sure."

That croak was his voice. He looked to see if she noticed, but she extracted a professional camera instead. "I'll also be taking pictures of the site."

He knelt by the hole and sized up the repair. He extracted pliers from his utility belt. After a few seconds, he laid them on the ground and rubbed his forehead.

"Will? What's wrong?" Kelsea strode beside him, her new jeans pristine, her penetrating gaze bright. "This must be a lot to digest. While you'll lose some of your usable land, EverWind is committed to its mission."

"How many acres?" Too much, and that might

eliminate his plan to introduce elk. It might even reduce the number of head of cattle at the Silver Horseshoe. "Too many could be a problem."

"EverWind will work with you to ensure as little interference as possible in your day-to-day operations."

Her plea was genuine, but he noticed how she referred to her company by its corporate name instead of using a more personal *I* or *we*. Something about her tone convinced him she didn't love her job as much as she loved everything else. Her promises might be for naught if she quit the company for a new adventure. Then where would that leave him without a contact he trusted at EverWind?

"There's something you should know," he said.

"You sound mysterious and foreboding. Why?"

She laid down her spade and vial beside the fence, and Rocket returned as if worried about the suddenness of her action. He sat beside her with his head tilted before he poked her out of concern. Even his dog was starting to change allegiance.

Will switched the pliers from one hand to the other and back again. "I want to introduce elk to this area. They'd suit this part of the valley, and they could help the ranch's financial woes."

"Come again? I missed something. Won't that involve start-up costs? How can expanding increase profit?"

"What profit? I'm operating at a loss and something has to change. This place would do a sight better with elk than wind turbines." But staunching the ranch's financial losses would only come with an infusion of consistent capital. The elk were a long shot; the turbines were a sure thing. His dilemma made his head hurt. He gripped the pliers and removed the old fencing.

Kelsea rose and gathered her supplies. "Have a minute? You look like you could use a friend with an ear to listen."

He might as well take a break before finishing the fence repair. "Why not?"

She gestured for him to walk beside her. Rocket bounded along on her other side. Only the shriek of a hawk broke the silence until they reached the pond's edge. Will gave Rocket his lead and the older border collie took off running, chasing ducks, his playful side coming out on this sunny morning.

"If you're trying to scare me off, it's not working."

Scare her off? Had he been so gruff she thought of him as some unapproachable cowboy who wanted everything to stay the way it was?

Was that how she saw him or how he saw himself?

"I'm just trying to tell the truth." He picked a blade of grass and split it down the middle. "If I sign, it won't be on account of EverWind's mission."

"So the environment isn't important to you?" She waved her hand at the vast expanse in front of her. "This is beautiful. Look at the puffy clouds against the backdrop of the craggy mountains. Listen to the soft hush of the rippling waves against the shore. Even Rocket is having some fun during his work break. I like his attitude."

Will fought the urge to call Rocket back to his side. Returning to work on that fence should be his top priority. He brought his lips together to whistle for the border collie when he stopped cold. The dog hadn't enjoyed himself this much in a long time. He deserved some fun.

His stomach did a flip. Once again, Kelsea had him all confused with the subtle way she made her point while bringing levity to the most mundane of tasks.

Her stare reminded him she was waiting for an answer. "Yes, I support the environmental mission of your company. Composting and up-cycling are big tenets of the Silver Horseshoe." He threw the two blades of grass on the ground. "There's something I don't understand. How will this area continue to benefit the environ-ment with big wind turbines in the middle of usable land that will lose its purpose?"

"Ah, my presentation tonight will cover how EverWind will only utilize the smallest acre-age possible." She smiled at him, a sight grow-ing more beautiful and more necessary for him with every waking moment. "And it'll be per-fect because the wind turbines will help the ranch and the residents of Violet Ridge since they are self-sustainable, something you should appreciate."

"You're not upset I'm listening to your pre-sentation for my personal gain? This might make the difference between the ranch becom-ing profitable and not."

She removed her Stetson and played with the brim. "While I'm relieved that we're communi-cating, this also presents an issue for me. If this isn't a choice you make without reservation, it won't start the partnership off well."

A friendly reminder this was a business relationship. There'd be no time for this to grow into something deep and meaningful. That might be beneficial for both of them. Absorbing her words, he reflected on how tenuous their connection was. He waited as the impact of what she'd said sank into him, but this arrangement didn't come with the same sense of the world closing around him as the moment Steve called with the news of his parents' fatal accident. In that split second, he knew he'd never return to the rodeo. His goodbye to his parents came along with a private farewell to the sport and the makeshift family he'd created with Lucky and Sabrina.

And hello to a mountain of inherited promises and debt.

He had to reassure her he was willing to make sacrifices for the good of the ranch. "The important part of that is having a strong professional relationship."

"Having something forced on you can harbor resentment," she said.

The wistfulness in her eyes gave him pause. "You sound like you're speaking from personal experience."

She reclined on the grass, and he accepted her invitation to sit next to her. Dew greeted his backside. This close to Kelsea, he inhaled her light scent of orange blossoms and vanilla. She almost made him yearn for new chapters and sweet days ahead. Everything about her, from her pink flannel shirt to the flowers on the brim of her cowboy hat, was fresh and alive.

It wasn't just the setting; it was also the company.

Her gaze followed a line of ducks at the water's edge. "Those ducklings are just so cute." One veered off the path, and the mother duck went over and corrected its course. Then they resumed their journey. "Isn't it wonderful how their mother took care of them?"

"They're one big happy family."

"I like the family you've created on the ranch. People looked at my house and saw a happy blended family, but that wasn't the case. My half sister once told me my father didn't know what to do with me. My two half siblings are like him, but having to deal with someone who's so different from himself didn't sit well. Still, I wish we were closer."

He'd never appreciated his uncle Barry more. He could say what he wanted about his uncle's dreams, but Barry had a pure heart. "I don't know how I'd have gotten through these past eight months without my uncle." Despite his bluster and talk of rainbow dreams, Barry provided stability.

He looked over at Kelsea. She stirred something in him, something deep. Talking to her about the past eight months brought him a sense of calm and acceptance that hadn't existed until now.

Until her.

He was happy, and almost didn't know how to handle it.

"My father's a little older than your uncle, but the two aren't anything alike. Once you meet Barry, you feel like you've known him for years." She plucked a clover from beside her and inhaled its fragrance.

"Uncle Barry and my father were best friends. They had a lot in common in some areas while being worlds apart in others."

"Well, my father pulled strings for me to land this job. I want my fellow employees to view me as someone who earned it. Please listen to my sales pitch at dinner with an open mind. EverWind might be your best solution."

"Without EverWind, I might have to go back on promises I made to keep up the ranch."

"Just so you know, other ranches approached my boss after the rodeo. I want you to have the first choice since there can be only one contract awarded within a set radius. Give me a chance. If you don't like the presentation, I'm out of here."

He blinked. Her loyalty astounded him, as did her enthusiasm. She extended her hand. He clasped it in his, the tingles from her mere touch impossible to ignore. There was a softness to her, but with a firm rigidity at its core. The steel butterfly was emerging from its cocoon.

Dare he open himself to her in a personal way? Make himself vulnerable to the possibility of another goodbye? There was only one way to find out, and she was worth the effort.

"I accept."

WHAT HAD KELSEA done early this morning? She might have doomed her employment with EverWind, for one thing. If word got back to her boss that she promised Will she'd accept his decision without argument or added pressure—probably not the most winning strategy—Mr. Mulroney might show her the door. Then she'd have to explain to her father why she parted ways with an employer once more. That was, if her father listened to her at all.

That made this dinner at Miss Violet's Fine Steak House and her presentation that much more important. She smoothed her floral silk dress, a favorite she'd chosen after discarding the more tailored suit, which would have matched the tone of this business occasion better.

She adjusted her eyes to the lower light but drank in the fine ambience of the restaurant. Located inside a historic carriage house, the brick walls drew her attention to the delicate stained glass window of a heart-shaped violet. The wooden backdrop on the far wall held what must have been local pottery with exquisite designs etched in the terra-cotta. On her right side, the bar's crystal gleamed with a mirror reflecting the interior.

"Do you want a drink while we wait for my uncle?" Will adjusted his bolo. She'd never seen one up close, but the black string tie with the silver horseshoe clasp suited him. It set off the chambray button shirt pulled tight across his shoulders. That, along with the slight scruff on his chin, gave every appearance of a genuine cowboy, and her chest tightened at the sight.

"I'll wait until after my presentation." She smiled as if either of them needed a reminder of the real reason they were here. As much as she'd enjoy a night on the town with Will, that wasn't why she was in Violet Ridge. "Your uncle was right in recommending this place. If I delivered my spiel at the ranch, you'd leave at every opportunity to check on either the horses or the cattle or even Churro. This way, you have no distractions."

His gaze held hers for a long moment. "I don't know if I'd agree with you." As if on cue, his phone pinged a text.

Kelsea gave him space, but she couldn't help admiring how attractive he was.

Business professionals did not make a play for their clients.

That would get her fired even faster than her offer to accept Will's decision and move on.

"That was Sabrina, letting me know she arrived safely at her next rodeo site."

"Admit it. You like feeling needed."

He shrugged, the dim light only adding to his ruggedness. "I'm the only family Lucky and Sabrina have. I take that seriously. That and the ranch."

"You love it there."

"I'm starting to realize just how much and why."

Before Kelsea could respond, Barry entered the establishment. The older gentleman looked rather dapper in a navy pinstripe double-breasted suit, although the smell of mothballs made her smile. She was touched he went to all that trouble for her. She hooked her arms into each of theirs. The maître d' led them to their table, the aged mahogany set with ivory place mats, fine bone plate china and gleaming silver.

Will held out the chair for Kelsea and then pushed her in before seating himself. She liked the old-fashioned gesture.

Kelsea unfolded the white linen napkin and placed it on her lap. Barry opened the menu set inside a black leather case. "The owners converted this place, one of the oldest structures in Violet Ridge, and named the steak house after the wife of the town's first mayor." He reached into his suit pocket and held out a shiny silver nugget to Will. "Look what I found on the way to the bunkhouse."

Will glanced at it. "But it's not the real thing. It's worthless."

"Sure is pretty." Barry tucked it in his pocket. "Fun to dream for an hour about a silver mine on our property."

That was the perfect opening. "Maybe no silver mine, but your property is a resource that can be tapped to provide energy and benefit the environment," Kelsea said.

She pulled out her work tablet and clicker. The server came over for their drink orders. Kelsea waited until she departed, then launched into her usual preliminary speech about Ever-

Wind. The evening flew by while they savored tender steak with all the trimmings. In between bites, she answered a multitude of questions.

She summarized her presentation while the server brought coffee. "EverWind goes to great lengths to minimize the impact of the construction on your livestock. Our engineers ensure the turbines fit into the landscape with minimal invasive effects. We also compensate you for any losses you incur during construction. We lease your land for twenty years, which will provide a continual income. That's especially beneficial if you have a bad year weather-wise or in case of falling livestock prices. That's when our subsidy ensures you pull through the tough times."

"You've made a compelling argument." Will thanked the server, who cleared their plates. All of them declined dessert.

Kelsea finally relaxed and soaked in the elegant yet charming ambience of the restaurant. Will's presence only added to the evening's appeal. What would it be like on a date with him? If she stayed here, it would give them an opportunity to act on this rare chemistry. She liked Colorado and could see herself living here. She especially liked Violet Ridge and everything around her.

Will leaned back and wiped the corner of his mouth with his napkin, drawing attention to his lips. She pushed away any thought of kissing him.

Business professionals don't kiss clients.

Barry cleared his throat and patted his stomach. "If I were thirty years younger—" he pointed to the silver strands gracing his hair "—I'd invite Kelsea for a stroll around Violet Ridge and walk off some of this delicious meal. As it is, I'm a bit winded, so I'll take my leave."

As he stood, Barry sent Will a pointed look, an obvious attempt to give Will and herself time alone together. But she seemed to recall Barry saying something about Regina. Perhaps she should return the favor and play matchmaker.

"If you're not too tired, it's closing time at Over and Dunne," she said. "A certain owner might enjoy seeing you're on the road to recovery."

Barry guffawed and donned his suit jacket. "Regina's too good for an old dreamer like me."

"Shouldn't she be the judge of that? I think the two of you would be great for each other." A little like her and Will if there weren't a question of distance, work and everything else.

"I'll give it a wee bit of consideration." Barry nodded at them and left the steak house.

Will laid his napkin on the table. "I don't want you to get his hopes up. It's not like he and Regina haven't had years to get together."

Kelsea accepted the check from the server and pulled out her business credit card. She tucked it into the black leather folder and smiled at the woman. "Isn't it better to expect the best and support them no matter what happens?"

Will's brows turned downward. "They're complete opposites. She'll break his heart."

"He's old enough to look after himself."

Will straightened his bolo. "Someone has to look after him."

Was there something in Will's past that caused him to jump to such a harsh conclusion? Kelsea longed to know more about this quiet but determined cowboy. Nothing like tonight, for starters.

"Maybe if Barry's advice proves to be right about you showing me around Violet Ridge, you'll start trusting him when it comes to his own feelings."

Before Will responded, the server returned and invited them to take their time, a nice but not surprising gesture given the steak house wasn't crowded. Kelsea added a generous tip on the company's tab.

Will waited until the server took her leave. "You probably think I'm overreaching or over-protective or one of those *over* words."

Not at all. She saw someone who wanted to earnestly do his best to look after his family and his ranch. There was something sweet about that, something that she could get behind. "Then let's change that impression. Let's push business to the back burner for the next hour."

At the end of that hour, she'd pick up the EverWind thread once more. For now, the town beckoned and her time here was too short to spend all of it discussing business.

CHAPTER TEN

To KELSEA'S DELIGHT, they hadn't missed the sunset while they ate dinner. The golden light of dusk reflected off the pastel colors of the wooden buildings. A romantic glow sparked something romantic in her, and she glanced at Will. They could be so much more than business acquaintances…

"I see what you're doing," Will interrupted her thoughts and directed them toward the sidewalk that led away from the carriage house restaurant and toward downtown.

Her heart raced as she feared he was about to address her lack of professionalism. "What am I doing?"

"Distracting me so I don't come up with a myriad of reasons to turn down EverWind's offer." Will tugged at his bolo tie.

The racing rhythm of her heart slowed to normal. "Uh-uh. We have fifty-nine minutes left on our business-free outing."

She strolled alongside him, allowing the contentment of a good meal and good company to take hold. Settling for that would have to be enough. The charm of the buildings with their purple, turquoise and pale yellow facades captivated her. So did the bustle of the visitors and locals. Even this late in the evening, the town was quite crowded. The window displays on Main Street caught her eye, and Will indulged her every time she stopped and stared at the unique offerings.

A group of teens, wearing flip-flops and shorts and laughing, entered Rocky Road Chocolatiers. A delicious aroma of sugar wafted Kelsea's way. Her mouth watered, but her full stomach rebelled against any more food. Everything about this night was charming.

"Violet Ridge is beautiful," she said. "What makes the town special for you?"

He was silent as he contemplated her question. Deliberative, he wouldn't rush anything. Instead, he mulled decisions like the fine glass of cabernet they'd savored with the filet. The dark stubble gracing his chin gave him a slightly mysterious aura that sent those butterflies soaring.

"I've traveled to other towns and states for the rodeo." He stopped to examine the display window for Corwin and Company Boots. Like the other facades, the purple storefront, pretty and bright, caught her attention. It had already closed for the evening, or she'd have entered and examined the fine quality leather boots. "Colorado's a part of me, same as the Silver Horseshoe was a part of my grandparents and parents. I never considered moving or leaving permanently, even when I was having fun with Sabrina and Lucky."

"I love traveling. There's always a new adventure around the bend."

What would it be like to be that attached to the place you lived? And for it to be a part of you no matter where you ventured? She hadn't found that.

Yet.

A couple with a golden retriever neared them. The dog veered toward Will, who obliged with a friendly scratch behind the ear. If anything, that endeared him to her even more. The owners waved goodbye and headed in the opposite direction.

"Linus and Violet Irwin hit on something good when they organized the town. There's something for everyone here."

"The town's named after Violet?"

"Rumor has it Linus would do anything for

his wife. It didn't hurt that her favorite flower happened to be violets, either."

"Aw, he was a romantic. Stories that revolve around love. They're my favorite." Ironic really, as she'd never figured out why or how Kristy and Preston Carruthers had fallen in love. They were complete opposites from everything her Mimi had said. A little like her and Will.

Kelsea yearned for a deep and abiding love of her own. And yet she found herself alone at the start of every new adventure.

She stopped at the next building, Weaving Wonders, where knitted gloves and hats dotted the glass window case. The fine caliber of the wool showcased the mastery of the craft. Her fingers touched the glass. "Those are beautiful."

He didn't take his gaze off the storefront, the teal wood burnished and glowing in the rays of the setting sun. "You're absolutely right."

"I'd love to buy something to remember my time here." Her father would have said it was a waste of money to buy a knit hat when she lived in the south. "Never mind. This isn't practical for an Atlanta winter."

"That doesn't sound like you." She faced him, noticing a hint of pink on those tanned cheeks. "You normally face everything with enthusiasm."

She laughed at how well he already knew her. "You're right." Suddenly, she didn't care what her father would say. She wanted to do this for herself. "I want a reminder of Violet Ridge."

She grabbed his hand and pulled him inside.

He hesitated in front of the first table. "Didn't you already buy a hat and boots?"

"Those are for everyday use. I want to buy something special. Something frilly and sentimental." A woolen purple cap with interwoven snowflakes caught her eye. "That's the one."

At that moment, her phone announced her father's ringtone. She excused herself to Will by mentioning Preston was on the line and hustled outside. "Alexis just called." He wasted no time getting to the point, as always. "She's receiving the Outstanding Student Doctoral Award. When are you flying to Boston?"

She wasn't surprised at Alexis's achievement. Alexis was a carbon copy of Preston, and they shared a close bond. She wouldn't want her half sister to have anything less. It was just that Kelsea wanted something more.

"I've been so busy at work that I haven't booked my flight yet."

He sighed. "I have a minute for you to book

the ticket. I'll read you my credit card number so you can pay for it." That familiar disappointment lurked in his voice.

"That's not the problem. This isn't a good time." That seemed to be the story of her relationship with her father.

"What are you doing that you can't take five minutes to make your sister happy?"

Shopping and having a marvelous evening with Will. "I'm with a client." A half-truth as they weren't discussing business, and the cowboy brought her happiness that had nothing to do with her career.

"This late at night?" His sardonic laugh came through loud and clear. "This is important to me, Kelsea. I expect you at your sister's graduation. Book your flight." He ended the call.

Kelsea texted her congratulations to her half sister while the pleasant glow from the dinner and the stroll with Will faded to indigestion.

BESIDE THE REGISTER, a delicate snowflake pin caught Will's attention. He added it to his purchase and handed his credit card to the salesperson. She glanced at it and then at him, her gray hair bobbing with the sudden movement. "Sullivan? Are you Rick and Polly's son?"

The name Rita on her name tag didn't ring

any bells, unlike most Violet Ridge residents whom he'd known since birth. For the life of him, he couldn't place her. "Yes. Have we met before?"

"Probably not. My husband and I were out of town when your parents died and we missed the services. Our sincerest condolences." She clucked her tongue and sent him a sympathetic look.

"Thank you." He tipped his hat toward her. "Nice shop you've got here."

"We fulfilled a lifelong dream when we opened it a couple of years ago. Some retire to Florida, but we wanted to be closer to our daughter."

"That's smart." He stared at the door, waiting for Kelsea.

"Best decision of our lives, especially since we love to ski. It's a life changer being so close to the slopes." Her light laugh trilled through the store.

"Violet Ridge is great for skiing."

She wrapped the hat and snowflake pin in teal tissue. "Your parents were so sweet and approachable. You look just like your father." The tissue crinkled as she placed it in a teal bag with handles and the store's logo. "Rick was such a character, always talking about his dreams for the town or other fresh business opportunities. He was thinking of running for mayor, you know. Before the accident."

"He never told me that." Another Sullivan pipe dream that never came to fruition.

"Rick's the person who persuaded us the town needed Weaving Wonders." She handed him back his credit card along with a pen covered with a fuchsia knitted sleeve and topped with a crocheted violet. "Best decision of our lives."

He handed Rita the pen back with a tight smile and uttered a weak goodbye. He walked out the door but didn't go far before Kelsea bumped into him. She wobbled, and he reached out to steady her. Her blue eyes didn't sparkle the way they had before she talked to her father.

What would Will talk about if he had five minutes with his father? The weather? The cost of cattle? Why he never followed through with his dreams of running for mayor?

"I guess our hour's up. Do you want to talk in town or at the ranch about EverWind?" Kelsea's voice wavered at first but ended strong.

"What about the rest of your tour? Larkspur and Lace seems right up your alley." While he had little reason to frequent the high-end women's clothing store, Sabrina had raved about their jewelry and jackets bedazzled with turquoise. "Rocky Road Chocolatiers has a great selection."

Admit it. You don't want the hour to end.

He led her toward one of his mother's favorite stores. Every Valentine's Day, whether or not he was home, he'd arranged with the former owner to deliver a box of their finest caramels to Polly.

Kelsea's ears perked up, and some of her color returned. "Is that the store that smelled so good when we passed by earlier? I love chocolate." Her gaze grew dreamy. "Wouldn't it be romantic to have a picnic with dessert from there?"

"It's one of the sweeter spots in Violet Ridge."

She didn't laugh or make any comments about his terrible pun, and he began worrying. He longed for the Kelsea of dinner to return, although for the life of him, that made little sense. Their connection centered around a business arrangement. A romantic relationship with Kelsea would be pure mayhem. Every day in every way, she'd challenge her partner, asking questions and delving into the bright colors of life around them. He and Kelsea could never work.

He wouldn't fall into the same pattern as his

father, laughing and joking through life, dreaming big and never following through with commitments.

It was for the best she was leaving at the end of the week.

She stopped and glanced back at Weaving Wonders. Will followed her gaze and found Rita changing the sign to closed. "I forgot to buy the hat."

"No one should leave Violet Ridge empty-handed." He handed her the parcel as concern that he might have overstepped his role as a client crossed his mind.

She squealed at the present. "For me?"

"A thank you for dinner."

She unwrapped the hat and snowflake pin, and her mouth dropped open. She traced the fine filigree of the silver, her eyes soft with wonder. "This is beautiful. I love it."

"Yeah, well, dinner was nice."

He groaned at his choice of words. Regular sunsets were *nice*, but Kelsea was like a Colorado sunset. In Violet Ridge against the backdrop of the Rockies, the oranges and pinks popped with an added dimension he'd found nowhere else. Sunsets here weren't just nice; they were unforgettable and exquisite.

Same as Kelsea.

His breath left him. That was the first time he'd thought in terms of color since his parents died. He stopped while she pinned the snowflake to the beanie and then donned it. It shouldn't have worked with a silk dress and turquoise boots, but on her, it did.

They fell into a slow step, his boots slapping the sidewalk, while her little strappy heels barely made any noise. Silence stretched out, but it was comfortable. That, too, was the rarest gift of all.

This stroll was nice, and he groaned at how that word was now stuck in his head. It was more than *nice*. It was unforgettable.

They reached the chocolatiers, and she grasped his arm. "Can I take a raincheck? I'm still full from dinner."

She reached up and rubbed the silver snowflake on her knit beanie.

Heat spread up his neck. "I'm sorry if I overstepped."

"Like you said, it's a thank-you for dinner. I love it in the glow of the sunset even more than when I saw it in the shop."

She stood on her tiptoes, delivering a kiss on his cheek, the warm imprint a brand on his skin. A small smile emerged on her face, along with some of her good humor. That smile would light up Violet Ridge more than a thousand wind turbines. He stopped short of kissing her back, an actual kiss that would test the waters.

Or blow everything.

The image of turbines on the acres he wanted for the elk was the reminder he needed. Those turbines were the key to the ranch's security. He had to quell these emotions. Stepping back from Kelsea was the only way he'd progress forward, so he'd leave behind something more substantial than the wisps of unfulfilled dreams like his father had done.

CHAPTER ELEVEN

WITH LAST NIGHT'S dinner a sweet memory, Kelsea drew a smiley face and doodled during the video conference call with the EverWind engineers and management team. On the screen, her boss reminded her too much of her father. For the life of her, she couldn't envision David Mulroney or Preston as college students, only as they were now in their early sixties. Maybe it was because David's red and gold tie was perfectly knotted and his cheeks held the paunch of a man who enjoyed fine cuisine with little exercise. No matter how hard she imagined an older version of Will, she only envisioned a man who would keep his athletic build and strong jawline.

Other colleagues delivered their reports, and she shadowed the outlines of the series of hearts she'd drawn in the margin, relieved Mr. Mulroney had called on her first for updates. She'd given a quick summary of her time in Violet Ridge, leaving out the good parts about Will.

"That's fine work everyone. We'll meet again on next week's video conference call." Mr. Mulroney's tone held a note of dismissal, and her finger approached the end button. "Kelsea, I'd like to speak to you."

Busted. She set aside her legal pad and nodded. Had he noticed her distracted state? The rest of the staff logged off before she folded her hands so she wouldn't doodle herself right out of a job.

"Good afternoon, sir."

"Your father and I have been friends for years." Someone, or something, caught Mr. Mulroney's attention, and he excused himself.

Uh-oh. That wasn't a promising start to their time together. That tone usually preceded a new employment search. What had she done this time? She braced herself for the blow of getting fired. Worse yet, she prepared herself for the fallout with her father.

He returned to the screen, and she defended herself. "I'm enjoying my time at the Silver Horseshoe, getting to know the Sullivan family." Along with the cowhands and animals on the ranch. Will was fast attaching himself to her heart, so she didn't mention him by name. "Getting to know my clients is the best way I can deliver a signed contract."

Mr. Mulroney tapped his pencil against his paper. "It's important to form connections, but it's also important to know when to move on. That area of Colorado has untapped potential. After we sponsored the rodeo, other ranchers and landowners have contacted us."

Kelsea should be ecstatic, but she wasn't ready to leave Will's ranch yet. "I can follow up on those leads after I deliver a signed contract with the Silver Horseshoe."

She saw the wheels turning in his mind. "We're in final negotiations for office space for our operations in the Rockies. We decided leasing office space near Gunnison rather than Grand Junction or Denver made the most economic sense. Any leads will be turned over to the sales team at that location."

A chance to stay near Violet Ridge? Her heart leaped with joy. She'd love to move closer to the town's down-home sensibility. The warm and welcoming residents were an added bonus. Then again, her father would look with disdain at her decision, shaking his head at how she followed her whims rather than buckling down at EverWind's East Coast operations.

Something Mr. Mulroney said, however, finally clicked. "Wait a minute. You're turning the leads I generated over to others?" All her hard work given to someone else? She deserved better. "Or are you considering me for the Gunnison office? After all, you sent me here rather than keeping me on the eastern seaboard sales team."

"So far you haven't made any sales. That corner of Colorado is crucial for our long-term growth. I need employees with a proven track record."

"Would you consider me for a transfer to Colorado if Will Sullivan signs with EverWind?"

"That, along with soil samples from those other leads, would make me more willing to discuss your future with whoever was in charge of the Gunnison operation." He tilted his head as if someone was interrupting him once more, and he muted the screen. Then he returned. "Get that contract with Sullivan signed, and we'll negotiate your future with the company."

He disconnected, and she sat there, stunned. Moving to Violet Ridge seemed like a real possibility if she could somehow convince her father this wasn't a whim but a measured response for her sustainable long-term employment with EverWind. However, the change depended on Will signing a contract in the end he might not be inclined to accept.

Once again, her future seemed to be in the hands of another person.

IN THE COMFORT of the bunkhouse's main living room, Will's mouth fell agape. He'd had his reservations about whatever Kelsea had stirred up when Doc and the Bayne brothers moved in temporarily. The three older gentlemen always sat in front of the Over and Dunne Feed and Seed, watching the world go by. He should have known better than to discount them so easily. That they went through all this trouble for him was mind blowing. Humbling, too.

Marshall poked his fingers underneath the suspenders holding up his pants and snapped the elastic. "I told you I still have contacts in the auction world. My buddies confirmed those figures as good estimates for starting your elk herd."

"Wait a minute, Marshall. It's not that simple. I crunched the ranch's historical data and created my financial projections." Glenn pushed four binders toward Will. "These contain four potential breakdowns depending on the number of head, weather outcomes and your present cash flow. Hmm, I forgot to account for some of your capital expenditures. You need an extra UTV. Two would work even better. I'll review the numbers one more time."

Glenn reached for the folders, his thick bushy

eyebrows curving inward, and Marshall slapped away his hand. "You've gone over it so much you talked about it in your sleep." Marshall glared at his brother and adjusted his brown bandanna. "You said the bottom line is that the elk expansion will help the ranch be out of the red in two years."

"I'll stay on site and be your resident vet for the elk. Make sure they're sound." Doc nodded. "This bunkhouse is a sight more comfortable than my daughter's house. I like feeling useful."

Will choked up, the guilt from walking past them day after day weighing down on him. If he was going to keep the ranch in the black, he had to swallow his pride and be totally honest with them.

"I'm not sure I have two years." This year's feed bill was higher than projected. Still, he was moved at the three of them coming together like this, especially Marshall and Glenn. "This is mighty generous of you."

Marshall waved away Will's praise. "It's our pleasure, and we love living here. Kelsea's cooking beats Glenn's every day of the week."

"I'm not that bad of a chef." Glenn pursed his lips.

"You scorched our grilled cheese sandwiches yesterday." Marshall leveled a look at his brother.

"Well, that made enough room for that mighty tasty pot roast, didn't it? Sure is nice of Barry to start cooking for us, too." Glenn said.

A knock at the door gave way to the squeak of the hinges. Kelsea entered, holding the handles of a metal pot with oven mitts. "I heard Jody and Jerome caught Barry's cold." She glanced at Will. "Is Sabrina feeling better? And did Lucky ever come down with it?"

Will shook his head. "Lucky's at the next rodeo. Feeling fine. He's coming back in a few weeks to help me with Domino. And Sabrina said she went to the doctor, who gave her a good report."

"Excellent." Kelsea hefted the pot and moaned. "This chicken noodle soup is getting heavy."

Marshall almost knocked Doc over in his haste to help Kelsea, a vision in a hot pink sweater and coordinated leggings paired with those strappy sandals from the first day she arrived. "It smells delicious," Marshall said.

Glenn scoffed. "I'm sure it's from a can."

Kelsea waggled her finger at Glenn. "I'll

have none of that. It's homemade from my grandmother's recipe."

Without his range rider and assistant herder checking on the cattle tonight, Will had best start on the extra tasks. Most likely he'd be under the stars later, watching over the calves. Even so, he'd be remiss if he didn't thank Kelsea first. "You're supposed to be here on business, yet you've stepped in and helped without complaint or compensation, almost to the point of being indispensable. Thank you."

Her cheeks flushed. "I love it here."

Was she just saying that, or did he dare think she might consider staying longer? He nodded at the group. "Tell Jody and Jerome not to worry about anything except getting better. I'm covering their shifts tonight."

Doc sniffed the air. "I haven't smelled chicken soup like this since my dear Stella made her last pot before she passed on." He wiped away a tear from his cheek. "How 'bout tomorrow I ride out with you and check on your herd? That'll give me a better idea of the impact of your reduced acreage on the cattle next year."

Glenn sniffed the soup and then joined Doc. "If he's staying on, I'd best stay, too. Your books

are in an awful mess. You need a full-time accountant."

"You two aren't having all the fun without
me." Marshall puffed out his chest. "I didn't
work forty years' worth of auctions for nothing.
I'll stay and make myself useful, too."

"I accept, and thank you." Something close
to awe silenced him at the three of them coming to his aid.

"Wait for our bill." Doc laughed and then
brushed Will's arm. "Neighbors stick together."

Marshall peeked under the lid. "Is that just
for Jody and Jerome, or is there enough for all
of us?" the former auctioneer asked.

"I wouldn't forget my three gents." She blushed.
"That slipped out. That's what I've been calling
you in my mind."

"I like it." Doc grinned his approval, and
even Glenn nodded.

Will started for the door when Kelsea blocked
his path. "Have you eaten yet? There's plenty."

Her concern brightened her eyes, those blue
flecks heightening the emotion. He couldn't go
there. Everyone was doing so much to save the
ranch. If he blew this, he could lose everything.
"I'm not hungry. The cattle are waiting. I'm

heading out to spend the night with the calves. Steve's joining me later and he'll bring food."

He excused himself and headed off to the stables. Besides, Kelsea never said she had any intention of staying. Goodbyes were always harder when they mattered.

CHAPTER TWELVE

MUCKING OUT THE stalls in the main stable hadn't taken long, so he had extra time to spend with Domino. Will brushed the quarter horse's mane, and the horse nickered. "What do you want to do? Are you up for some ranch work? It's not the rodeo, but I love it. Maybe you will, too."

Domino whinnied, the sound almost masking the grumbling of Will's stomach. He'd worked up an appetite with all his chores. Why hadn't he accepted Kelsea's offer of soup? Probably his stupid pride. He reached for the bucket and filled the water trough.

"I brought sandwiches for you. If you're staying out all night, you need something to eat." Will jumped at the sound of Kelsea's voice.

He turned and rubbed his eyes. "I could have sworn you were wearing something different at the bunkhouse."

Forget the old saying about a person's eyes. Kelsea's rosy cheeks were the windows to her soul. She rubbed the edge of her pink flannel shirt left untucked from her dark denim jeans. "You noticed."

He noticed almost everything about her. "Why did you change your clothes?"

He grabbed Domino's blanket and currycombs.

"You're doing the work of two people, so you need someone to help you. At least until Steve can join you. For now, I'm coming along."

For someone who hadn't owned a pair of boots or ridden a horse before arriving at the ranch, she seemed to take to ranch life almost too well. A natural cowgirl at heart. "Thank you, but no. You're a guest, not an employee."

"So are the three gents, but you accepted their help. Same with Lucky and Sabrina."

True enough, but he grasped at straws. "You're not an experienced rider."

"Barry and Kurt have been giving me lessons, remember?" Her cheeky grin was too appealing. "I'm a fast learner."

"Does that smile always get you what you want?" He slipped on Domino's bridle, leading him out to the corral.

"You'd be surprised." She bumped Domino on the nose and winked at him. "Talk him into it, okay? I'd like to see the sunset at the ranch."

"A new adventure to add to your list?" He didn't know whether he liked being a box she'd tick off when she left.

"No." She backed away and sat on the fence railing. "Your ranch is more than an adventure or something new. It's your way of life, and I respect that. I want to help, that's all."

Every time he thought he was close to figuring her out, she surprised him. Her lack of pretense was refreshing, to say the least. Rocket approached her, and she jumped off the railing and scratched him behind the ears.

"Rocket and I accept," he said. "We'll saddle Calico next."

Afterward, they set off for the pasture with the cows and calves. He kept a close eye on Domino, who had worked at the ranch over past winters and had some experience with this type of terrain. Still, there was a difference between taking part in the rodeo practically year-round and living at the ranch full-time. The quarter horse didn't seem to mind just then. In fact, his ears perked up, and he seemed like his old self again.

Will dismounted and tied Domino to a post. Kelsea did likewise with Calico. He checked the cattle watering station and filled it to the top.

"What do you want me to do?" Kelsea approached him. "And when are you taking your dinner break?"

His stomach grumbled at her words. "Once I check on the calves, I'll eat."

"Let's get started. Two of us will make for lighter work, and that's a great thing because I haven't had dinner, either."

Will handed her a small medical kit from Domino's saddlebag. "In case we come across any issues." Coming to the pasture every day helped him keep abreast of each calf and their developing personalities. So far this spring, everything had been fairly routine.

Several cows lounged while others congregated at the licking station. Once he poured feed into the troughs, some lumbered his way. Kelsea tapped his arm. "What's that over there? The thing that looks like a giant scratching post for a cat crossed with big toilet scrubbers."

Her chuckle meshed with his laughter as they observed a black-and-white cow going to town, her happiness evident while she rubbed her sides along the bristles. "That's a cow brush. I added it last month, and they love it."

"Does it hurt?"

"On the contrary. It helps their circulation and gives them a place to scratch. It keeps them safe from possibly hurting themselves on exposed nails on fences."

"So something new actually benefited the ranch, huh?"

He dipped his Stetson toward her. "Point well taken, Miss Carruthers."

"Thank you, Mr. Sullivan." She touched the brim of hers in return. "Dinnertime?"

"As long as I can keep watch over the cows and horses." He laced her fingers through his, and they walked toward Domino and Calico. She broke the contact, and he missed her soft delicate skin. She reached into her saddlebag and brought out bags of food.

"And as long as you don't mind me talking."

Never. He already found himself looking forward to her stories about her encounters with the cowhands and the town residents each day. She made the simplest conversation seem like a cherished event. "It's growing on me."

Why was it so hard for him to express himself around her? Did it have to do with that bull that stampeded on his chest whenever she was near, making him feel breathless and invigorated at the same time?

She laid a blanket on the ground and unwrapped sandwiches from the bags. "Turkey or ham?"

"Turkey, thanks." He lowered himself and reclined on the blanket, then accepted the sandwich and took a big bite. This was no ordinary sandwich. She'd mixed basil with mayonnaise and sprinkled the homegrown tomatoes with a touch of pepper. The lettuce came from Barry's garden, and it was delicious.

That was something else he'd noticed about Kelsea. She put her own touch on everything, even this seemingly simple picnic dinner. If he were going to trust anyone with something as big as EverWind on the Silver Horseshoe, she was that person.

From beside him, she waved toward the scenic view that greeted them, the low-lying clouds tinted with deep orange as the sun hovered near its dipping point on the horizon. The gentle lowing of the cows provided an interesting symphony. And yet the beautiful backdrop of the calves nestling against their mothers faded compared to her. His heartbeat raced while he polished off his sandwich.

"Breathe in this crisp air. This is the perfect spot for dinner."

He agreed even with her voice weaving daydreams about pots of gold at the end of the rainbow.

"What happened to Miss Violet's Steak House?" he teased.

She giggled and moved closer, her scent of oranges and spring filling him with calmness. He'd had his share of relationships, even a broken engagement, but this connection with her? This could be an adventure of a lifetime. She was making him reconsider his thoughts about dreamers. He wasn't sure that was a good thing.

She gave his words consideration, the long pause drawing out her response. "They both have advantages, but this?" She placed the rest of her sandwich on the bag. "Miss Violet's is great for a special-occasion dinner, but this setting for a picnic meal? This is life. It's special every day. I see why you love it. I wouldn't tire of it, either."

"It's easy to see why my great-grandparents decided to stay here."

"When something's right, it's right."

Her leg bumped into his. He tingled from her touch even with the layers between them. In the slight breeze of the topsy-turvy season that was Colorado's spring, her blond hair fluttered in the breeze. Her cheeks flushed, her breath came in quick spurts. His gaze was drawn to her pink lips, so appealing and so kissable.

She smiled and drew nearer. He entwined

his hands in her hair, stroked her cheek and put his lips on hers. The silkiness of her mouth was soft and appealing. The sweetness of her was more than he could have ever imagined. She deepened the kiss, the world spinning around him. Her arm circled his back, and no distance separated them.

This was right, and he savored feeling the emotion after cutting it off for too long. That bull in his stomach did a full number on him, flattening him on the ground, leaving him as breathless as any rodeo ride. This kiss was the start of something rare and unexpected.

Except she lived in Georgia, and his home and heart were here in Colorado.

With effort, he separated from her but couldn't take his eyes off her. She blinked and then licked her lips. "Wow!"

An understatement, but he had to pull himself together. She was leaving soon, and she didn't need to take his heart with her.

"Kelsea—"

"Will—"

A deep blush came over her cheeks. "You go first. What's your dream for the ranch?" she asked.

A few seconds ago, he wouldn't have thought

anything could have destroyed the moment. He was wrong.

"Dreams don't pay the bills." He had to be honest with her. She deserved that and more.

"Dreams provide hope when everything else is haywire." She reached into the sack and pulled out an apple for him and then one for her. "I know that for a fact."

He munched on his, the sweetness paling after that kiss. He kept watch over Rocket and the bucolic scene on the other side of the fence. Even Domino seemed relaxed for the first time since he'd been back at the ranch. All of this happiness surrounded him, yet his stomach tensed. Why was she so insistent on believing in dreams?

She bit into the apple, and juice dripped down her chin. Will reached into his pocket and whipped out a clean bandanna. She accepted it and wiped away the droplets.

"What's your dream?" he asked.

"To see what's around the next bend and greet whatever it is with a smile and love." She tried giving him back the bandanna, but he curled her fingers around the cloth. More tingles shot up his arm. Why did this woman who invested so much in everything flimsy and fleeting make him feel this way?

"Keep it." Was he insistent about that so she wouldn't forget him?

Why did that thought hurt as much as never seeing her again?

She stuffed the bandanna in her pocket. "Surely, you have a dream." He shook his head. "What were you talking about with the three gents earlier?"

He hesitated and then elaborated on his vision of elk and cattle coexisting on the ranch. Enthusiasm poured out of him. He outlined what the three gents had incorporated into a business plan that held the potential of turning hard work into saving the Silver Horseshoe.

This was a lot for one person. For the first time, he wanted someone by his side during the process, to share the ups and downs. What would it be like to have this vibrant woman beside him, not just for a week, but for always?

The sun dipped below the Rockies. How had he lost track of time talking to Kelsea? The grass and pond were now covered in a blanket of shadows rather than dripping with color.

The sound of a motor disrupted the calm. Steve pulled up in the UTV and announced he'd take Kelsea's place with the task at hand. After promising she'd let them know she arrived at the ranch house safely, Kelsea drove away.

Will checked on the horses. Domino seemed like his old self. With that happy thought, he removed his bedroll from the saddlebags. Then he paused. Tonight, he'd enjoyed every second of Kelsea's kiss. Her positivity was winning him over.

The issue was he wanted more evenings like this with Kelsea. Someone who lived on the other side of the country.

CHAPTER THIRTEEN

EVER SINCE THE night of their dinner in Violet Ridge, Kelsea possessed a hankering to find out if the treats at the Rocky Road Chocolatiers were as good as they smelled. To her delight, a trip to town presented her with an opportunity to do just that.

She entered the small candy shop, and the aroma of chocolate filled her nostrils. She bent over and peered through the opaque glass at the shelves of treats. Truffles and fudge occupied space alongside luscious chocolates filled with cream fillings or nuts. Then there was the display of chocolate-covered apples. All of it was as tempting as that left dimple in Will's cheek.

She straightened and explored the shelves behind her. Every inch of space was covered with stuffed animals, oversized lollipops and bottled soda. She picked up a stuffed elk and then put it back. Somehow, she didn't think Alexis would appreciate this small token along with her actual graduation present, although Kelsea liked the whimsy.

"Can I help you?" a woman's voice called from behind and Kelsea startled.

Turning around, she planted her hands across her chest. "You scared me."

The saleswoman offered a crooked smile. "I was in the back. Would you like a sample?"

Kelsea didn't have to be asked twice, and she savored a raspberry cream chocolate. "That's heavenly."

"Thanks. You look familiar, but I don't think we've met before." The woman slid the tray back into place.

"I'm here on business at the Silver Horseshoe." Speaking of the ranch, she wanted to get them a present to express her thanks. "I'd like to purchase a thank-you gift for the Sullivans and the cowhands. What would you recommend?"

"Barry Sullivan?" She waited for Kelsea's nod. "He loves my chocolate habanero truffles and the Irish cream ones, too. Jody and Jerome are frequent customers here. They're both fond of the chocolate bacon."

Kelsea scrunched her nose at the last, but ordered a box of truffles for Will and Barry and enough chocolate bacon for the whole bunkhouse as a get-well-soon present. As the salesperson wrapped it up, Kelsea asked, "Is chocolate bacon popular?"

The woman, who appeared to be nearly the same age as Kelsea's twenty-seven, taped the sides of the package and laughed. "Especially with teen males. At least that's my experience in the two years since I bought this shop. I'm Emma Graham, the owner."

"Kelsea. Nice to meet you."

"Oh, you're the rodeo princess." Kelsea's face grew as hot as a chili pepper. "My daughter, Macy, is about to enter pre-K. Thanks for all you did with the fundraiser."

"I loved every minute." Kelsea handed over her credit card. "What would you recommend for someone who loves all things chocolate?"

"I'm out of my famous molten lava cakes for the day. I make them once a week, and they sell out pretty quickly. My recommendation is to go with the dark chocolate cherry fudge or the turtles."

Kelsea selected some of each. On the spur of the moment, she glanced back at the stuffed elk and added one to her purchase. Before she left, she'd give Will the elk as a reminder to keep dreaming.

She thanked Emma for all her help.

"You're a delightful addition to Violet Ridge, Kelsea. I hope you come again."

Kelsea didn't correct Emma's misperception. She loaded her purchases in her rental car and drove to the feed and seed.

Minutes later, she grabbed a cart at Over and Dunne, list in hand. She whipped off her sunglasses and her eyes adjusted to the dimmer lighting. How hard could it be to buy goat feed? After all, she just bought chocolate for the cowhands and Barry. Her jaw slackened as she stared at the different varieties. She read over Barry's notes, searching for the name of the brand and finding nothing.

He didn't respond to her text, but she wasn't surprised, as he was busy. She'd also noticed he had a tendency to forget where he'd placed his phone. If only she'd taken a picture of Snow and Flake's regular feed, she'd have her answer. Then again, she'd have never appreciated the variety and selection of goat food. Grains and pellets, young goat and old. This was actually fascinating stuff.

She wanted to share this latest adventure with Will. But she'd seen little of him over the past couple of days, and she was almost to her two-week mark of time allotted for her stay. Still, she'd been busy driving to ranches in other parts of the state to collect soil samples, since the delays here couldn't be helped. With the ranch being shorthanded, he and Steve had spent the night in the meadow, riding range and moving the cows and calves.

That night, she should have mentioned Mr. Mulroney's bombshell while they were discussing dreams. Then again would telling Will about EverWind's Gunnison office constitute exerting undue pressure on him? That didn't even cover the possibility of other ranches being under consideration for the contract.

All of that was moot, anyway, since he was everywhere at the Silver Horseshoe except in the same room as her. She touched her lips and remembered the kiss. Hard to ask someone for a second kiss if he wasn't around.

A loud crash from behind her broke her reverie, and Kelsea searched out the source. A clerk swept up a broken bag of cattle feed. "Excuse me."

He glanced her way, an exasperated look on his face. "I'll be right with you."

"I'll be on aisle four." She went back and waited. Reading the descriptions was more fun than she'd have thought possible. Finally, the clerk appeared, bits of feed on his sleeve. "You have some feed, right there." She waited until he brushed it off. "Can you help me decide what goat feed to buy?"

"You look familiar. I know you from the rodeo. You're Kelsea, right?" The clerk snapped his fingers. "Regina wants to see you. Follow me."

Perfect. Regina would know better than anyone the brand of goat feed the Sullivans usually bought. Not only that, but the store owner had her pulse on everything that went on in Violet Ridge. If anyone would know of a long-term room to rent or someone looking for a roommate, it would be Regina. If Kelsea ended up moving here, and that was a big *if,* she'd need a place to live.

The clerk knocked on the storeroom door, and Kelsea entered once bidden to do so. Piles of boxes of varying height occupied most of the space, and Regina crouched in front of them. She stood and swept her long plait of coppery hair to her back. "Look at what you've done."

"Me? I did nothing." Kelsea's eyes widened. Had she ordered the wrong number of T-shirts at the rodeo? No, she was sure she hadn't. Besides, those were supposed to be delivered to the customers and the ranch. That delivery was one reason she hadn't moved into the Violet

Ridge Inn yet. She patted the top box. "Are these the T-shirts?"

Regina handed her a box cutter. "See for yourself."

Kelsea walked over and peeked inside a box. She found it full of Stetson hats. "What does this have to do with me? These aren't mine. I only own one cowboy hat."

She picked out the one on top, a weathered but serviceable brown hat, and placed it on her head. It was a good three sizes too big, and she tipped it back into the box.

"Vern told one of his ex-wives, who told her friends and so on. Word spread through Violet Ridge faster than a bucking bull that I was accepting cowboy hats and Western apparel for consignment."

Kelsea's mouth formed an *O*. "I was right?" A slow smile spread across her lips. "People do have hats in their closets with plenty of wear left in them."

"And belts and boots and shirts and buckles." Regina let out a deep breath. "Everyone who dropped off a box wanted me to thank the rodeo princess. So, when are you coming to work for me?"

Kelsea's fingers froze on a gray cowboy hat. Part of her objected to the presumption she

would change ships in midstream, but something stronger pulled at her. Flattery for sure,
but a feeling akin to relief that someone recognized and appreciated her worth. It was nice to
be offered a job out of the blue. That had never
happened before.

She caressed the soft brim of the hat, her
throat tight. "Thanks, but I already have a job.
In Atlanta."

With every passing day, her ties to Violet
Ridge grew stronger and more genuine. In the
past, whenever something good came into her
life, it didn't last long. Perhaps that was how
she'd put aside the disappointment, by moving
on to greener pastures.

Perhaps Violet Ridge was her pasture.

Was it the town itself or a complex cowboy at
the root of it all? Emotion swirled in her heart
about Will. His strength and sense of purpose
propelled his every move. He didn't fool her.
Underneath his gruff exterior beat a compas-
sionate heart that would do anything for the animals under his care. Same for his friends and
family, including his uncle. Despite his grum-
blings about Barry's big dreams, a generous
heaping of love poured out of Will every time
Barry was in the same room.

This was how families acted around each

other. This was how they showed they cared. Moving to Violet Ridge might provide her with a family of her choosing, the same way Will had bonded with Sabrina and Lucky.

And yet committing to EverWind would prove to her father and half siblings she was a responsible adult. If they saw that, the same way Regina and Will acknowledged her worth, she wouldn't feel inferior anymore.

"Earth to Kelsea."

She hadn't realized she was that deep in her thoughts. "Sorry, come again?"

"This job of yours with EverWind." Regina propped her elbow on one of the boxes. "You don't seem to love it much. After all, you've helped at the rodeo, organized a T-shirt drive and sparked residents to clean out their closets while you've been here. Why don't you come work for me? I've never had a partner, but we could arrange some sort of deal. You could use part of the building for a consignment store."

"Thanks, but you're the reason this feed and seed is so successful." She stepped away from the hat with reluctance. "This place is the heart of the ranching community, isn't it?"

Regina patted the top of the nearest stack of boxes. "You say you don't want to work here, but your eyes say otherwise." She whipped out a box cutter and peeked inside. Then she rolled her eyes. "More belt buckles."

Kelsea came over and held one to the light. "They're beautiful."

"They're a nuisance. I can't tell what's my merchandise and what's not." Regina reached for the packing tape and sealed the box before muttering something unintelligible under her breath. She stopped and stared at Kelsea. "You seem like someone who follows her heart. Guess I was wrong."

Actually, she was right. What's more, Regina didn't make that sound as if she was a nuisance the way Preston would have. "I'll think about your offer and get back to you." She opened the flap of another box, revealing a turquoise necklace, leather belts and spurs. She ran her hand along the edge of the spur, the rasp of metal echoing in the room. "If Will signs the contract, I might end up transferring here. Maybe I could work for the Gunnison office and you at the same time."

"Sounds like there's a condition attached to your move." Regina put her finger on what had been bothering Kelsea since her talk with Mr. Mulroney. "You can't control other people's decisions any more than you can control your heart. Why don't you leave EverWind and put your talent toward something you love?"

Kelsea stilled the circular motion of the spur. "EverWind is a sure thing, and my father is set on my keeping this job. I promised you I'll think about your offer, and I will." Presenting her father with a plan might show him she wasn't doing this on a whim. "If I were to move to this area, do you know of any rooms for rent?"

"There's a high demand for housing here. Seasonal work, you know. We're done with the skiing season, but the summer activities are about to kick into high gear. Hiking and white-water rafting, and then there are the mineral springs resorts." Regina bustled around the storeroom.

"Is anyone looking for a roommate? I can't stay at the Silver Horseshoe forever."

Regina huffed. "Honey, the Sullivan men wouldn't notice if you stayed or not."

Kelsea read between the lines and discerned there was something under the surface as far as Regina and Barry were concerned. "Did something happen in the past between you and Barry?"

Regina pursed her lips. "That's exactly the point. Nothing has happened in ten years!"

"You're direct, and you know what you want. Why don't you ask Barry out?"

Regina laughed and then sighed. "I've given that man every signal I'm available. I've hinted and I've cajoled. He's not interested, and I have my pride, especially after my last disaster of a marriage."

A knock stopped Kelsea from responding, and the clerk ducked into the room with two more boxes. Regina pointed at the door. "No, no, no. We're returning those to whoever brought them." She glared at Kelsea. "You, come with me. We're ending this now."

Regina strode out of the room, and Kelsea helped the clerk by taking one of the boxes. "I only came here to buy goat feed."

By the time they reached the front, the only customer around was Will. Kelsea's heart raced that much faster. Reminding herself she owed it to him to tell him about the new twist with EverWind didn't slow down her heart rate. She had to tell him. It wouldn't be right to hold back any longer. That kiss offered a promise of something she wasn't sure she could deliver, but maybe she could. She wouldn't know unless she was honest about this development. EverWind first, more kisses second.

Regina reached Will before Kelsea did.

"Don't tell me my new employee got your order wrong again?"

"Nope, I ran out of goat feed. They'd butt me for sure if I didn't make a special trip into town for them." His gaze connected with Kelsea's. Dark circles lined his brown eyes, drawing attention to the hours he'd been devoting to his ranch. "Wish I'd known you were here. It would have saved me time."

Time he needed to sleep.

"Barry sent me here. Didn't he tell you?"

Will hefted three bags of feed into his cart. "Nope. He told me this was top priority."

"Regina?" The cashier ducked her head. "Another car pulled up and the driver's unloading boxes on the curb."

Regina muttered under her breath and stormed off. Kelsea waited until the older woman was out of earshot before she laughed. Will hefted one more bag of feed into the cart and added some supplements. Her laughter faded away when she caught sight of those dark circles once more. "Barry's right. You need some time away from the ranch. You're killing yourself doing the work of three people," she said.

"I can sleep when everyone's well. The cowhands depend on me." His voice broke with equal emotion. "The ranch is all they have."

He rolled the cart toward the register, but she slid her foot in the way. "Life is more than work. Look at my father. He never stops to appreciate what's around him." Unless it was Alexis or Adam. Come to think of it, though, she'd never expressed to Preston her feelings about the constant comparisons and subsequent disdain.

Had her pride prevented her from asking him if he realized he treated her differently?

"I appreciate…" He rubbed his eyes but stopped as if he knew he couldn't knead away the lack of sleep.

Regina came toward them, a fierce gleam in her eye. "Kelsea, you have to tell people you're not starting a consignment store here."

"I never said I was starting one!" Her indignation rose to the surface. She was getting tired of everyone running her life for her. Although she didn't mind Regina doing it quite as much as her father. Her meddling was appreciated. She hoped Regina felt the same way regarding her suggestions about Barry.

"Well, my office says otherwise." She strode off, muttering something about the Sullivan men and Kelsea.

Chastised, Kelsea moved her foot out of the way. "I'm stopping at Howard's Grocery for ingredients for more pots of chicken soup. When I get back to the ranch, put me to work."

"It's not—"

She walked over and placed her finger on his lips. They trembled under her touch. "If you say it's not my responsibility, I'll buy canned soup and then you'll have a bunkhouse of cowhands after you."

The edge of his eyes crinkled, a proper smile breaking out on his lips. "They'd take your side."

She flipped her blond hair to her back. "Darn right they would." She started for the front of the store. "I'll meet you at the goat shed."

ONCE THEY STORED the goat feed in a secure location, Will saddled the horses with Kelsea's help. He rode Domino to the middle pasture for a check on the cows and calves with Kelsea beside him on Calico. She fit in well on the ranch, almost too well.

Finding a person to share all this with him hadn't been something he'd considered much, but since they'd kissed two days ago, he couldn't think of anything else.

Were the good times worth the goodbyes?

They continued riding until they arrived at the meadow. Cows and calves lowed from their new location with fresh grass. He dismounted and tied Domino's reins to the closest post. Kelsea did the same. In ten short days, she'd proven a natural for adapting to ranching life.

"Kelsea."

"First things first." She came over and jabbed him on the chest. "You need to relax more."

"I can't afford to relax." Not with a bank balance near zero. Guilt rocketed through Will. Had his time on the rodeo circuit kept him from knowing the truth earlier? Would his presence on the ranch have helped get out of the hole before it became a chasm?

That indignant stare morphed into something softer. "Will, what's wrong?" She touched his forearm. "Are you okay?"

"I couldn't help but wonder if I was part of the problem. If I'd come home sooner…"

She rubbed his arm, her softness easing some of the ache in his bones. "From everything I've heard, your parents were proud of your rodeo days. They wanted you to pursue something that made you happy. Not everyone is so lucky to have such support."

Be that as it may, the guilt still weighed on him. "And now I have even more support. Thank you."

Her cheeks flushed and she walked over to Calico's saddlebag. "I didn't do anything."

"The three gents are working hard on my behalf. Doc and Marshall helped move the cattle, and Glenn has transformed my books into working order." He let out a rough breath. He decided to tell her everything. "Introducing elk would have been a boost a while back, but now it might be too late."

Failure tasted dustier than the dirt he swallowed whenever he fell off a horse at the rodeo.

"Did he factor in EverWind's current offer? That's a windfall." She frowned, a most unusual Kelsea expression. "I have a confession. There's been a development."

Her hesitation gave him pause, but he forged ahead. "Go on. Tell me."

"While it will take months for the actual installation, EverWind wants your answer about whether you're signing the contract by tomorrow. Otherwise, there are ranchers who've said they're open to signing with us. I've even visited a few other places and gotten samples from some of them."

Had his delay cost him the offer? "I'm almost ready to sign. Doc is calling some friends to check on the impact of the turbines on the stock. I have to look out for them. He's supposed to get back to me tomorrow. Then I'll have my answer."

"That's good enough for me." Kelsea buttoned her denim jacket and pointed toward the far end of the pond. "Walk with me?"

He nodded, then jammed his hands in his pockets. They strolled along the shore that stretched from here to the northeastern pasture where the cattle had grazed last week. The gentle sound of the water lapping against the grass reminded him of the land's resilience. He bent over and picked up a stone, sending it skipping along the surface until it sank.

"I've never skipped stones before. How do you do it?" Her eyes lit up in the rosy glow of the afternoon sun.

He reached down and collected several smooth stones, handing her one. "It's all in the flick of your wrist."

Kelsea faced the water and threw one overhanded. It plopped straight into the water. "I don't think that's the way it should be done."

He laughed, the feeling sweeping over him. He'd missed the spontaneity of doing something just for fun.

"You'll get the hang of it. You have a persistent way about you."

"You say that like it's a bad thing." Her raised

eyebrow told him he'd best tread water carefully.

"Not at all. You're a breath of fresh air." He scuffed his boots on the ground and then picked up more flat stones. "Here. I'll show you."

"I'd love that."

Nestling behind her, he planted a stone in her hand while pocketing the rest. Her light scent sweetened the air, and her silky smooth hair tickled his chin. There was something about her thirst for new experiences that meshed well with his pragmatic self. Her mere presence made him come alive and look forward rather than back.

He reached for her arm. "You dig your feet into the ground like a baseball pitcher."

"I thought pitchers moved their feet when they threw the ball."

He laughed again, the sound rusty from lack of use. "You're right. Tilt yourself so you're at a slight angle with the water." She moved with him, and he brought her arm back. "The key is a quick flick of the wrist."

She did so and released the stone. It skipped twice before sinking. She seemed to wait a moment, then turned and launched into him for a full hug. Her softness pressed against him. He leaned into her before her gaze lifted, the connection instant and electric. Unlike the stone, this force was unsinkable.

He moved his lips closer to hers.

"They've told me I can ask for a transfer to the new Gunnison office if you sign."

He didn't think any words could spoil this tender moment, but these did.

"What?" He backed off.

"Any possibility of my transferring to Colorado is contingent on your signing the contract."

The stones now weighed down his pockets. "If I sign, you move here. And if I don't?"

Anguish played across her face. "A new sales member will get the contacts from the rodeo. There's a good chance they'll sign another ranch, especially now that they have those samples. If they do that, they could lower the offer to you or even walk away altogether." She hesitated, wringing her hands. "I feel like I'm only adding more pressure to your decision."

This company's tactics seemed underhanded at best. "I'm not sure whether I want to do business with a corporation that's holding something over your head."

"Oh." The muscles in her cheek relaxed, and she exhaled. "You're the second person today to question the company's tactics."

She'd talked about this to someone else? That knocked the breath out of him. "What? Who?"

"I asked Regina if she knew of anyone in town with a room to rent. I mentioned Ever-Wind and the contract." Kelsea's sweet lips twisted into a frown. "Will, it's not a secret why I'm at your ranch."

She was right, but the fact she'd brought this situation up with Regina before him sent a ripple of hurt through him. "Did you talk about my financial troubles with her?"

"No, I didn't. I asked Regina for a recommendation about a place to live and why I wanted to know. The only way I can convince my father I've given this serious consideration is to create a plan. So he'll be proud of one of *my* accomplishments." A burst of wind almost sent her hat flying, and she held it down with both hands.

Silence stretched around them, tension thickening with each second, until he realized what she'd said. "You'd really consider moving here? That would be…" He searched for the right word but couldn't express how light, almost giddy, he felt. "I'm sorry I jumped to conclusions about your talk with Regina."

"See? Letting me in isn't so hard, right? You

don't let many people in your life except for
Lucky and Sabrina. Why not?"

He glanced at the horses, contentedly munch-
ing on their dinner of oats. Then he scanned
the cows and calves, equally content in the new
pasture. "Is that a roundabout way of asking
about my past relationships?"

"There's a difference between dating and letting someone in." She grinned and picked up
a stone, sending it skipping along three times
before the water swallowed it. "Now that you
mention it, I'm curious about both."

"You're more relentless than you look."

"You live with Preston Carruthers, and then
we'll talk about relentlessness." She veered
away from the path and plopped in the grass
near the pond. "You're not off the hook. If you
care to share, that is."

One more glance confirmed everything was
in order with the herd. He sat on the ground beside her. "Haven't we done this before?"

"Yes, but this time, we're talking. No kissing. You mess me up, and I have to stay professional." She scooted over and added distance
between them.

Too bad. It was more fun to talk to her when
she was closer. "Hmm, you want to be profes-

sional, yet you're asking about my past romantic relationships."

She reached over and bumped his arm. "Even business associates can be friends."

"You pack a pretty heavy punch." He laughed as he pretended to rub the spot. He picked a blade of grass and split it down the middle. "I've had a few relationships here and there. For the most part, it turns out I'm not a good catch." Or at least that's what he'd heard enough times.

"Who said that, and why?"

"My last girlfriend. I've been known to lose track of time when I'm on the rodeo circuit or looking after Domino." He concentrated on the grass. He glanced over at her, noticing how much more relaxed she was, her blue eyes cheerful and conscientious. "It wasn't uncommon for me to show up a couple of hours late to a date, or even forget about it."

"Hmm, the absent-minded cowboy? Not so popular, huh?" Her chuckle was delicate enough to know she wasn't making fun of him, but enough to show she'd push him to want to do better.

"I was engaged a couple of years ago, but she broke it off. She said I tended to shut her out. According to her, I acted differently around Lucky and Sabrina, more open and carefree.

After that, it was easier to spend time with them or Domino." Would he fall into his old habits if a relationship did develop between him and Kelsea? Judging from how often ranch business distracted him and he'd excused himself from talking about EverWind with her, he knew the answer. It wasn't the right one. Then again, she'd held her own and found ways around his excuses. That gave him hope he could change, or make room for her in his life. "What about you?"

"Being Preston Carruthers's daughter was enough of a deterrent for the boys in high school. Then when I started hopping from one job to another, I'd have a boyfriend here and there, but none of them stuck. My half sister says it's because I'm a romantic, but what's wrong with a candlelight dinner and music? Little touches like that. Ones that show someone you care."

And that was why they could never work. He'd get caught up in the ranch, and she'd wonder if he cared. This was why it was better to keep an arm's length.

Yet, the ranch had come alive in the past week with Kelsea's cheerfulness. She brought in light and made it feel like a home. Somehow, she didn't see herself like he saw her. A sweet, good-natured person who formed instant bonds and made everything better even in the face of adversity.

"There's someone out there who can give you all of that." Too bad it couldn't be him.

Unless it could be. That optimism of hers stirred something deep within him, stoking something that made him feel he could be that person.

She stared at him as if she could read him like he could read the cows and calves by their tone and body language. "What if there was someone here who could give me so much more?"

Behind them, the lowing of the cows grew more insistent, and his responsibility for the ranch flared into full flame. The animals depended on him. He rose and dusted the grass and dirt from his jeans. She followed suit.

The spell was broken. "EverWind shouldn't base a possibility of a transfer on my decision, Kelsea. What's more, if you made contacts from the rodeo, you should be the one who pursues them. Are you prepared to walk away from them if they send you back to Atlanta?"

Those expressive cheeks deepened to a rosy pink in the light of the setting sun. "Are you ever going to let your guard down and just be?"

"On a ranch, taking your eye off safety could have serious consequences." Just like in his case, it could result in the loss of his heart.

"You let me in more than you intended, and you're scared." Her steely look of determination saw through him.

"We won't work, Kelsea." While he longed for someone to share the everyday life of the ranch with him, she wouldn't be around long enough to be that person.

"Why not?" A slow smile spread across her beautiful pink lips. "Because guess what? You just skipped stones, shared your life with me and sat in the sunshine. It's time to stop running, cowboy, and face up to what's happening between us."

She strode away, and he stared at her back in disbelief. Somehow, she'd managed to find a way for him to be near the cattle yet relax at the same time. He wanted to protest, but it was to no avail.

She was right. He found himself smiling as he followed her toward Calico and Domino.

CHAPTER FOURTEEN

NEARING THE GOAT PEN, Kelsea pressed the red button and ended her phone conversation with Martha at the Violet Ridge Inn. Starting tomorrow afternoon, she'd be staying at the lodge for four nights until her return flight to Atlanta.

Business professionals keep a respectful distance and don't kiss their clients.

Putting physical distance between her and Will while the contract was under negotiation was for the best. But if he signed, and she moved to Colorado, she'd see if he wanted to close the gap between them. Perhaps permanently.

He made the ordinary extraordinary. Who knew skipping stones was a contact sport?

Snow came over and butted her in an obvious ploy for attention. She hurried into the pen, taking care with the gate so the three animals wouldn't escape. "Hello, goats and Churro. What do you think? Should I stay? I want to move here. Isn't that enough?"

She found the goat brush. Snow wiggled

with delight as Kelsea stroked her back with the brush. Flake came over, demanding equal time, while Churro guarded the group, accepting Kelsea into the fold. Snow wandered away while she brushed Flake. From her vantage point, she saw Will exiting the stables.

Now was the perfect time to tell him about the thank-you present she'd decided upon for letting her stay at the Silver Horseshoe.

"Will!" Flake nudged her with his horns. "Point taken about the loud shouting. Sorry, Flake."

She put away the brush and hurried toward Will, taking care to close the gate behind her.

She caught up with him on his front porch. "Doc and I are about to talk." He didn't waste any words. "I'll have my decision tonight about the contract."

"I have a meeting with the engineers later today about the soil samples and photos I expressed to them. Then I'll review the selected site with you for your final decision. That's not why I wanted to talk to you, though." Although after she conveyed the engineers' thoughts, she'd need to pin down a time for the signing. They'd also need a notary as a witness. Ever-Wind was in the midst of changing over to electronic document signing, and this was one of the last paper contracts. "I'm leaving tomorrow, and I want to do something as a thank-you for letting me stay here."

That muscle in his jaw tightened. "I thought your flight wasn't for a few more days."

"EverWind okayed my four-night stay at the Violet Ridge Inn. I'll be here in the daytime, working out the details of the contract. I'm not leaving Colorado yet." Slow delight spread through her that he'd miss her. "You're probably counting down the minutes until you don't have a houseguest."

Her small chuckle didn't have any real oomph in it.

"You're probably counting down the minutes until you don't have goat poop in your hair." He reached up and pulled out a black pellet.

That deep laugh of his reached down and twisted her insides something fierce. These feelings were genuine: a little scary and totally wonderful.

"I'll miss the goats." Her admission was sincere, but the animals weren't at the top of her list of who'd she miss most at the Silver Horseshoe. Topping her list was a certain cowboy. She decided to launch into details of her gift to him. "The chocolates were a small gesture, but there's something else I'd like to do before

I leave. I want to paint the living room and spruce it up for you."

"That's too much." He shook his head, his dark eyes becoming shadowy as if he wanted to accept, but couldn't bear to let someone else take care of this. "All I did was let you use a vacant room. I'm doing the same in the bunkhouse for Doc, Marshall and Glenn."

His gruffness might, in fact, fool others, including himself, yet she knew better. Why couldn't he trust his feelings? "It was more than that, and you know it."

She'd miss waking up to the glorious sunsets. She'd miss Barry bringing up his next big idea whenever they cooked dinner for the cowhands.

And then there was Will.

The connection between them could be scary if she let it, this type of soul-searching bond that didn't exist with anyone else. Like her first attempt at skipping stones, any chance of a lasting relationship might sink before it took flight. Atlanta or Violet Ridge? A relationship with her family or with Will? Staying at EverWind as the staid sales representative or embracing life as a cowgirl? Those were her dilemmas.

She was almost out of time here, and leaving this glorious place filled her with sadness. But she knew what she had to do.

That muscle in his jaw, the one that gave his true feelings away, tightened and then released. "You don't owe me anything, Kelsea. The pleasure was all mine."

Every minute it was harder and harder to turn her back on this, but she and her father deserved one last chance to fix their relationship. She'd seen how Will mended fences on the ranch with hard labor, grit and the right materials. He didn't give up. There was too much at stake for the animals and people he cared about. She couldn't give up on her father, either, without telling him what he stood to lose by turning his back on her.

Will headed for the front door and entered the living room. She followed and reached out for his arm. The sturdy muscles reminded her of all he did for others on the ranch. She wanted to do this one thing for him. "A fresh coat of paint. A little color, but not too much as to overwhelm the magnificence beyond those picture windows."

"You're an interior designer, too?" He stopped and stared at her.

She shrugged. "I worked for a design firm for two months before I spilled coffee on some important sketches." That hadn't ended well, and dismissal had been her fault. "After that,

I worked as a wall painter for a few months."
Until she accidentally mixed up the colors for
two houses.

"How many jobs did you have before Ever-
Wind?" Will frowned.

Too many to count. "A lot. That's why I'm
committed to this one. My father pulled strings,
and I won't let him down." *Not again.* "Painting
is fun and soothing for me. Barry said you already have all the supplies."

He rubbed his hand along a faded rectangle
on the wall. "This is more than a mere thank-
you present. It's too much."

"Let me be the judge of that. I know what I'm
capable of doing." She ran her hand over the
same section. "What was hanging there? It must
have been in that spot for a long time." She'd
been curious about this ever since she arrived.

"My mother was an artist. After the accident, I couldn't bear to look at her watercolors
every day." His gaze grew distant. "I'm doing
her a disservice by storing them in the basement. They belong here."

"There's no time like the present then. Let's
go to the basement." She reached for his hand,
and it felt cold, unlike previous times.

"What about lunch?"

She interlaced their fingers together. "Sometimes we have to face something head-on. This is one of those times. Reacquainting yourself with your mother's paintings is too important to put off any longer." She knew a thing or two about avoidance; she'd been running on excuses about talking to her father for years.

They both had to confront the emotional hole left by their parents before they could move forward. Was it easier for her since her father was alive? She hadn't expected to come to Violet Ridge and discover a place where she fit in, any more than she honestly expected her father to come around to a relationship with her after all these years.

Helping Will might be the best way she could find the courage to express herself.

WILL FLICKED ON the lights to the basement. To his surprise, Kelsea hadn't let go of his hand.

They walked downstairs, and she shivered. He let go and wiggled out of his jacket, placing it over her shoulders.

"What am I going to do when I don't have you to lend me your jacket?" she asked.

He remained silent and then pulled away the dust covers from his mother's paintings.

In the past eight months, he'd forgotten the breadth of her talent. He caught a glimpse of the one featuring the aspens set against the Rockies. She'd painted it in the northwest pasture. Then he flipped to the next one, a stark winter landscape. Kelsea reached over when he got to his favorite, a meadow with wildflowers. She gasped. "Will, these are breathtaking. You can't keep them down here."

"I don't know why I haven't hung them back on the walls already." He clenched his fist and let go. "That's not true. It's just hard to understand why they both went out with the weather changing by the minute. They probably never saw the patch of ice."

"From what I know about you, you'd have done the same. You'd do anything to watch over the animals."

It wasn't an accusation or anything other than a plain, simple fact. "You're right."

"I'm surprised these aren't in a gallery." Her gaze lingered on the masterful strokes, the vivid colors.

"All of Mom's friends said the same thing."

Until now, he'd forgotten a conversation he overheard at one of the many parties his parents hosted. Someone asked his mother whether she felt like Violet Ridge held her back.

This is my home and my family. This is where I draw my strength and inspiration.

His teen self had scoffed at the words as sickly sweet sentiment. Now, though, he wasn't so quick to dismiss them. Rather than holding her back, this ranch gave her a place to express her creativity, and Dad had always given her room to fly.

He flipped through the rest of the paintings until he found one he'd never seen before. His breath caught as he lifted the oil painting of a tender moment between Domino and him. Mom had painted it so his hat obscured his face. She'd captured the scene with poignancy and skilled technique. The artwork was magnificent, and probably her last and greatest masterpiece. He reeled with shock and amazement.

He pulled out the painting and something on the back caught his eye. A sticky note with his mother's handwriting: *Will's Christmas gift*. The basement swirled around him, and he reached out and steadied himself. This one had to come upstairs now.

Kelsea faced him and grasped his arm. "What's wrong?"

"This was going to be my Christmas present."

Will let the grief wash over him. The goodbye he'd said with words was now goodbye in his heart.

Although he mourned the Christmas that might have been, he couldn't dwell on it. The real question was how would he rise up and meet future holidays? Happiness was in his grasp.

She hugged him. A longing for something permanent flickered inside of him, a longing for something real and meaningful. To have someone else in his life, even if he risked having to say another goodbye. Not just anyone, though. Kelsea.

He lived in this moment, her silky hair caressing his chin. Her light orange scent reminded him of spring and life and hope. Her soft arms surrounded him, and he leaned into the embrace. She stood on her tiptoes, and he weaved his hand around her slender back, his arm fitting perfectly in the curve on her side. He lowered his head until his lips met hers. This kiss proved the others were no fluke. Her soft lips probed his. Time stood still as he found what he didn't even know he'd been looking for. Someone who pushed him but wasn't pushy. Someone who supported him and accepted him for himself, faults and all. Someone beautiful and willing to meet any challenge.

The kiss deepened, and color flooded back

into his soul. This woman brought so much into his life.

She released him. "She wanted it to bring you happiness. Grab on to that feeling."

Was there a way to be happy and be a responsible ranch owner?

He owed it to his parents, and himself, to find out the answer.

CHAPTER FIFTEEN

IN THE BASEMENT, Will scanned the storage area, generations of lamps, furniture and other household items everywhere. "If there's anything else you want to take upstairs for the living room, be my guest."

"Thanks. It's not every day a girl gets an offer like that." Kelsea winked and lightened the mood, as if instinctively knowing he needed that bright spot of sunshine and hope. She looked at the paintings and then at Will. "We need help getting these upstairs."

"I'll do it myself." It would take longer, but he didn't want anyone throwing out their back for him. "It's not a problem."

"Don't be afraid to let the cowhands and the three gents help and support you."

A message he was finally believing and living thanks to her. He reached out and fingered a strand of her silky soft hair. "There's hope for me yet. I've let a certain someone get close." Come to think of it, his parents had always welcomed Sabrina and Lucky to the Silver Horseshoe as if they were family. Maybe to his parents, they were. From what Kelsea said, her father wouldn't be as accommodating to her friends. "Who's your support network?"

She glanced at the floor, silence his answer.

"The tiled floor's not that interesting."

"My half siblings try their best, but we're not that close. I like to think they'd be here in a minute if I needed them."

These things worked both ways. More than anything, he wanted to be part of her support system. Her resilience struck him. Here she'd traveled more than halfway across the country for a new job, learned how to ride a horse and discovered she was a goat whisperer. Every day, he was finding more and more remarkable aspects of this woman. He'd love a lifetime to find out everything. Will lifted her chin until her bright blue eyes met his. "It takes a strong person to be positive and spread that feeling when support isn't always there for her."

The door squeaked. "Kelsea? Will? Are you down there?" Uncle Barry's timing broke them apart.

"Hey, Barry," Kelsea called up. Will bit back his chuckle at the odd note in her voice. "Are you feeling well enough to help me with a project this afternoon?"

She lifted the wildflower painting and started up the stairs. She glanced backward over her shoulder. He paused, his hands still on his Christmas gift. "I'll be up shortly."

He needed a minute to be alone. The truth stared him in the face. His parents were gone. They'd left behind a financial mess, but they had loved him and the community surrounding them. What's more, Violet Ridge loved them back. Mom and Dad's unwavering love and encouragement had meant more than he'd known or expressed.

He looked again at the print with the aspens and kept himself from calling Kelsea. Just as it was his mother's choice to live in Violet Ridge, so, too, did it have to be Kelsea's choice to stay and build something real of her own.

KELSEA HELPED WILL and Barry take the lunch dishes into the kitchen when the front doorbell rang. She offered to find out who was there and found five big boxes addressed to her on the porch. The T-shirts!

"Will, I need your help."

In two seconds flat, Will was by her side,

alarm in those brown eyes as he prepared to defend her. "What's wrong?"

She chuckled, but her insides felt a different kind of funny. No one had ever come at her beck and call. Will not only arrived, but he'd sprinted. "Nothing. The T-shirts are here. They were a great success in raising more money for the early education fund. Help me carry them inside, please."

In no time, Will moved the delivery boxes into the living room and handed her a box cutter. Barry ventured their way, dish towel in hand, leaning against the doorframe. She ripped into the first box. The gold circle with the Violet Ridge Rodeo Roundup logo popped on the burgundy. She turned it over and found the list of sponsors look even better than she'd expected. She squealed and launched herself into Will's arms. "These turned out so pretty. I can't wait to show Regina and hopefully persuade her to start selling T-shirts with the feed and seed's logo at her store."

Even though she still didn't have a definitive answer to the shop owner's job offer.

The reality of being in Will's arms spread a deep hum of contentment through her. For a minute, she allowed herself to revel in the luxury of his embrace.

This gruff cowboy with a heart of gold was so close to lassoing her heart.

Barry clapped from the doorway. "This is big, really, really big."

She loved Barry's familiar catchphrase. Somehow, she knew he wasn't referring to the boxes of T-shirts. Barry was talking about her and Will. She'd miss hearing that mantra.

Will eased away from her, and she longed for another moment in his muscular arms. "I'll be back after I finish my chores." His gaze promised more to come, and she looked forward to his return. He reached for his cowboy hat. "Thank you, Kelsea."

"You'll want to hurry back once I tell you what's coming." Kelsea looked at Barry for confirmation. "Should I tell him or let it be a surprise?"

Barry rubbed his hands on the dish towel. "Go ahead."

"We arranged everything. All you have to do is show up. After dinner, everyone's helping me prep the room for painting. Barry, the cowhands, the three gents. Then we're baking cobbler outside on the fire. Barry's making homemade ice cream this afternoon. I've never had cobbler cooked over a pit fire before."

"As long as the livestock cooperate, I'll be

here." Will sent her a lingering glance before taking his leave.

Barry stuffed the dish towel in his back pocket. He reached for a T-shirt, nodding his approval. "Will was an old soul as a kid. Your spirit is just what he needs in his life." His gaze landed on what was over the hearth. His mouth dropped. "Polly's painting."

"Will and I went down to the basement. He's given me carte blanche to spruce up the living room." Kelsea folded the edges of the box together.

"You're good for him, Kelsea." Barry ran his hand along the frame before holding it toward the window, the light reflecting off the canvas. It was as if she could smell the fragrance of the flowers, they were that lifelike. "You'd make a great addition to Violet Ridge. So would a consignment store at the feed and seed. You have a way of bringing out the best in everything others cast aside. Regina sure perks up whenever she talks about you."

While part of EverWind's attraction was her father's approval, she believed in the environmental aspect of the company, lowering the carbon footprint and lessening air pollution. How could running a consignment store compare to that?

Reusing and upcycling existing materials would give new life to something old. Spreading happiness also had its benefits.

Her phone rang, and Mr. Mulroney's number popped up on the screen. She excused herself and walked out onto the front porch.

"I have some news." Dave Mulroney wasted no time getting to the point. "The soil sample and photo from the Silver Horseshoe are a no-go. There are ranchers on the other side of the state that have requested a pitch. I'll send you the details of the leads we've prioritized so you can schedule those appointments before you return to the East Coast. Our best field scientist is leaving for Colorado in a couple of days. She'll relieve you and narrow down our options."

Kelsea's mouth dropped, and it was as if a herd of cattle rode hard along her chest. "Should I return to Atlanta now?"

"Your return flight is in four days?" She confirmed it during his pause while trying to absorb everything he'd said. "You can stay in Colorado until then, as long as you approach those other ranches."

"Hold on. I've sent several samples from the Silver Horseshoe in two different packages. Didn't you receive all of them? Or are you still awaiting analysis of the others?"

Papers shuffled in the background. "I only

have records for one. I forwarded you the analysis."

She opened the file and frustration bubbled at the incomplete review. "I sent another package, and that one had the more promising sample. One must have been lost along the way. This analysis covers the northeast site, which I didn't think was viable because of the lack of easy access and the tree break. The one I recommended for the contract belonged to the vial from the northwest site." The one Will wanted for the elk expansion.

More silence, followed by a pencil tapping out the beat of a popular disco song from before she was born. "I can't find any record of the second shipment. Express a new one as soon as possible and resend the photos. If another suitable property comes up in the meantime, I'll put that one at the top of our list. Sullivan is dragging his heels too much for my liking."

Beeps signaled the end of the conversation, and she tried wrapping her mind around what had just happened.

Worse yet, how would she explain all of this to Will?

WILL ENDED THE phone call and brushed his hair away from his forehead with an exasperated sigh. The farrier had a last-minute emergency with a horse rescue and postponed Domino's appointment until later in the week. Now Will had no choice but to leave Domino behind and ride Tuxedo. Ranch horseshoes differed from the rodeo ones. For months, Will had fostered a faint glimmer of hope buried so deep inside he didn't even know it was there that he'd return to the sport he loved someday. Attending the rodeo ended that for good. His hips thanked him, and even the roar of the crowd had spurred no desire to reunite with what had once been his passion. If Domino was going to adjust to his new life here, he needed the right shoes. At least, Will hoped that was the problem. Domino had given every impression he was perking up but now he'd reversed course again.

It must be the shoes.

If not, he'd have to face the fact his quarter horse missed the rodeo too much to hold him here. By the time Lucky arrived next week, Will should have a sense of what was truly best for Domino.

For now, though, he was content on heading home for cobbler and ice cream. With any luck, he'd be there in time to score a bowl. Kelsea was bringing fun back to the ranch. His mother would have approved.

Reining in Tux, Will approached the northwestern pasture, the one that bordered the Double I Ranch. He wanted to make sure that the predator hadn't ripped a hole in the fence again. He dismounted where there was a supply of grass for Tuxedo and checked the repaired site. Sure enough, whatever had caused the hole had returned. He pulled out his pliers and set to work.

Once he repaired the fence, his stomach rumbled its discontent. He looked around. Somehow, the day had slipped away from him. He soaked in the rays of the late afternoon sun, the orange glow spreading through the valley, making the aspens glimmer as if silver.

Would he have stopped and appreciated this moment if Kelsea hadn't happened onto the ranch? It was like he'd found his way back into the world. Her happiness imbued him with a feeling of peace that he was grateful for.

Whether or not he liked it, Kelsea impacted every particle of his life. She brought people together, and the animals on the ranch sought her out. She made the day brighter, just by being her. He was happy. The pinkish-orange glitter reflecting off the craggy mountains couldn't compete with the red of her lips or the blue of her eyes or the spun gold of her hair. Every time he was around her, his senses almost buzzed with a new awareness.

Falling in love with her would be easy, if he let go enough to do so. Still, he knew she sought her father's approval about her current job. If she moved here, would she regret any unfinished business with Preston? For so long, he'd felt as if he'd left so much unsaid with his father. Difference was Kelsea's father was alive and well.

"Sullivan!"

He recognized the voice and waited while Elizabeth Irwin, one of the owners of the Double I, rode up on a magnificent Appaloosa. The Irwin family were admired in the community, their ranch a model of executive planning, their word platinum. That might have been why Violet Ridge still buzzed about Elizabeth's brothers deciding to move out of state with careers that had nothing to do with ranching. Still, no one in town broached the subject with Elizabeth or her father. Folks had too much respect for them to bother with gossip.

"Good evening, Elizabeth."

She was only two years younger than his thirty-two, but she held herself in such a polished way he'd have thought her older. Her auburn hair hung to her shoulders, mostly hidden by her brown cowboy hat, and her green eyes missed nothing. Cautious and proud, she relished her position on the Irwin ranch. "Glad I found you. You're a hard man to pin down."

She rarely minced words, taking after her father, Gordon, a man many believed hard as flint.

"You know as well as anyone it's calving season." He hesitated. As it was, he'd probably arrive too late for dinner, but he might make it in time for the cobbler and homemade ice cream. The neighborly thing to do would be to ask Elizabeth to join them.

She dismounted with grace, years of practice training her well. She led her horse over to Tuxedo, who let out a soft whinny upon their approach. "Have a minute to talk?"

"Yes, but before I forget, Kelsea's organizing an evening of campfire cobbler and ice cream if you'd like to join us at the Silver Horseshoe."

This night was all Kelsea's doing. She had a way of shaking up everything around her, and that was what he'd needed.

She was what he needed.

"Sounds like a plan." Elizabeth mounted her Appaloosa before he swung into Tuxedo's saddle. "Kelsea? She works for EverWind, right? I came by because I was curious to know what you think of this turbine business? My father's interested in the prospect."

"I'm talking to Doc Jenkins tonight about the impact of the turbines on our herd and Glenn Bayne about the financial aspect."

Elizabeth brought her horse around until they both headed in the direction of the ranch house. "I'd like to talk to her."

"You should. She's bright and intelligent, funny and easygoing. She makes sunsets a work of poetry. You'd like her." He stopped talking. Even the tips of his ears felt hot.

"Wow. She's made some impression on you." Elizabeth scrutinized the fence and the surrounding land with the same meticulousness she gave to everything. "You know, my father was hoping we'd end up together, eventually merge the two ranches." She shook her head, dismissive of the very idea. "I have a strict policy of not dating people who knew me while I wore braces. No offense."

"None taken. Come to think of it, we've known each other all our lives." Their relationship was more like distant cousins than anything else. It was always easy to pick up where they'd left off as if no time had passed. Even so, he'd never felt the slightest attraction to her, unlike the powerful tug toward Kelsea.

"Long enough for me to know you've never talked about anyone like this before. Does Kelsea live around here?"

To his regret, he answered in the negative. Then Elizabeth let her Appaloosa have its lead. They trotted in silence until they reached the stables. After they tended to the horses, Will led Elizabeth toward the lively gathering. Rocket bounded over and greeted them.

He'd expected the cowhands, Uncle Barry and a few others, but it was as if half the town showed up for this impromptu gathering. The sweet scent of cinnamon and peaches infused the air. Groups of people milled together, bowls in hand, laughter livening up the festivities.

Kelsea spotted him and rushed over, her long blond hair in two braids under her colorful straw hat. She'd paired her long skirt with a white tank top that sent his pulse racing.

"Isn't it wonderful? When I went to the grocery store for extra peaches and other supplies, I ran into Rita from Weaving Wonders and some people who remembered me from the rodeo. I invited them, and they came!" Will wasn't surprised. Her gaze fell on the woman beside him. "Elizabeth Irwin from the rodeo, right? Great to see you again. Hope you like cobbler and homemade ice cream, but you better hurry because we're almost out of ice cream. I underestimated for sure."

Elizabeth excused herself, and he found himself alone with Kelsea. Well, as alone as they could be with forty people surrounding them. He glanced around in wonder. Kelsea had turned the ranch into a home in the short time she'd been here. "This is something."

"I hope you don't mind. I really didn't expect this many people." Her blue eyes registered some apprehension.

He absorbed the lively atmosphere. He didn't mind. "Not at all. This reminds me of my mother's parties, celebrating the end of calving season. It's been too long."

She led him toward the dessert line, and he scooped cobbler and ice cream into a bowl. She smiled at him. "I've had my share of delicious desserts, but the way your uncle's ice cream melts around warm cobbler cooked over a campfire? It might not cure everything, but smiling helps the world go round."

He took in the joy surrounding them. Kelsea had done this. Like a moth to a porch light, she drew people to her presence, himself included. Friends came over and winked at the both of them. The thought of people believing they were a couple should have given him pause.

Yet, this was a moment for happiness. She was here for now, and he'd take that.

He inhaled her fresh scent. From here on, he'd always associate the sweet smell of oranges with her. He wanted to put his arm around her. Make what was as plain as the horns on a bull to everyone else a reality. That they were a happy couple with a future ahead of them.

Yet, that couldn't be. She deserved a chance to make everything okay with her father. He couldn't deny her that.

This beautiful evening, though, was all due to her. Mere words didn't seem enough. "Thank you. I—"

Laughter and applause broke out. He and Kelsea looked at each other. Shouts came from near the bunkhouse. The crowd shifted enough for Will to see what was happening. Doc held out his fiddle, and Glenn polished his harmonica. Marshall lifted his guitar from the case. The three gents huddled together before they started playing a reel.

Whoops accompanied the rhythm of the country music. Kelsea held out her arm. "How do you feel about dancing?"

Her bright blue eyes glinted in the gloaming. Will accepted her offer. "You haven't danced until you've danced in the dusk."

Her cheeks blossomed into a dainty pink. "I do believe that's the most romantic thing anyone's ever said to me."

He whisked her off to the makeshift dirt dance floor. Before long, Steve cut in, and Will watched her from the sidelines with a glass of cool lemonade. Kelsea took turns with the cowhands, each with a unique style of dancing. She laughed while being twirled and dipped. Each ceded to the next, happier for the time with her. Finally, Will placed his empty cup on the nearest post and tapped on Jody's shoulder. Kelsea met his gaze, the electricity sending his pulse racing. The three gents announced one slow song to end the night.

Will swayed along to the music with Kelsea's cheek on his shoulder. Life didn't get any sweeter.

CHAPTER SIXTEEN

THE CHILL OF the early morning braced Will, and he hurried to the stables. First up, morning stable chores followed by a check of the cows and calves.

The hair on the back of his neck rose. Something was off, but he didn't know what. "Hello?" Slight sniffles caught him by surprise, and he found Kelsea talking to Endora, the stable cat. "Kelsea? What are you doing out here so early?"

Endora gave him a disdainful look before heading into the shadows. Kelsea stood and shuffled the dirt with the tip of her cowboy boot. "You looked so happy last night. I didn't want to upset you."

"About what?" His defenses prickled all the more.

"A recent development with EverWind. Mr. Mulroney called. The first sample came back, and we can't use the northeastern pasture." She walked toward him, her hands fidgeting.

In one swoop, he might have lost a chance

at signing the contract that would have helped him save the cowhands their jobs. The elk expansion was a long shot, after all, a dream in the grand tradition of Sullivan schemes, but EverWind came with money upfront. Kelsea's news cut deep. There went any hope of holding on to the ranch as it was and building a relationship as well.

He pulled back, unsure of what to think. Last night he'd gone to bed on cloud nine. That dance had given him hope everything might go his way.

Now, in the shadows of the early morning, the reality of a failing ranch settled deep. "I see."

"Will?"

His throat tightened. He couldn't ask this beautiful woman to take a chance on a ranch that might soon be bankrupt. On him.

"I have to get to work. Thanks for everything, Kelsea."

THE SMELL OF fresh paint usually cheered Kelsea. This time, however, it signaled the end of her time at the Silver Horseshoe. She just had to collect and send off that one last sample and she'd be on her way.

She glanced around the living room at her helpers. The three gents argued in a convivial way, each convinced he was right, while Barry bustled back to the kitchen.

The doorbell rang. The three gents continued talking, and she didn't see Barry. As the second peal echoed in her ears, Kelsea found Regina on the doorstep, her boot tapping. "I'm here for the T-shirts and to plead my case with you." She hustled inside. "This time with some cold hard numbers."

This was sweet of Regina, but after she left the stables, Kelsea had faced some cold hard facts. She'd fallen into her familiar habit of plunging right in and then backing out when circumstances became too hard to handle. If she quit EverWind and moved here, she'd be continuing that cycle.

"Thanks for going to all that trouble, but check-in time for the hotel is four this afternoon. I'll be there until I return to Atlanta." Everyone in the room stopped what they were doing at her pronouncement and she could have heard a pin drop.

"What do you mean you're going back to Atlanta?" A frown replaced Marshall's usual grin.

"Told you she wouldn't stay." Glenn fussed and shook his head.

Regina reached into her back pocket and pulled out a sheaf of papers. "Hear me out. I wrote everything down all official-like. I want you to run the consignment shop with the belt buckles and hats. We'll be partners and you can buy me out after five years. Here are some numbers for you as far as making a living at this."

Kelsea walked over and accepted the papers with her blood racing. A partnership implied permanence. Her father might respect that.

Barry emerged from the direction of the kitchen, his glasses fogged over. "Kelsea, did I hear you utter some nonsense about leaving?"

"How have you stayed in one piece all these years, Barry Sullivan?" Regina reached for his glasses and wiped them with the corner of her flannel shirt. "And why didn't you invite me for peach cobbler last night?"

"Regina." Barry hemmed and hawed. "Um, I didn't know you like peach cobbler."

He gave a slight chuckle, but Regina was having none of it. Kelsea almost felt sorry for him.

"There's a lot you should know about me. I'm right here in front of you." Regina pushed the glasses back on Barry's nose. "What are we going to do about this?"

"This? Us?" Barry paled and glanced at the kitchen. "About what?"

"This attraction we've been skirting around for years now. To use your words, we could be big together, Barry. Really, really big."

Kelsea found herself hanging on every word that passed between them, same as the three gents. A fine sheen of sweat popped out on Barry's forehead. Seconds that seemed like minutes passed by, and Kelsea worried Barry was going to miss out on the best and biggest adventure of all.

Barry removed his glasses and stood his ground. "Tonight, perhaps you might, if you're interested, that is, we could—"

"Seven o'clock. Dinner at my place. You like chili?" Regina put the poor man out of his misery.

"The hotter, the better." Barry nodded and looked as if an enormous boulder was lifted off his shoulders. "I'll bring the corn bread."

"With jalapeños?"

Barry nodded. "That makes it pop. Really, really pop. Almost as much as the blue flecks in your eyes. I'll see you at seven."

"About time," a male voice sounded.

Kelsea jumped. The whole of her attention had been on Barry and Regina, and she hadn't heard Will enter the living room.

"I agree," she said. She turned and found Will taking in the changes to the living room.

"I thought you were leaving for the inn." His eyes gave away too much. He'd let her into his life, and she was leaving. What she couldn't tell was if he regretted doing so.

"I promised you I'd paint this living room and leave it in better shape than when I arrived." She understood Will felt betrayed by EverWind, and she couldn't blame him. Still, she wouldn't back down from this obligation. It didn't even seem like an obligation with all the fun they'd been having. "The new me finishes everything I start."

"When the paint dries, we're hanging your mother's painting of wildflowers over the fireplace. It was your father's favorite." Doc went over and removed the drop cloth protecting the painting. "Whenever we stayed up all night with the cows or a mare delivering her foal, Rick would light up talking about Polly."

Regina moved away from the boxes and ran her hand over the frame. "Polly Sullivan was my best friend since kindergarten. It's still hard to believe she's gone. Her painting of the feed and seed hangs above my bedroom dresser. It's the first thing I see every morning." Emotion coated her words, and she wiped away a tear from her cheek. Barry reached into his pocket and pulled out a bandanna, handing it to her. "Thanks. She and Rick had a hand in so much of this town."

"How so, Regina?" Kelsea asked, keeping a close eye on Will.

"You've been to Weaving Wonders, right?" Kelsea nodded, and Regina continued. "Rita Ortiz stayed in touch with Polly after they met at an art show. When Rita mentioned moving here, Rick and Polly called in a favor so Rita could rent the store. Then they spread the word about the store's grand opening."

Kelsea's gaze didn't leave Will, who played with the brim of his hat.

"I can attest to their generosity." Doc nodded. "I know of a couple of Violet Ridge High graduates who worked on the ranch over their summer breaks. Rick made sure their tuition and board were covered for the entire year if they went to college. For those who chose the rodeo route, he paid their entry fees and let them use Will's equipment and training area. That doesn't even begin to cover those he helped if they needed a little extra for a down payment for a ranch of their own. And just so it's clear, Rick mentioned none of that to me. I've picked up little bits here and there at the feed and seed over the past few months."

Will frowned. "But people always laughed behind my father's back."

Marshall ripped off a piece of painter's tape from the fireplace mantel. "Of course, we did. Rick told funny jokes, and Polly had a kind word for everyone, even my brother." He nudged his brother's ribs. "Glenn always opened the door for Polly at the feed and seed. He wouldn't allow anyone else the privilege."

"Polly rounded up the dinner brigade after my wife Marlo's death. I didn't make supper for years. Now, Marshall complains I can't cook." Glenn swiped at the corner of his eye. "The paint fumes are too strong in here."

Regina pursed her lips at Will and sized him up. "You think we laughed behind their backs because we didn't respect Rick and Polly? You're a fool if you really think that. I can either laugh or cry when I remember them. I choose laughter." Regina hefted a box of T-shirts. "I've left the feed and seed for too long as it is."

Barry rushed and picked up the second box while Doc opened the front door. Marshall and Glenn grabbed the last of the boxes before Will could beat them to it. Kelsea found herself alone with the handsome cowboy, who stared at the wildflowers in the painting.

"I guess that's the reason the ranch fell on hard times. Your parents invested the profits in the community rather than in their own place." Kelsea joined him, so close to him that their shoulders touched.

"Too bad there wasn't a way they could have done both." Will's voice sounded unsteady, the past few minutes affecting him as much as everyone else in the room. "I wish someone told me this earlier."

"Would you have listened?" she prodded with a gentle voice. He shook his head. "Speaking of not listening, you didn't hear me out in the stable this morning. EverWind only tested one sample. I have to collect more soil and new photographs of the northwestern pasture."

"If that's the place for the turbines, where will the elk graze?"

"Maybe you should think about that after the tests come back? Do you have time to take me up there?"

His shoulders stiffened, and he nodded. "I'll make the time." He met her gaze, and his cheeks softened. "Thank you, Kelsea. You're fighting for me and the ranch."

She knew that admission was from his heart.

She wasn't sure if she should laugh or cry. In the near future, in Atlanta with EverWind, she saw herself doing both over the stoic rancher, sometimes even simultaneously. She waited for the adrenaline that always came with a new adventure, or in this case, restarting an adventure, to make her heart race and prepare her for the hard reality of leaving Violet Ridge. *Nothing.* Her fickle chest squeezed tight at the prospect of saying goodbye. The loss left her weak in the knees.

"Kelsea?" Will's worry came out in his voice.

"I'm fine." She ignored his concern with a breeziness she didn't feel. "Your parents made a real difference around here."

"They did." This time, his voice reminded her of the whisper of seeds carried on the wind. "Kelsea, have you thought of staying and making a real difference around here?"

She didn't dare look at him. "I'd love nothing more." But in doing so, her resolve to finish what she'd begun at EverWind and build a strong relationship with her father might dissolve in a hurricane force wind.

Barry and the three gents returned, laughing and taking turns patting Barry on the back.

"My first date with Regina is tonight." Barry's

eyes glistened with promise. "This could be the start of something—"

"Big. Really, really big." Everyone else in the room finished his sentence for him, and Barry's face flushed a deep red.

"I was going to say special." Barry nudged the carpet with his boot.

Laughter spread through the room except for Will and her. She'd found something special here at the ranch with Will. For the life of her, she didn't want to let it go, but too often she didn't finish what she started. Ending her time here was the only way she could prove to herself she could go the distance with EverWind.

UNCLE BARRY YANKED on Will's arm until Will had no choice but to stumble into the kitchen. He rubbed his arm. "For someone who has a date tonight, you sure are acting funny."

"What did you do to Kelsea?" His uncle's eyes were blazing.

"Nothing." On the contrary. He'd asked her to stay, and her silence on the matter said everything.

"Whatever you did, undo it." Barry bustled around the kitchen until he pulled out an insulated bag.

If only it were that easy, but this was one

time hard work or fancy words couldn't change reality. It wouldn't be fair to her or her career or her family to stay. "Uncle Barry…"

His uncle glanced over his shoulder at the open refrigerator. "Chicken or roast beef?"

"I'll have whatever everyone else is having. I have a full afternoon ahead of me." Calving season gave rise to a busy summer. Hard work was what he needed. Anything so he wouldn't think about what could have been with the beautiful blonde.

"Kelsea likes chicken, so I'll pack that." Barry filled reusable water bottles and stuffed the bags with food. "You need to settle this once and for all with her. She should stay here."

Will went over and stilled Barry's busy hand. "I'm glad you and Regina have finally got whatever's going on between you in the open, but that doesn't mean it will work out with Kelsea and me."

Her decision had to be hers and hers alone, and he respected that.

Barry tilted his face toward Will. "Regina divorced her cheating husband ten years ago. I wasted all that time because I didn't have the courage to speak up."

"Kelsea came here on business. Regina made her an offer, and now the ball is in Kelsea's court." There was more he had to tell his uncle. All the cowhands deserved to know. "Our ranch might no longer be in contention for the Ever-Wind contract. If that doesn't come through, I can't keep everything intact. I'll break Dad's promise and my personal pledge to honor his commitments." He hunched his shoulders as the admission was wrenched out of him. He had failed the legacy that his great-grandparents had entrusted to himself and future generations of Sullivans.

Uncle Barry laid his hand over Will's. "We've made it through hard times before. We'll keep dreaming, same as you have to keep the dream of something beautiful with Kelsea alive. You'll regret it if you don't."

His throat clogged, and the comfort from his uncle seeped into him. It wasn't lost on him that the word *dreaming* didn't send him running anymore. "I can't promise anything."

"That's a start." Barry rubbed Will's hand.

"What's a start?" Kelsea wheeled her suitcase into the kitchen. "Never mind. I want to thank you both for having me."

Uncle Barry crooked his arm and elbowed Will in the ribs, not holding anything back.

"Oomph. Ouch!" Will almost lost his balance. His uncle didn't know his own strength.

He composed himself and stared at the bags. "Would you like to take a horseback ride?"

Kelsea glanced at her suitcase. "Rocky Road Chocolatiers announced its special on Facebook. Molten lava Bundt cakes. I thought I'd snag one before I check into the hotel."

Barry bustled over and pulled out a pan from the refrigerator. He cut two slices of his peach crumb bar and added them to the bags. "A horseback ride will do you both good."

He handed Will a bag and Kelsea another and pushed them out the front door. Kelsea paused. "What did I miss?"

Will held out the crook of his arm. "Calico could use a good ride today. We could go to the northwestern pasture."

"That's pure romance right there, Will." Kelsea frowned and popped her hands on her waist. "Want to try again?"

Always pushing him to do a little better. He valued that almost as much as he valued her. He bowed and removed his hat. "Kelsea, would you do me the honor of escorting me on a ride around the Silver Horseshoe this afternoon? I'd like the pleasure of your company."

She wound her arm through his. "That wasn't so hard, was it?"

Not as hard as the day when he'd have to face

the fact that she was gone from his life. "A little, but if you say yes, it'll be worth it."

"With an offer like that, I have no choice but to put you out of your misery and accept." She smiled. "I'll meet you at the stables after I load the suitcase in my rental."

If the ride and the ranch worked its magic on Kelsea, that might give her a reason to stay. And Will wouldn't mind at all.

KELSEA SLAMMED THE trunk of the black Mustang, and the wind changed direction so she smelled the goat and donkey pen. She couldn't resist a chance to see her favorite animal trio.

Scurrying into the pen, she closed the gate behind her. Flake ran toward her, catching her before she could move out of the way. She stumbled and fell backward on the ground. Churro and Snow hurried over. Whether they were checking on her or joining in the fun, she wasn't sure.

They made soft sounds as if chatting to each other while she picked herself up and a few too-familiar black pellets fell out of her hair. "One last hurrah, huh?"

She chuckled and patted each of them, trying to show her love for them in the gentle touches. Her father's ringtone blasted from her jacket pocket. Of course, he'd call now. It was as if he had a sixth sense about her visiting the goat pen.

"Hello, Dad." Snow came over and butted her before sending up a series of uninterrupted bleats.

"What's that? That doesn't sound like an airport to me."

Didn't her father observe conversational niceties?

"They're goats. I'm still at the Silver Horseshoe in Violet Ridge." Kelsea held the phone between her shoulder and ear while slipping the goat brush on her hand. She pressed the speaker function and then started brushing Snow, whose bleats turned from dismay to contentment.

"Hold on a minute. Traffic up ahead." Tense words, but she'd been in Atlanta rush hour and understood too well.

She glanced around at the mountains rising up and the aspens blowing in the wind. Crisp air filled her lungs. She hadn't missed traffic one bit. What had she missed about her life back home? Not much.

Seconds ticked by, and she checked and made sure the connection wasn't broken. "Dad?"

"Someone cut me off. I'm back and not moving in this blasted construction zone." Frustration fueled his words.

"That's not why you called, though, is it?"

"My schedule is quite hectic, and I should be mentally reviewing tomorrow's surgical procedure. Instead, I need to know if my assistant should pay for an airline ticket from Grand Junction to Logan Airport." That incessant tapping was back.

"If I come, I'll pay my own way." Her pride ruffled, she stiffened and received an immediate nudge from Flake. She brushed his coat, the rhythmic strokes soothing and bringing more pleasure to the goat than this phone call was providing to either her or her father.

The hard truth was that nothing she did was ever going to be good enough for her dad.

What was she going to do about it?

"If I can spare the time away from surgery and the practice, you should be able to do likewise."

He never had approved of her choices, and chances were good that he never would. Was it time to form her own path? "Is this really about molding me into the person you want me to be rather than the person I am? I'm not like Alexis or Adam, and I can't follow in your footsteps."

"The chief oncologist is calling. I have to take this. Text me your flight info." He hung up, and she kept brushing Flake.

"Kelsea? I knew I'd find you here." Will entered the pen, and he stopped short. "I thought we were going for a horseback ride. What's wrong?"

"Nothing." She brushed away any moisture on her cheeks with her sleeve. "It's the goats. Who'd have guessed I'd have become attached to a donkey and her friends?"

His raised eyebrow confirmed he wasn't buying her story. He came over and rubbed the soft flesh between her thumb and index finger. "Is that the only living thing you've become attached to on the ranch?"

What could she say to that? If nothing would ever be good enough for her father, maybe she should at least entertain Regina's offer. Violet Ridge made her happy. Wasn't that enough?

Her chest ached at the thought of leaving the ranch. Leaving Will. And she wasn't sure she'd be the only one left unscathed when she returned to Atlanta. Hurting him was the last thing she wanted to do.

Except to stay, she'd be leaving yet another job, quitting when circumstances with her father became too tough for her to handle.

"Even if I am attached to the ranch and the people here, I made a commitment to Ever-Wind. I have to see that through. After that, however, I hope to be as free as an eagle. Am I still invited on that horseback ride?"

He nodded. "Let's go."

WILL SAT TALL in Tuxedo's saddle, this ride torture and paradise at the same time.

He'd had every intention of taking Kelsea to the pasture so she could collect the soil sample. Then, he'd discovered the recent rain had caused flooding in the building where they stored the cattle's grain reserves. Will wasted no time in adjusting the saddlebags for a different ride. Kelsea had agreed to hold off a little longer so they could investigate this newest problem together.

He glanced at Kelsea as the horses trotted southeast. A relative newcomer to horseback riding, she looked at ease on the animal. Calico responded to her, and Kelsea came alive whenever she mounted the mare. Even now, it was hard to believe this was the same person he'd encountered in the goat pen earlier today. Thirty minutes on the trail had changed her posture, and color finally returned to her cheeks. Her back was already more relaxed and natural. She needed this ride as much as he had after Glenn had approached him in the stables with the latest update about the revised books.

While the accountant had a tendency to dwell on the negative, he'd come prepared with solid facts and figures.

The ranch's reserves had withered away, and they were running on fumes.

If he borrowed money and introduced elk to the ranch, and that gamble lost, Will would lose part of the acreage. And he only had to hope those grain reserves were intact. Somehow, he had to find a short-term way of replenishing the bank account until late summer rolled around and they sold off some of the stock.

"I don't think I've seen this part of the ranch before." Calico guided Kelsea along the rocky and steep incline. "There might be a silver lining to our detour. I might find another site to collect a sample."

"You can see if any of it looks promising for EverWind, but I doubt it will. The trail to the southern tip is rockier with a steeper climb, but you and Calico have a good rapport. Trust her, and she'll keep you safe."

Calico had that type of calming impact on everyone, even Domino. Will could have sworn Calico had looked for Domino when they set off on the ride. However, Domino was still in his pasture. Until the farrier reshod the quarter horse, Will was keeping him on the sidelines.

Kelsea held the reins in one hand and patted the horse's neck with the other. "Calico's a sweetheart."

"She's a happy spirit, even in rocky territory." He shifted the reins to one hand and rubbed Tuxedo's withers. "Tux is determined and a mite stubborn. He never lets anyone down."

"So I'm more like Calico and you're similar to Tuxedo?"

"There's no way I'm comparing you to a horse." Her light chuckle, soft enough to ripple through him but not sudden or loud enough to startle the horses, was more proof of how she'd adapted to the ranch. He was this close to getting caught by the cowgirl. "The hill's getting steeper. Ride in front of me. Just give Calico the lead. She knows the way, since she often came this route with my mother."

Will guided Tuxedo until the two horses formed a straight line, stepping over the dirt and rocks. The air thinned out as they climbed in elevation.

"Like this?" Kelsea kept her voice modulated and calm.

"Yes." From here, it seemed to Will that Kelsea had one clear path ahead of her, the same as the trail they were currently navigating. With Calico to guide her and keep her on level footing, she couldn't go wrong. Could he convince Kelsea she had all of Violet Ridge behind her should she decide this was her new path?

Or was it selfish of him to want her to stay here? This spark between them. Was it enough of a reason to plead with her to give them a chance even if they started a relationship long distance?

Too soon, they arrived at his chosen destination at the southernmost tip of the ranch. Brush and pines clustered around the old cabin, originally intended as a home for his grandfather's sister and her husband. They left Colorado for Wyoming, preferring to chase their own dreams. In recent years, Polly had used this cabin as a painting studio. When Will was a toddler, she'd load them on her horse and ride to this space. Once Will started riding in the rodeo, she stayed closer to home and his parents transformed the cabin into more of a storage shed.

He led Kelsea to the clearing in front of the porch. Will dismounted Tuxedo and tied him to an old post, taking care the horses had oats and water. Asking her to wait for a minute, he hurried inside and found the damage not as extensive as he feared. He could still show her around. Returning to the horses, he helped

Kelsea down, his hands on her hips. Electricity coursed through him. As always, her presence brought out the best in him. He relished being happy again. They both stood there as if transfixed by each other's presence. They were so close he could see the dark blue tint in her irises. Her shallow breathing echoed his. He could kid himself that it had something to do with the elevation, but in reality, he wanted to kiss her. Not just once, but again and again.

An eagle swooped overhead, squawking for joy at gliding in this majestic area. Will broke away from Kelsea. "A long time ago, my family built this as a home for my great-aunt." He grasped her hand, her fingers interlacing with his, her touch soft. If only it were this easy to have a permanent connection with her. "In the end, she and my great-uncle settled elsewhere. They followed their own dreams."

They walked over to one of his favorite spots on the ranch. While he loved every acre, this bird's-eye view took his breath away. It had been too long since he'd been here.

"Is that our pond? Skipping Stones Pond?" Her voice echoed with delight as she pointed her finger toward the pond nestled in the valley.

He nodded. Aspens waved their silvery boughs as if greeting Kelsea. Wildflowers swayed in the breeze, the purples and reds a beautiful sight. Sharing this with someone made it even more special. "Yes. See how it curves and borders each of the pastures? I thought you'd appreciate the ranch from this vantage point."

"It's beautiful." Her eyes grew misty as she stared at the valley in front of them. "Is everything okay with the grain reserves?"

"I don't think we lost too much. It'll take me a little bit of time to repair the bins. Thank you for being flexible yet again," he said.

"I won't back down from getting my soil sample. That's my priority." She continued looking forward. "I'll go ahead and scout out this location while I'm here. See if it will work."

"This is an underutilized part of the ranch. Maybe it could be the best site, after all." They could move a grain storage shed much more easily than reconfiguring space for the cattle.

"Good point. Thank you for bringing me here."

"If anything, though, Uncle Barry is the one who engineered this." Will believed in giving credit where credit was due.

"Don't cut yourself short. You're as persuasive as he is." She swayed their hands back and forth in an arc, her gaze not leaving the valley.

"My uncle and I just have different ways of looking at things…" They caught sight of each other and started laughing.

Then she grew serious. "I think you're both afraid to show your grief around each other."

"I sometimes forget he and my father were best friends. Many of his mannerisms remind me of my dad." A big admission he wouldn't have been willing to make before Kelsea arrived in town.

Her sigh spoke volumes. "Speaking of fathers, mine called earlier today." She glanced at their joined hands and then let go. "I envy you the family you've created at the ranch."

"I hadn't thought of it like that before, but we *are* a family." He rubbed his fingers, her touch lingering. "Each cowhand is like an uncle to me. They're so different. Steve is a big believer in conservation. Kurt and Lyle are quiet, so when they speak up, it's important to listen. Jody's rather blustery, whereas Jerome is more mischievous and keeps the bunkhouse on their toes. The three gents are our newest additions, but they're becoming like honorary grandfathers."

"Y'all look out for each other." Her faint Southern drawl came through.

"Never thought of it that way."

Kelsea turned around and faced the cabin. "Can we go in?"

It had been some time since he'd been inside, but Jody rode out here every so often and would have reported anything that needed immediate attention. "Sure. I'll see what I need to fix the hole in the grain storage area. Watch your step, though."

They headed toward the front door.

"I'm not sure my father understands that families look out for each other. He's been so mired in his world that he hasn't taken the time to get to know me. It's like he can accept my half siblings, Adam and Alexis, because they're like him, but he doesn't afford me the same privilege."

Her expression grew somber, and he stilled. "You're stronger than you know, Kelsea Carruthers." She glanced at him, those eyes wide and luminous, her pink lips radiant. He was a goner.

One step became two. Then he closed the distance between them. He wasn't ready to say goodbye yet and wasn't sure he ever would be. "You're full of surprises and adventure." His voice cracked at the end of the sentence.

"How can someone who craves adventure fit with someone who craves the status quo?"

Her words, quiet yet assured, hit him hard. It was clear they were no longer talking about their families, but about themselves. He reached over and pulled her close. She leaned into his touch as if she didn't mind that his fingers were rough with calluses or that he was rough at the edges.

Maybe the best way to convince her he could accept change was with another kiss. He bent down as she rose on her boots, meeting him in the middle as their lips tentatively joined. Then everything spun out of control. He wasn't sure when or how it happened, their arms around each other, the feel of her familiar yet not familiar. He'd always find some new facet of her personality, something fresh and surprising. He'd never tire of the taste of her, sweet like a sip of mountain spring water on a hot day.

They stayed that way for minutes, exploring, not holding back, until they came up for air.

"You should know appearances can be deceiving. I'm responsible for this ranch, but there's adventure in every corner. Adventure is where we find it, in little everyday details." Will found his voice as he was now finding himself again after a long winter.

"I guess someone who's ridden in many a rodeo knows a thing or two about adventure."

He rubbed his hips, the days of seeking glory in the competitive arena gone forever. They stood there, and he soaked in her presence.

"For once, I'm living in the here and now."

"Not the past?" Her voice teased. How well she already knew him.

"Or the future." This moment was what he needed, a time to focus on what really mattered, and who. He pulled her to him, the softness of her accenting his rougher manner. "Sometimes the person in front of you is where you need to keep your attention."

"Why, Mr. Sullivan, you have a spark of the romantic in you, after all." She let the words roll off her tongue, and she moved onto the first step of the porch, bringing her face-to-face with him. "You might be the biggest surprise in Violet Ridge."

This time she kissed him, and he focused on this moment. He might not be the romantic she deserved, but despite that, he might be the right person for her.

CHAPTER SEVENTEEN

KELSEA AND WILL exited the cabin, and she looked out at the sprawling valley. The path here was too treacherous. Without a heavy investment in infrastructure, this section of the ranch wouldn't work. That left the pasture where Will wanted to introduce elk to the ranch as the best and only prospect. She took a long hard look at Skipping Stones Pond.

"Will, how many pastures have you carved around the pond?" From here, it seemed like all the little dots representing the cattle occupied one side.

"There are several." He adjusted the saddlebags and brought out some tools. "Now I have everything I need for the grain storage repairs."

"Remind me why they're grazing on one pasture and not the other?" Learning the ways of the ranch was slowly but surely coming along. She wished she had more time to become a cowgirl, like a lifetime.

"We leave that other side fallow so the grass

has time to root. It's part of the ecology of the ranch." He reached for her hand, and they settled down on a grassy spot that was dry. She listened while he elaborated on the wildlife of the area. Then he opened up about his revised business plan. "The three gents and cowhands stayed up with me last night. We covered what needs to be done and how to do it while keeping the integrity of the ranch intact."

His face lit up, and his voice grew more animated while he outlined the differences between elk and cattle management. She picked daisies from where she reclined and began a chain while he talked. This wasn't a big scheme or dream. He was going into this venture with a firm grip on what he'd have to do and what it would take to make it succeed.

His support network, a family of sorts, would see he not only succeeded but thrived.

How far he'd come in just a short time. She'd like to think she had a hand in that. The fact he'd opened up to her and revealed all of his plans wasn't lost on her, either. This bond was a little scary, but wonderful.

At a break, she presented him with the chain. "It's not a snowflake pin, but I think it's pretty."

"That it is." He stared at her, and she knew he wasn't only talking about the chain.

Business professionals don't fall in love with their potential clients.

"You mentioned pastures on the northern ridge. What do you do with this section of the ranch?"

"That's part of our plan. Finding a way to utilize the rockier parts of the ranch over the next few years. More cattle, more revenue, so we can upgrade the equipment and keep promises."

Would Will become a workaholic like her father? Or would he learn to rest and relax rather than run himself ragged? She'd love to be the person to remind him of the importance of taking time for himself and others, but she couldn't do that if she was halfway across the country.

That didn't mean she couldn't, or wouldn't, help Will gain his financial footing so he could make his plans a reality.

"Unfortunately, until you have better access to and from this part of the ranch, that northwestern pasture is the only one I see as a feasible option for the wind turbines. There's no point in even taking a sample here. Can we go on?"

"Sure. It shouldn't take long to right everything with the shed." The wind picked up, changing in direction. "We best get started. There's a storm coming."

Her bones felt the cold, and she knew he

wasn't kidding about the storm. "Will you take me to the meadow tomorrow morning? Then I'll ask the lab to rush the results." She still wanted him to have first choice at the contract, and time was running out. "I'll arrive at the ranch as early as you need me to be here."

"Can't get enough of me, huh?" His voice sounded almost light, enough for her to smile.

"Why, Mr. Sullivan. I do believe you're flirting with me."

He smiled back. "I do believe I am. Is it working?"

Absolutely. She might have to leave this ranch, but this ranch would never leave her.

"The sooner I submit the soil for analysis, the sooner I might be able to present you with a contract and a check." A contract with Ever-Wind could still provide needed funds, so the bunkhouse remained as it was with more job security for the crew who'd been so sweet to her.

That would be her real farewell present to Will.

He fingered the daisy chain and then stared at her for a long time. "I'll be ready to leave when you arrive."

AFTER THEY RETURNED from the cabin, Will tended to his chores. The wind was getting stronger, and a crackle of thunder sounded in the distance. He forked the old hay onto the vegetable beds behind the house while Churro stared at him. He finished the job and smiled at the personable donkey. "You earned your favorite treat for watching over the goats."

After storing the shovel, he entered the pen and reached into his pocket for an apple slice. Churro gobbled the treat with gusto, her rough tongue tickling his palm. The donkey brayed and gave him a second look, as though he was a pale substitute for Kelsea.

"What else can I do to make her stay?" The donkey brayed again as if the answer should be obvious.

Tell Kelsea how you feel.

Without Kelsea arriving on the ranch and adding her touches everywhere, he'd be the same jaded cowboy he'd been for too long. She'd reminded him of the beauty all around him and why every breath was a testament to what surrounded them. She'd left her mark on every part of the ranch, but that was chicken feed compared to their potential for something happy and lasting.

Without Kelsea, would he lapse into his old familiar habits? Had her presence and sheer force brought him to the brink of, dare he even think the word, *change*?

Suddenly, a strong smell, almost overpowering, reached Will. That was saying something, considering he was in the goat and donkey pen. He turned and found Uncle Barry there. Will waved his hand under his nose.

"That's some aftershave, Uncle Barry."

His uncle grinned. "Isn't it great? I was afraid Regina might not like me smelling like the ranch, so I used extra."

"She won't be able to mistake you for anyone but you." He couldn't bear to hurt his uncle's feelings.

His uncle's grin only grew larger. "Don't wait up, son." That grin faded as if he'd realized his error. "Don't pay any attention to my lapse of the tongue. I'm not trying to take my brother's place. I'm just an old dreamer, still hoping for the day when I can hang up my gone-fishin' sign."

That forlorn look wasn't the way Will wanted his uncle to start his date. He went over and threw his arm over his uncle's shoulder. "You're a Sullivan, through and through."

"And don't you forget it." Some of his uncle's spirit returned.

Good thing, as Uncle Barry had waited for this date for so long. "I love you, you big dreamer.

Thanks for staying on the ranch and putting up with me."

"Same right back at you."

His uncle whistled and headed toward his truck. A few weeks ago, that sentence equating him with the rest of the Sullivan family would have caused dread to pool in his stomach. Now? Not so much. Dreams were the first step into making something become reality. But what if his dreams now centered on skipping stones, daisy chains and work picnics?

Could he ask Kelsea to dream big with him? No, he couldn't ask her to give up her life for a ranch that was hanging on with hope and a prayer.

Could he?

She'd been honest with him from the beginning. Her home was in Georgia with her family. Despite that, he'd fallen for her, anyway.

He'd finally accepted what he'd feared all along. He was a dreamer, just like his family. Accepting his true nature was the easy part.

The hard part was letting go of someone whose dreams could only be fulfilled two thousand miles away.

WILL GROANED. In the middle of the night, Steve had contacted him with an emergency call about the cattle. The deluge from the storm damaged the fence in the northeast section. The cattle had scattered all over the range. While he was saddling Tux, Doc had seen the light and ventured into the stables. Without a second thought, Doc volunteered to help. The three of them spent the early morning rounding up cattle, some of whom had headed back to the northeastern pasture.

It was a good thing Doc came with them. They discovered a cow giving birth, unusual, since it was late in the season. The vet had called on every ounce of his forty-plus years of experience to save the life of the calf and its mother. If Doc hadn't been available, the outcome could have gone the other way. Now there was new life and new hope on the ranch. Seeing the calf take its first breath made ranching so worth the hassle and long hours.

He'd take Kelsea to meet the calf after they collected the soil sample. She'd love that.

He hoped Kelsea had received his text that he was running late. She was normally great about answering him. Was she that upset he hadn't returned when he said he would? He'd only postponed the ride to the northwestern pasture until he returned rather than cancelling altogether. That was life on the ranch.

Then again, her father was a workaholic and that had added tension to their relationship. This latest delay probably reinforced Will's status as someone who cared for his job more than other folks, particularly special ones. It was hard to let someone into your inner circle if you didn't make time for them.

There wasn't much he could have done differently, though. Not with that storm.

Halfway between the stables and the ranch house, the skies opened up once more. By the time he reached the porch, he was drenched. He removed his soaked coat and left it on the railing. It was getting colder by the minute, not rare in May. He had to love Colorado with spring temperatures in the eighties one minute and forties the next. After he changed into dry clothes, he headed to the kitchen. Sniffing, he started sprinting down the hall. Something was burning.

Will turned off the oven, billowing smoke clearing to reveal a pan of burned muffins. Waving the mitt around, he coughed, but his uncle was nowhere in sight.

"Uncle Barry?" he shouted.

"The muffins!" His uncle ran inside, waving his arms in a weak attempt to dissipate the smoke. "My second burned batch in one day!"

His uncle moaned at the mess. "What's wrong?" Will reached up and felt his forehead. He must have relapsed. This time the symptoms must be worse, if he'd forgotten about the food in the oven.

He knocked Will's arm away. "I'm fine. I went outside under the eaves since my phone wouldn't work inside. I kept trying to call Regina, to no avail. Then I remembered the muffins."

Alarm bells rang loud in Will's mind. "Has the cell service been spotty all day?"

"Yep. Ever since last night's storm. Why?"

"Was Kelsea able to drive in from town, or were the roads washed out?"

"She made it in just fine."

"Where is she? Have you seen her in the past few hours?" Will already knew the answer. Somehow, she'd gone to the northwest pasture on her own. If she'd been at the ranch house, she'd have greeted him already.

"She talked to Jerome earlier." Uncle Barry halted in the middle of the kitchen. "She headed off to the northwest pasture in the UTV."

"When was this?"

Uncle Barry tapped his chin. "Around nine. Have you seen my phone?"

"The one in your hand?"

His uncle rolled his eyes, but Will started doing mental calculations. "She should have been back by now," he said, glancing at the kitchen clock. A bad memory of Steve's phone call delivering the sad news about his parents and their UTV accident surfaced.

His face suddenly grim, Uncle Barry stilled. It was one of the few times Will had seen him without his familiar grin. He couldn't blame his uncle. Kelsea meant so much to everyone around here.

"You don't think..." Barry left the rest of the sentence unspoken.

"I think I should have gone and collected that sample myself last night," Will said.

"I'll try texting Regina again. This time, I'll tell her I'll be late. We have to find Kelsea."

"I bet Kelsea just came up with some new idea about where to locate the turbines." There was a satellite phone in the UTV. "I'll call the satellite phone."

"Good idea."

The squeak of the front door alerted Will to the cowhands arriving for dinner. A minute elapsed as they removed their raincoats. His stomach lurched when he spotted Jerome next to his brother. Kelsea was nowhere in sight.

Worry about her safety tore at him. "Have you seen Kelsea?"

"Isn't she back? She took the UTV out a couple of hours ago. She knew you were busy after the storm, and her boss called last night. He wanted that sample today."

Phones pinged with incoming texts. The tower must finally be working again.

Uncle Barry looked down, and his face blanched. "Kelsea texted me. Something about the UTV's tire and…"

Will didn't wait. He grabbed a dry raincoat from the hook and ran to the stables. He willed away the memory of Steve breaking the news about his parents. Kelsea had to be fine.

He saddled Domino in record time. In an emergency, there was no horse he trusted more. Watching out for slick spots of mud, he urged the stallion to go as fast as possible. Safely. The rain tapered down to nothing, but the temperature plummeted. He spurred his stallion toward the fallow pasture. No matter what, he'd find money for two new UTVs. The ranch couldn't survive on one, especially in case of emergencies.

This was an emergency of the worst sort, though. He reminded himself he didn't know for sure anything bad had happened to her.

Overthinking and believing the worst were old habits. Besides, Kelsea showed him anything was possible with a little ingenuity and a lot of spunk. He already knew better than to underestimate her.

Suddenly, he had the wind knocked out of him.

He'd fallen in love with Kelsea Carruthers, who'd never stepped foot on a ranch until two weeks ago. She was so enthusiastic it was easy to forget she'd never ridden a horse or driven a UTV before this visit.

They arrived at the pasture, and Will's stomach lurched at the sight ahead. The UTV listed on one side near the Skipping Stones Pond. He dismounted, tying Domino to a post, then braced himself as he ran to the vehicle. He stared at the two flat tires both on the left side. This was an easy patch for anyone with experience. Everything else appeared intact, except for one thing.

Kelsea was nowhere in sight.

He yelled her name. Nothing. Worse yet, she hadn't appeared when he'd arrived on Domino. Where was she? His chest felt empty, a dull ache spreading through him. There were many dangers on a ranch. Predators. Unpredictable weather. A wayward bull. He knew all too well.

Will was almost out of his mind with worry.

A nearby shed caught his attention, the only shelter in his line of sight. He rushed over, and there she was, huddled inside, sound asleep.

"Kelsea?" He kneeled beside her. Her eyes flickered open. A beautiful sight, indeed. "Are you hurt?"

She sat up and rubbed her eyes. "Will, I'm sorry I scared you, and I'm sorry about the UTV." She shivered. "This must be especially traumatic for you after your parents."

That was an understatement. Losing someone else to a UTV accident? He calmed his breathing and focused on her.

Like the ranch, the equipment was in serious need of updating. A little like his attitude over the past few months, something Kelsea had slowly caused him to acknowledge. "That UTV is on its last legs."

"And only has one spare."

When they got back, he'd give Jerome a strong lecture on making sure a guest didn't use the UTV alone.

Kelsea was more than a guest, wasn't she? Then again, in the two weeks since she arrived, she'd become such a part of the ranch that everyone, including her, seemed to forget she wasn't a born cowgirl.

Ranching life wasn't for the faint of heart. The true consequences of what could have happened to her made him second-guess her staying on. He leaned against the wall of the shed, unsure whether or not to hug her. "What are you doing out here by yourself?"

His anger flared at the number of calamities that could have befallen her. Ultimately, everyone and everything on the ranch was his responsibility.

"Are you prepared in case of a coyote? Or a moose or a bear?" he asked.

"Jerome was busy, and I needed these soil samples and pictures today. The other results are in, and Mr. Mulroney gave me an ultimatum." She rose and dusted herself off, along with her cowboy hat.

"Didn't you get my texts?"

"No, I didn't." Kelsea came so close that her light orange scent replaced the peaty smell of the shed. "But the UTV isn't the problem here, is it?"

She was right. Here Kelsea was riding without a full understanding of ranch life and its dangers. "My parents loved every inch of this spread and knew it by heart, and an accident still claimed their lives."

"I can take care of myself." Kelsea tipped

her cowboy hat higher off her forehead. "I've been doing that for years, whether or not anyone wants to admit it."

"Nothing is so important that you go off without being prepared."

"No one can prepare for everything, Will. Not even you." She kept her voice in check.

"You could have been seriously hurt. The UTV, an animal attack, a storm." She never did carry a spare jacket. He stopped talking, his voice too raw with emotion.

It was a good thing he did. She shivered, her thin coat not providing enough protection from the frigid air. He shucked his coat and placed it over her shoulders, her hands rising to meet his, her unexpected warmth searing him.

She touched his hand, but he couldn't deal with all these emotions, worry and fright the least of them. He had to do something, anything, to get moving. Striding out of the shed, he stopped at the UTV. He rummaged in the rear until he found the repair kit. He would plug the tires and patch them. He watched while Kelsea checked on Domino. He had finished the first and started the second tire when Kelsea arrived at his side.

"I found watermelon rinds in the saddlebag and gave them to Domino." Kelsea stuffed a hand in his pocket. She then pulled out a scarf and wrapped it around her neck. "Thank you for the coat. I'm sorry I frightened you."

His emotion spent, he took a good hard look at her. At them. The image of her being hurt out here in the elements crashed over him. Her health and welfare mattered to him, and he wanted her to live a long life.

If it happened to be in Colorado with him? All the better. He stood and moved toward her. "I don't want to lose you."

"Is that an offer to stay?"

She walked closer. Before he knew it, they reached for each other. He drew her into an embrace, her softness absorbing his hard muscle. She felt good. She felt right. "It's an offer for you to think about staying. Of course, it has to be your decision."

"You're not going to make this easy, are you?" She paused, while he nodded. He reached out and touched her cheek. "You'll be the first to know."

That was enough for now.

CHAPTER EIGHTEEN

KELSEA RUBBED HER back from her crouched position on the tiled floor of the ranch house basement. Even though she had been scheduled to leave yesterday, she postponed her departure, taking vacation days, after sending off the Silver Horseshoe's soil samples and marking them *urgent*. The engineer received them yesterday morning, and now she waited for the results. While she was considering Will's offer to remain in town, she was putting the final touches on the living room.

She needed to do this for herself as much as for him. Kelsea stood and eyed the huge vintage trunk. She knew the exact spot for it upstairs. Situated between the two leather sofas, this would make the perfect coffee table. The burnished wood was in serious need of furniture oil and a good polish, but it looked promising under the layer of dust. She tried moving it on her own. The trunk wouldn't budge. She tried to open it, but a lock prevented her from doing just that. She needed someone to help her haul it upstairs.

Same as she'd need someone to pick up the shattered pieces of her heart if she left Violet Ridge. She'd never expected to meet anyone like Will. Decent, kind, intelligent. He wasn't a man of many words, but the chosen few carried substance and meaning. *Forget chocolate or candlelight*. All she needed was Will.

Kisses that made her knees buckle and toes tingle didn't come along every day, and yet that was exactly the type of silly emotional outlook that her father expected of her. He wouldn't see the offer from Regina as the reason for her move if she followed her heart. No, he'd only accuse of her of not living up to her promises or her potential.

Either way, she couldn't win. She'd either lose her father's approval or Will.

The worst part of it was she'd always come in last with her father. No matter what she did, she never seemed good enough to claim the name of Carruthers. And yet, she couldn't be sure she wouldn't finish second to the Silver Horseshoe either if she left Georgia for Colorado. Always landing as second best wasn't the way she wanted to spend her life.

Putting the final touches on Will's living

room became imperative. If she chose Georgia, she wanted him to remember her. She went upstairs and found Barry in the kitchen, pulling out a loaf of bread from the oven.

"How was last night's date with Regina?" She cared about their relationship, same as she cared for the man who'd become like an uncle to her, same as the three gents were like the grandfathers she never had.

How could she leave all this behind?

Barry placed the loaf pan on a trivet and removed the oven mitts from both hands. A glimmer of light animated his face. "It was magic, sheer magic. Tonight, I'm taking her to Pham's Asian Fusion. We've both always wanted to try their pad Thai. Even really big things have to start somewhere."

"I'm so happy for the two of you. I was hoping, if you have time, could you help me move a heavy trunk upstairs?"

He stood tall and then flexed his arms. "Regina might like a man with muscles." He chuckled. "But then, I'd have no choice but to inform her that man isn't me."

She joined in the laughter as they headed downstairs. Barry grasped one end of the trunk while she lifted the other. It took some time, but they finally installed it in its new place. It fit perfectly. Barry traced his finger through a line of dust before glancing around the living room. "This looks perfect, Kelsea. You've made this house a home again."

His approval meant a lot to her, given how close he was to his brother and Polly. "The elements were already here. It just needed someone to pull it together." She could easily say the same about Will. "Do you think there's anything in there?"

"It's too heavy to be empty." Barry confirmed her suspicion.

"As long as it's not anything creepy crawly, I'm good." She bent over and pointed to the lock on the latch. "Oh, drat. Do you happen to have a key?"

"There's a master set somewhere in the kitchen. Let me find it and grab some furniture polish. A dust rag, too. I'll be right back."

With Barry gone, Kelsea walked over to the expansive picture window with a gorgeous view of the mountains. Leaving this would be impossible.

Then why leave?

Out the window, she saw Will talking to Steve. The morning sun reflected off the metal silver horseshoe on Will's cowboy hat brim. His oval face guarded much of his inner self, but she was becoming familiar with the small details that revealed so much. The tic in his jaw. How his eyes changed from dark brown to green when he relaxed. Her gaze wandered to his denim shirt stretched over muscles formed by hard work. There wasn't a task on the ranch Will wouldn't step in and do if need be.

He loved his job and this whole spread. Guarding his feelings was just part of his personality. Even though he didn't express everything out loud, he cared deeply. That came out all too clear yesterday at the scene of the UTV accident. It had taken all her strength and concentration not to flip over.

In spite of that scare, that cowgirl spirit wanted more time in Violet Ridge. This was where she'd found contentment and an inner calm that grounded her. No matter where she might go in the future, she'd want to come back here. Was it time to accept that she followed her whims, and that was part of her? Her personality was uniquely hers, and that might not be a bad thing. In fact, it was wonderful.

WILL ENTERED THE ranch house and found Kelsea and Barry kneeling by a trunk situated between the two leather couches. The warm hue of the creamy white paint enhanced the natural wooden timbers of the room without distracting from the view. His gaze was drawn to the mantel where his mother's artwork once again occupied center stage. The vivid colors made the Colorado spring day come alive. The ranch was awash with color once more, thanks to Kelsea, the vibrant woman who'd captured his heart.

As much as he wanted to settle everything this minute, he had to make sure that staying in Violet Ridge was what she really wanted.

"This room is beautiful. Thank you."

She smiled with those pink lips, a wonder as beautiful as the surrounding ranch.

"You're welcome." She motioned him over. "I can't wait to find out what's inside, although I sure hope it's not anything icky."

He chuckled. Barry brandished the key with a flourish and handed it to Kelsea. "You can do the honors, ma'am."

"Thank you very much." She twisted the key in the lock and gasped. "Photo albums!"

His breath escaped him, and Will sank onto the couch. "So that's where they went."

Kelsea looked at him, then Barry, as if seeking an explanation.

"We couldn't find any of the old photo albums of my parents or grandparents." Barry reached in and traced the embossed lettering on the first cover. "They've been here all along."

Barry glanced at Kelsea, then at Will and

excused himself. Will reached for one of the albums.

He thumbed through the pages. Grandfather next to his tractor. His dad and Barry, arms linked, standing shoulder to shoulder next to a cow with a blue ribbon. His mom holding him up to see his first birthday cake in the shape of a barn. The pictures were a time capsule of the Sullivan family through the years. Was it truly goodbye when all of the past Sullivans lived on in him?

Kelsea brushed his hand. "If this is too upsetting, we'll close the trunk." She reached for the lid.

Will kneeled beside her and halted her progress. "No, I'm okay. I loved my parents and I always will. These bring everything full circle. This is the ranch's past and I'm the future. I belong here, and so do you."

He leaned over and she did the same. His callused hands wound themselves through her hair, her familiar light scent filling him with a peace he hadn't thought possible. Their lips locked, and he lived in this moment. In the future, wherever Kelsea was, she would carry his heart.

He only hoped she would consider sharing that future with him.

Will entered the tack room the next morning and closed the door for more privacy for his phone call with Lucky. "What do you mean you haven't heard from Sabrina? I thought she was coming with you so the two of you could look at Domino?"

"She transferred to the women's circuit, remember?"

"I'll text her again." This time until he received a response. "Now, what was this about you falling off your horse last weekend? One of my cowhands is a huge fan of yours and asked me how you're doing. I would have liked to have heard about that from you."

"I didn't tell you because it wasn't a huge deal. I still landed in the money and am on track to make the national finals." Will didn't miss the edge to Lucky's voice, an edge he'd never heard before.

"I'm always here for you, Lucky."

"I know. Thanks."

What was happening to his best friends? Sabrina wasn't responding to texts, and Lucky wasn't responding to reason.

He started cleaning tack.

"There you are." Doc entered the small room with Marshall and Glenn. "We've been elected by the bunkhouse crew to give you advice on ways to keep Kelsea here."

Will's head snapped up, and he didn't know whether to laugh or just keep on working. Still, he nodded his appreciation to the three gents. "It's sweet of you to want to get involved, but I can't keep Kelsea here. It has to be her decision to move to Violet Ridge."

Just like he couldn't keep Domino here if this wasn't the best place for him.

"You have to woo her." Marshall smiled and nudged Will's arm. "My Sadie was fond of chocolates, and Kelsea brought the bunkhouse a tin of chocolate bacon. You should go into town and buy her some candy. Show her you're sweet on her."

Glenn rolled his eyes. "Marlo would have seen through that in a minute."

"Stella loved flowers, and so does Kelsea." Doc entered the fray. The three were trying to help, and Will loved them for it. "A bouquet of wildflowers would mean something to her."

Glenn harrumphed and folded his arms. His brother shot him a look of exasperation. "Why did you come along?"

"Because I knew the two of you were stepping in where they need to tread alone." Glenn nodded his head for emphasis.

"You don't have any suggestions, then?" Will tried to keep his voice from shaking with laughter. He didn't want to hurt their feelings.

"Marlo would have thought I cheated on her if I'd brought her flowers and chocolate out of the blue." Glenn sniffed after saying his late wife's name.

Curiosity got the better of Will. "Then how did you propose?" The three of them gasped, and Will's cheeks flooded with heat. "Not that I'm at that stage."

Glenn came over, his hand trembling. He reached for Will and took his hand. "I told her how I felt. I gave her my heart."

Kelsea loved romantic gestures, but was it possible she could love him even if he was just a plain rancher? Sometimes words spurred on a reality that was bigger and stronger than any dream imaginable. Combining dreams with substantive action was Will's next step in convincing Kelsea to stay.

He'd give her his heart.

IN HER HOTEL ROOM, Kelsea mopped up the last of the blueberry syrup and polished off her delicious pancakes. Her phone buzzed. To her surprise, Alexis's name appeared on her screen. "Hello, Alexis."

"Are you coming to my graduation?" Same as Preston, Alexis rarely minced words.

"I'm fine. Thanks for asking. I love Colorado. I'm making new friends, and I've fallen in love with a handsome rancher. The weather's beautiful, and you'd love the rafting and rock climbing." That was one thing they had in common. They both loved the outdoors. "I know grad school's kept you busy, but have you taken any personal time to be you?"

"Which of that did you want me to address first? Never mind. I want to ask you something. I found a job and a house in Atlanta. Will you move in with me?"

Kelsea blinked, unsure she'd heard Alexis correctly. "You want me to live with you?"

"I'd like to get to know my little sister better." One thing about Alexis that Kelsea appreciated was how she never referred to her as her half sister. It was all or nothing in Alexis's book. "That is, if you're not moving to Colorado."

"I'm not planning on it."

"You never plan anything." Kelsea bristled at Alexis's tone. "But you said you fell in love with a rancher."

"Huh? I said no such thing." Heat flooded her cheeks as the truth revealed itself to her.

She loved Will Sullivan. "That was a slip of the tongue."

"If you say so, but for the record, I don't believe it was. Getting back to the reason I called. I want you to move in with me regardless of whether you attend my graduation." Alexis chuckled. "If you can't get away because of work, I understand. Don't let Dad snowplow you into coming."

"Is this important to you, Alexis?"

"It's a day just like any other."

This was the hard part of being a Carruthers. They didn't like to admit something was special, which went against every fiber of Kelsea's being. She preferred shouting her feelings from the mountaintops to bottling up her emotions.

"It's okay to tell me the truth, Alexis. You won't hurt my feelings." Kelsea winced. "Much."

"Yes, I'd like you there. You're the one person who's always supported me."

There it was. That concept of a support system. No matter where she turned, that kept coming up as if the universe were trying to tell her something. She hadn't expected this new twist of Alexis asking her to move in with her. Now she had yet another reason to return to Georgia.

Her heart broke. The thought of leaving Colorado sapped the warmth out of her with only an icy chill remaining. In proving to her family that she was a responsible adult who took her job seriously, she'd have to say goodbye to Uncle Barry and Regina, the Silver Horseshoe, the three gents.

To Will.

"I'll be there. And I'll think about us living together. We'll talk about it more then," she promised and disconnected the call so she could book her flight.

There was always another adventure around the bend.

Except love was the best adventure of all.

CHAPTER NINETEEN

WATCHING DOMINO PACE at the fence line of his corral, Will braced himself. His horse had been off his feed and a shadow of his former self ever since the farrier had come out to the Silver Horseshoe. With a glance at the proud stallion, Will knew what he had to do.

He had to say goodbye and let Domino live his best life. That it happened to be with Lucky instead of the Silver Horseshoe hurt so much. He texted Lucky and waited.

It wasn't long before Lucky called. "I'm on my way."

"With your horse trailer, right?"

Lucky huffed out a breath. "Yes. Look, I gotta go."

That wasn't a strong confirmation that Lucky would take Domino with him, but Will would convince him of the urgency of doing just that once he arrived. The stallion would perform in front of rodeo crowds again in no time.

Domino stared into the distance and pawed

at the ground. Will reached into his pocket for the stallion's favorite watermelon rinds, but the horse simply trotted to the other side as if disgusted with the attempt.

Knowing Domino would be safe and satisfied with Lucky was enough for now.

Dejected about the upcoming farewell, Will walked toward the ranch house. He perked up when he caught sight of Kelsea's rental heading up the long path. He hurried into the house for the bouquet of wildflowers and the box of chocolates. This was it. He'd offer these along with his heart. Covering all the bases couldn't hurt in this last-ditch effort to ask her to stay.

Will greeted Kelsea's rental with his hands behind his back. She was barely out of the car when he asked, "Walk with me?"

Her smile cast away some of the pall weighing him down over the impending loss of Domino. "Can we say hello to Churro and the goats?" she asked.

He extended the flowers to her with his left hand. "Here you are, visiting Colorado, and you lose your heart to a donkey and two goats?"

She laughed and then caught sight of the bouquet. "Blanketflowers. They're beautiful."

He thrust them toward her with one hand and almost hit her in the chest. *Smooth, Will, smooth.* "Um, that's not all." He brought forth the box of chocolates. "Emma said the truffles represent the best of Colorado—habanero, mint, peach and dark chocolate."

Bemusement crossed her face as she stood on her tiptoes, her turquoise boots no longer looking new but still fashionable. She brushed his cheek with her lips, the lightest of kisses that didn't have the lightest of reactions. He swooned.

"Thank you."

She placed them in the car before they walked to the goat pen. Here went nothing and everything. "Kelsea, I know this isn't much, and life might get a little harder before it gets easier."

She frowned and laced his fingers with hers. "You're not making much sense."

The goats came over and even Churro gave him a look that told Will to up his game. "The ranch needs a lot of work." *A little like the owner himself.*

"You don't shy away from that." The compliment pleased him, especially since it obviously came from her heart.

"I know, but you've made me think about why I'm doing what I'm doing. And the answer is all around me. You've made me dream of continuing my family's legacy with new family members to come. It's a lot to ask of you to consider such a big change in your life, but the cowhands and the gents and I are going to the auction and introducing elk to the ranch this summer..."

She released his hand and threw her arms around him. "That's wonderful, Will. I have just the thing to celebrate." She unzipped her purse and rummaged about before pulling out a stuffed elk. "For you. It can be your mascot."

As long as she was his silver horseshoe, that suited him fine. "Kelsea."

Her phone pinged, and she held up her index finger. "Hold that thought." She excused herself and came back, her face a shade paler.

"Are you okay? What's wrong?"

"The northwestern pasture, Will. It's perfect for the wind turbines. I've been authorized to offer you a substantial package." She outlined the terms and then shook her head. "No, I can't let you do this. You have other plans. The elk."

He leaned against the fence. It all came down to this: the sure windfall or the dream. If he signed with EverWind, would she still consider transferring here? "If I sign, you can apply for a transfer?"

A shadow crossed over her eyes. "My sister,

Alexis, called earlier today. She asked me to live with her when she moves to Georgia."

Will reeled at Kelsea's admission. Her sister's offer was a chance for Kelsea to be accepted into the fold of her family. He couldn't stand in her way. He couldn't ask her to give all that up for him.

Cold seeped into his bones and he reached for Churro. He stroked the rough bristly coat, the stiffness exactly what he needed. "I accept EverWind's offer, and you should accept Alexis's."

Kelsea searched his gaze. "The chocolates, the bouquet. Were you going to say something to me, Will?"

Tell her how you feel. Give her your heart.

She already had it, and she'd take it to Georgia with her, along with a signed contract for the wind turbines. Holding her back from this chance with her family? He couldn't do it. Just like he couldn't risk the ranch's future on a dream rather than a surefire way to increase revenue and honor his father's promises as his own.

"Just goodbye."

Kelsea gripped the signed contract in her hands, the reason she came to Violet Ridge fulfilled.

Instead of joy, she felt a deep emptiness inside her. "You don't have to do this."

"You and Alexis need time together," Will said as he capped the felt-tip pen. "We knew you were here for your company."

"Give me a reason to stay," she repeated what she'd said not even a minute earlier. Will's jaw clenched, and he left the room.

Kelsea kept from crying. She walked away from the ranch house. With a last lingering look at the goat pen and stables, she set off for Grand Junction, where she'd board the plane to Atlanta. There, she'd deliver the signed contract to Mr. Mulroney before flying to Boston for Alexis's graduation.

Minutes later, she found herself entering the Over and Dunne Feed and Seed rather than hitting the open road. Whether she needed to compose herself or say goodbye to the woman who'd been as much of a mentor as an aunt, Kelsea wasn't quite sure. She collected herself outside of Regina's office and then knocked.

No answer. She tried one more time without a response. With a puffed exhale, Kelsea turned and then heard Regina's command to enter.

Barry stood on the other side of some boxes

and Regina pushed her plait of hair to her back. "Hello, Kelsea. Here to take me up on my offer?"

Kelsea shook her head and reached into her purse for a tissue, offering it to Barry. "You have lipstick all over your cheek."

He only laughed. "When something's really big and right, you know it."

That was true Kelsea knew what was big and right. Moving here where she had people who backed her and took her into their hearts was what she should do. Disappointing her father once more? Her throat tightened, and she stopped from shedding any more tears.

Regina came over and rubbed her arm. "You've been crying."

Kelsea tried denying it, but Regina harrumphed. "I know what red-rimmed eyes mean. What's wrong?"

Kelsea patted her purse. "I didn't think he'd sign."

Barry's face fell, and he kicked the stack of boxes. "My nephew is too obstinate for his own good."

The top one tumbled down, and silver candlesticks and bronzed baby shoes fell beside Kelsea's boots. She bent down and picked up the shoes. "They still make these?" She looked at

Regina. "You're going through with the consignment shop?"

"Yes and yes." Regina jotted something on a clipboard and placed the candlesticks in one pile and the shoes in another. "Like Barry said, when something's right, it's right. Are you here to accept my job offer?"

Kelsea straightened and then shifted her feet. "I came to say goodbye."

"Stuff and nonsense." Regina folded her arms, her clipboard clasped to her chest. "Why?"

Kelsea blinked. She'd expected words of wisdom and a fond farewell, not this. "I don't know. I started for Grand Junction and ended up here." A little like how her luggage had started in one place and reached another destination instead. It finally found its way back to her.

Regina brayed out a laugh. "That's a sign you're meant to be here in Violet Ridge. Permanent-like."

"My father and sister expect me back. It's my way of proving I'm a *responsible adult*." She used her fingers for air quotes.

It was Barry's turn to scoff. "That's overrated. Besides, you and I are dreamers. Denying your true self isn't responsible."

Regina went over to him and batted his arm. "And taking years to get around to fulfilling a dream isn't good, either." Her face became serious as she stared right at Kelsea. "Don't wait as long as we did to figure out what you want and go for it. You're strong, Kelsea Carruthers. You came here not knowing anyone and captivated everyone at that rodeo, pulled off a fundraiser and made Will happy."

Regina and Barry looked happy. Kelsea's stomach lurched at what might have been between herself and Will. "He doesn't want me around."

Barry burst out laughing. "Oh, darling, if you believe that." He shook his head and then stopped laughing. "He needs you. No matter what havoc a storm wreaks, there's something beautiful when a rainbow appears. You remind him there's a pot of gold at the end of the rainbow."

Kelsea tapped her watch. "My flight." She couldn't say anything else.

Barry and Regina encircled her and gave her a fierce hug. When they broke away, Regina lifted Kelsea's chin. "Your job will be waiting here for you, along with my offer to be partners."

"Thank you."

Kelsea didn't say goodbye this time, and she didn't look back. If so, she'd never leave.

CHAPTER TWENTY

REGINA'S WORDS STAYED with Kelsea through the flight and subsequent drive home. The businesswoman obviously had Kelsea confused with someone else. Her father had often called Kelsea the irresponsible sister and Alexis the strong one. She'd always believed him, too.

But Regina had stirred something in Kelsea. People in Violet Ridge believed in her without putting her down. They offered encouragement, the type that made her reexamine everything she'd thought about herself. She might not be like her half siblings, but she was pretty darn worthy of love and respect.

The residents of Violet Ridge had taken her into their fold and become her support system. In return, she left them high and dry.

She'd think about that later. In no time, she'd travel to another place for a sales lead and find something else that was great.

Except she didn't want another town. She wanted Snow and Flake and Churro. She wanted

another truffle from Emma's Rocky Road Chocolatiers.

She wanted to see Will and have him admit
she was important to him.

Tomorrow was Alexis's graduation, and her
sister needed someone in her corner. After a
brief trip home for clothes, the Atlanta airport
and a flight to Boston were her next stops. Kelsea turned the key in the ignition. Nothing. She
tried again. Not even a tiny whir. She rested her
head on the steering wheel. Of all days for this
to happen. She only hoped her father hadn't
left for the airport yet so she could catch a ride
with him.

He arrived ten minutes after she'd left him
a voice mail and with that ever-present look of
exasperation. To her surprise, he'd aged in the
past few years. Seeing him on a constant basis
hadn't driven home the changes until now. In
his early sixties, his gray hair was thinning
and there were new wrinkles on his forehead.

"What did you do this time?" He huffed out
a breath and shook his head. "You forgot to
fill your gas tank, didn't you? Or did you leave
your lights on and drain the battery? I'll fix it
later. We can't miss our flight."

"I filled up the tank last night and checked
my tire pressure like one of the cowhands taught

me. I already called a tow truck." Kelsea took in her father's appearance in his navy suit with the knotted red and gold tie. She leaned over the luxury car console and kissed his cheek. She buckled herself into the passenger seat. "You look very distinguished and handsome, Dad."

He blinked as if he'd expected none of that. He started the car and pulled out of her driveway. "Uh, well. Okay. It's your sister's weekend, so we won't mention this to her."

Kelsea sighed. He wouldn't like what she was about to say, but she had to get this out into the open as soon as possible. "It's Alexis's graduation, but I don't know when we'll speak next, so here goes. I'm resigning from EverWind."

"What?" The stoplight turned from yellow to red, and he slammed on the brakes. "Kelsea Arianna Carruthers. What did you do?"

I found myself and fell in love in the process. The light changed, and he accelerated. She inhaled and poured out her heart. "I'm not Alexis or Adam. I have to be myself. If that's someone who goes through jobs, so be it. I'm happy, and something good is waiting for me in Violet Ridge. An opportunity to do something I love. And that's not all. I met a man you'd like if you give him a chance. He's obstinate and loyal.

He's solid and wonderful. I'm in love with him, and I think he's in love with me."

The buildings passed by in a blur while she waited for some response. Preston turned the car onto I-285, the traffic and constant construction a familiar sight. "That sounds like something Kristy would have said."

She fidgeted with the gold chain link of her purse. "I wish you two had been closer so you would have talked about her more."

His head whipped around, his dark eyes blazing, and then he concentrated on the traffic once more. "Is that what you really think? Your mother was the love of my life. She's the reason I give so much of myself to my patients. She's the reason I want you to be settled and happy." His voice trembled for the first time Kelsea could remember. "If I prevent one family from living through the same sadness I've been dealing with since Kristy died, then I've done my job."

Kelsea blinked, having never seen this type of emotion from her father before. He always seemed so distant. Was age mellowing him or just the moment? "You don't return my calls because of your patients? It's not me?"

His face contorted, almost as if he were in

pain. "You're the spitting image of Kristy. You're even older now than she was."

When her mom died. "I've always thought you wanted nothing to do with me."

"That's not true. That's not it at all."

Somehow, her father had managed to get stuck in a vortex from which he'd never escaped. He'd never sought out reinforcements to assuage his pain. He'd never reached out to her for comfort. Unlike her father, she'd seen changes in Will over the past couple of weeks with help from the three gents, his cowhands and his uncle.

"I'll admit I'm shocked about why you act the way you do. I had no idea I reminded you so much of Mom. I hope you'll take time to get to know the real me. But it will have to be from a distance. Violet Ridge makes me happy." This wasn't a whim, but even if it was? It was her life. "I'm going into business with an enterprising woman who doesn't pull punches. I'll be breathing life into a business that treasures objects that can provide value for a new owner. It may not sound like much, but it's important to me."

Her father pulled into the airport's long-term parking lot. "Dave said you're doing a good job. He's invested in your future."

Kelsea reached over and squeezed his hand. "It's my future, and EverWind doesn't make me happy. I believe in their cause, and they do something constructive and vital. But it's not who I am."

After he applied the emergency brake, he stared out the window. "Your mother would be proud of you."

She noticed he didn't mention his own feelings. "I'm proud of me."

"What about Alexis, though? I thought you were moving in with her."

"I'd love it if she visited me. I'll show her Colorado." She squeezed his hand again. "When was the last time you had a vacation?"

"Twenty-six years ago." There was no hesitation whatsoever.

"You can visit me, too." She was moving to Violet Ridge because it was right. If she and Will acknowledged what was between them? That would be right, too.

Still, she was glad she came back to Georgia. Whether or not her father ever expressed his pride in her, this conversation was long overdue. Her mother meant something to him.

She knew deep down, she did as well.

"We'll see."

"Please try to return my calls, okay?"

He nodded, and Kelsea decided to leave it at that. Today was progress, of sorts.

NEAR DOMINO'S CORRAL, Lucky pulled Will close and gave him a pat on the back. "How are you holding up?"

Will separated and shrugged. Everyone from the three gents to the cowhands had asked him the same question. What did they want him to say? That he'd acted a fool, signing the contract on the spur of the moment? That he'd let the best thing that had ever happened to him go without a fight? That he'd fallen in love with Kelsea? Yes, to all the above. "I don't know what's worse—losing her or having everyone look at me like it's my fault she didn't stay."

Lucky threw a sympathetic glance at him and then focused on Domino. "You didn't tell her you love her, did you."

Of course not. "It wouldn't have mattered. She needs her family." Will leaned his arms over the wooden rails of the corral.

"Isn't that for her to decide?" Lucky mimicked Will's pose. "So you didn't say the words everyone knows you feel?"

"I couldn't come between her and her family. If I had ten more minutes with my parents…" Will's voice trailed off.

"What if you had ten more minutes with Kelsea?" Lucky kept his voice low, but the question had the impact of a bull crashing down on him with twenty thousand rodeo fans watching in horror.

Ten minutes wouldn't be enough. "Not gonna happen. She went home. To her family."

Will watched as Domino stayed on the other side of the corral, a shadow of his former self, the same way Will had felt this past week. Lucky nudged his arm. "Family isn't just the people who are related to you. It's the people who love you and accept you and have your back. You should know that better than anyone. You form a family wherever you go. So does Kelsea. She deserves the right to decide where she wants to be."

"Speaking of family, I thought Sabrina was supposed to come with you." Will changed the subject on purpose and faced Lucky, genuine concern for their best friend rising to the forefront.

Lucky sighed. "There's something going on with her. Has she told you what's wrong?"

He might have to track down Sabrina himself and make sure she was okay. "I'll find out."

"Afterward, you can leave the ranch in the capable hands of your cowhands and go to Kelsea.

Tell her you love her. Let her make her choice." Lucky turned his focus back to Domino. "I've never seen anything like this."

Neither had Will. "He must miss the rodeo."

Domino's ears perked up, and he started trotting toward them. If that wasn't a sign, Will didn't know what was. Will's already shattered heart broke into even smaller pieces at having to let the stallion go.

Steve's voice came from behind. "Calico and I are heading out to check on the cattle."

Lucky looked at Domino, then at Calico. Then he burst out laughing. The hair on the back of Will's neck bristled. "This isn't funny," Will said.

Lucky grinned. "Are you still not getting what's right in front of you? Watch the horses."

Will glanced at the sweet mare, then his feisty stallion. Domino pranced around the corral, and Calico responded with a nicker and soft whinny.

All this time, Domino had been pining for Calico?

"I just assumed…" Will let his voice trail off. He'd been assuming too much. He'd assumed Domino was pining for something, and he was. Only thing, though, it was the mare in the next pasture and not his former life.

He'd assumed Kelsea wanted to live with her sister rather than hearing her out.

Steve rode Calico toward Domino. The two bumped noses, and Steve laughed. "They're bonded, all right."

Domino already seemed like a different horse, and Lucky shook his head. "Seems like my horse trailer's going to be empty when I leave."

Will faced the truth. "Need to have a conference with everyone tonight. I'll be taking a trip soon."

He'd made so many assumptions. It was time to tell Kelsea how he really felt. What if it was too late?

It had almost been too late for him and Domino. Maybe it wouldn't be too late with him and Kelsea. He wouldn't know unless he put his plan into action.

Love happened when he'd least expected it. It could only flourish if he did what Glenn said to do in the first place. Tell Kelsea she had his heart.

CHAPTER TWENTY-ONE

WITH HIS CARRY-ON packed and waiting, Will tapped his fingers along the goat pen railing. Where was Uncle Barry? His uncle had texted that he had something really big to discuss with Will, but Will had to leave for Grand Junction in less than ten minutes to make his flight to Atlanta.

There were some things in life you had to do in person, and this was one of them. Whatever happened, Will wouldn't live with regrets about not telling Kelsea how he felt.

He whipped out his phone. "Come on, Churro, Snow and Flake. Look adorable, so Kelsea can see what she's missing." He wasn't below using the goats as an incentive for her to return. He snapped the picture.

Uncle Barry came running up to him. "Thank goodness I caught you. You gotta come quick. It's the ducks."

"Slow down." Will tried to concentrate on his

uncle's ramblings but eyed his truck. He had to get moving. "You're not making sense."

Uncle Barry waggled a finger at him. "You can't leave yet."

"Steve or Doc can handle it."

He opened the truck door and Uncle Barry shut it for him. "I need you."

Will held his breath for a moment and looked up at the sky. "We've been through this. Everyone blames me for Kelsea leaving. I'm flying to Georgia and telling her I love her. I can't miss this flight."

His uncle ignored him. "I thought we could make money on the ranch by opening it to weddings. It was going to be epic."

Will paused with his hand on the door, and his jaw dropped. "What did you do?"

Uncle Barry scuffed the ground with the tip of his boot. "Um, I ordered ducks and swans for the pond. I thought we could turn it into a wedding destination. I might have gone a little overboard and ordered too many. Now they're everywhere."

The image of ducks everywhere sent Will into a peal of laughter. "They'll still be there when I get back."

"They'll destroy the fence."

Will froze, muttered under his breath and took off for the stables. "You're paying for the next flight to Georgia. As soon as the duck situation is under control, I'm taking the first plane to anywhere near Atlanta."

KELSEA REINED IN Calico next to the pond and inhaled a deep breath. Where was Will? Barry and Regina had assured her he was on his way, but she'd been here for over an hour with no sight of him.

He deserved to hear she was moving to Violet Ridge from her and no one else. She had more to say to him as well, including how much she loved him. She patted her jacket pocket and let Calico have her lead. She'd missed riding during the past week. This gentle mare was only one of the animals she'd missed, in fact. Everything about the Silver Horseshoe had imprinted itself on her innermost self, Will most of all.

Suddenly, a speck appeared in the distance. Without any warning, Calico was off like a prize thoroughbred, and Kelsea held on for dear life. The meadow passed by as hooves thundered underneath her, almost as fast as the speed of her heart hammering in her chest.

"Kelsea!" Will galloped toward her on Domino.

She planted her head close to Calico's mane, bracing herself for impact. Instead, the mare stopped and Kelsea waited for the world to stop spinning. Will repeated her name, and she slowly straightened in the saddle.

"Hi. Funny meeting you here. I just happened to be in the neighborhood," Kelsea began blabbering.

Will dismounted and then reached for her, helping her off Calico while holding the reins of both horses. Solid ground never felt so good or so wobbly. He tied the two horses to the nearest post, and Kelsea stood there in shock. Domino and Calico were nuzzling noses.

She'd survived the ride of a lifetime. Best of all, Will was in the same zip code again. She shivered at the sheer nearness of him.

He laughed and approached her. "I'm going to go broke buying extra jackets." He shucked out of his and put it over her shoulders.

His scent clung to the fabric, and she reveled in it, missing it along with everything about him before she'd come back. "You're assuming something, aren't you?"

He nodded and looked up at the sky. Then he glanced to his right and then his left. "Wait a minute. There are no ducks in sight."

Ducks? She'd traveled all this way, and he wanted to discuss *ducks*? "What are you talking about?"

A smile transformed his face, showing off that dimple. "You let Uncle Barry in on this, didn't you?"

She nodded. "He suggested the pond as a place where we wouldn't be distracted."

"I was about to leave for the airport when he told me he'd ordered ducks and swans for his new really big idea of hosting weddings at the ranch."

She grinned. "Where were you flying to?"

"Atlanta. I was going to find you."

"Why?" She had an idea, but she wanted to hear it for herself.

He shuffled his feet but then gazed right at her, as if he were staring into her very soul. "When you left, I didn't just say goodbye to you. I said goodbye to my heart. I love you, Kelsea."

She leaned up and kissed him, adding all the love in her heart and more. Knowing there would be more kisses in their future, she broke away. "You have to let me be me. I might go through a lot of jackets and jobs, but I will always love you, Will Sullivan. That will never change."

His face lightened, as if the weight of the world had been lifted off him. "I can't offer you much, but the wind turbines will help the ranch break even—"

"About that." She reached into the inside pocket of her own light jacket. She pulled out an envelope. "I talked to Elizabeth Irwin. This is a lease for acres on the Double I. Acres that border the Silver Horseshoe and would be perfect for your elk." She held out the envelope to him. "So if you want to introduce elk to your setup like you agreed to do with the blessing of your cowhands and the three gents, there's nothing to hold you back."

Will opened the envelope and examined the documents. His face lit up with joy. "This is affordable."

"Elizabeth and her father agree that your wind turbines will help them reduce energy costs, so they wanted to return the favor. The terms are beneficial to everyone," Kelsea said.

"So, you're staying with EverWind?"

"I turned in my resignation. I'm no longer employed with them. I'm working with Regina now."

"And your father and sister?"

"If they visit me in Colorado, I'll teach them how to skip stones and feed goats while selling them a used cowboy hat and boots." She produced a pen for him to sign the lease.

He picked her up and twirled her around the meadow. Her laughter carried into the wind and rustled through the aspens. He lowered her into a kiss that was as unforgettable as her first trip to Colorado. This was the adventure of a lifetime, and she'd cherish every minute.

EPILOGUE

WILL RAISED HIS paddle and bid on the elk Doc recommended. He relaxed when the auctioneer's "sold" echoed in the outside auction venue. For better or worse, he was now the proud owner of twelve head of elk. From the seat beside him, Kelsea entwined her fingers in his before leaning over and kissing him.

"What do you think of your first auction?" Will asked.

She released her hand and twirled her engagement ring on her left hand. "I love it." She rubbed the platinum band of amethysts and diamonds. "Almost as much as I love you."

Emotion swept over him. He intended to make every minute count with this woman. So far, the consignment store was a success, mostly due to Kelsea. "Are you sure you want to wait a month for the wedding?"

"I'd love if it were today, but we needed a plan. Everyone is happy with how things turned out, including the three gents and the cowhands." She leaned over for another kiss. "Besides, the last time we talked to Sabrina, she said she can make it then. I know you've been worried about her."

Ever since Sabrina took a leave of absence to care for her grandmother, he'd been concerned for his friend. Only Lucky's promise that Sabrina had confided in him and would reveal all in time kept Will from flying to see her with his own eyes.

"And your dad set aside that time to take his first vacation in years. I'm rather nervous about meeting him."

Kelsea grinned. "I can't wait to introduce my father to everyone. Adam's coming, too. Alexis is standing up with me, along with Regina." She nodded. "Their visit will be better than good. Our wedding is going to be spectacular."

Uncle Barry came dashing toward them, Regina on his heels. "Barry!" Regina's voice held a note of caution. "I left you alone for five minutes."

"Will, did you see the alpaca? Their wool is hypoallergenic and odor-resistant. This could be big, really, really big, so I figured you wouldn't mind…"

"Mr. Sullivan," the auctioneer came over to join their group. "Do you have a different trailer for your alpaca? They need to ride separately from the elk."

Kelsea laughed while Regina glared at her fiancé. No matter what Uncle Barry dreamed up, Will would always thank him for bringing Kelsea to the Silver Horseshoe. Adventure didn't come any bigger than the many days he'd share with Kelsea. Their love was stronger than anything he'd ever imagined. A lifetime of dreams in vivid color was just beginning.

* * * * *

For more small town, feel good romances from author Tanya Agler and Harlequin Heartwarming, visit www.Harlequin.com today!

Get 4 FREE REWARDS!

We'll send you 2 FREE Books plus 2 FREE Mystery Gifts.

FREE Value Over **$20**

Both the **Love Inspired**® and **Love Inspired**® Suspense series feature compelling novels filled with inspirational romance, faith, forgiveness and hope.

YES! Please send me 2 FREE novels from the Love Inspired or Love Inspired Suspense series and my 2 FREE gifts (gifts are worth about $10 retail). After receiving them, if I don't wish to receive any more books, I can return the shipping statement marked "cancel." If I don't cancel, I will receive 6 brand-new Love Inspired Larger-Print books or Love Inspired Suspense Larger-Print books every month and be billed just $6.49 each in the U.S. or $6.74 each in Canada. That is a savings of at least 16% off the cover price. It's quite a bargain! Shipping and handling is just 50¢ per book in the U.S. and $1.25 per book in Canada.* I understand that accepting the 2 free books and gifts places me under no obligation to buy anything. I can always return a shipment and cancel at any time by calling the number below. The free books and gifts are mine to keep no matter what I decide.

Choose one: ☐ **Love Inspired**   ☐ **Love Inspired Suspense**
                   Larger-Print   **Larger-Print**
                   (122/322 IDN GRHK)   (107/307 IDN GRHK)

Name (please print)

Address   Apt. #

City   State/Province   Zip/Postal Code

Email: Please check this box ☐ if you would like to receive newsletters and promotional emails from Harlequin Enterprises ULC and its affiliates. You can unsubscribe anytime.

Mail to the **Harlequin Reader Service:**
IN U.S.A.: P.O. Box 1341, Buffalo, NY 14240-8531
IN CANADA: P.O. Box 603, Fort Erie, Ontario L2A 5X3

Want to try 2 free books from another series! Call 1-800-873-8635 or visit www.ReaderService.com.

Get 4 FREE REWARDS!

We'll send you 2 FREE Books <u>plus</u> 2 FREE Mystery Gifts.

FREE Value Over $20

Both the **Harlequin® Special Edition** and **Harlequin® Heartwarming™** series feature compelling novels filled with stories of love and strength where the bonds of friendship, family and community unite.

COUNTRY LEGACY COLLECTION

19 FREE BOOKS IN ALL!

Cowboys, adventure and romance await you in this new collection! Enjoy superb reading all year long with books by bestselling authors like Diana Palmer, Sasha Summers and Marie Ferrarella!

YES! Please send me the **Country Legacy Collection!** This collection begins with 3 FREE books and 2 FREE gifts in the first shipment. Along with my 3 free books, I'll also get 3 more books from the **Country Legacy Collection**, which I may either return and owe nothing or keep for the low price of $24.60 U.S./$28.12 CDN each plus $2.99 U.S./$7.49 CDN for shipping and handling per shipment*. If I decide to continue, about once a month for 8 months, I will get 6 or 7 more books but will only pay for 4. That means 2 or 3 books in every shipment will be FREE! If I decide to keep the entire collection, I'll have paid for only 32 books because 19 are FREE! I understand that accepting the 3 free books and gifts places me under no obligation to buy anything. I can always return a shipment and cancel at any time. My free books and gifts are mine to keep no matter what I decide.

☐ 275 HCK 1939 ☐ 475 HCK 1939

Name (please print)

Address   Apt. #

City   State/Province   Zip/Postal Code

Mail to the Harlequin Reader Service:
IN U.S.A.: P.O. Box 1341, Buffalo, NY 14240-8571
IN CANADA: P.O. Box 603, Fort Erie, Ontario L2A 5X3

Get 4 FREE REWARDS!

We'll send you 2 FREE Books <u>plus</u> 2 FREE Mystery Gifts.

FREE
Value Over
$20

Both the **Romance** and **Suspense** collections feature compelling novels written by many of today's bestselling authors.

#471 HER ISLAND HOMECOMING

Hawaiian Reunions • by Anna J. Stewart

When by-the-numbers accountant Theo Fairfax arrives in Nalani, Hawai'i, to evaluate free-spirited pilot Sydney Calvert's inherited tour business, he just wants this assignment behind him. Until he begins to see Hawai'i's true beauty. And Sydney's, too...

#472 THE LAWMAN'S PROMISE

Heroes of Dunbar Mountain • by Alexis Morgan

Shelby Michaels wears several hats in her professional life, including museum curator in Dunbar, Washington, and acting as protector of the town's most prized possession. But after clashing with police chief Cade Peters, she'll have to guard her heart, too!

#473 HER KIND OF COWBOY

Destiny Springs, Wyoming • by Susan Breeden

Hailey Goodwin needs a cowboy to help her run trail rides at Sunrise Stables, not the big-city businessman who volunteers for the role. Opposites may attract—and Parker Donnelly is *certainly* attractive!—but can they find a happily-ever-after?

#474 HIS MONTANA STAR

by Shirley Hailstock

Cal Masters can't stand to see his temporary neighbor and former Hollywood stuntwoman Piper Logan feeling sorry for herself after a stunt gone wrong. He hopes re-creating it with her will help—but now he's falling for her...